THE SCHOOL AT

CHARTRES

David Manicom

OOLICHAN BOOKS
LANTZVILLE, BRITISH COLUMBIA, CANADA
2005

National Library of Canada Cataloguing in Publication

Manicom, David, 1960-
The school at Chartres / David Manicom.

ISBN 0-88982-222-0

I. Title.
PS8576.A545S36 2003   C813'.54   C2003-910635-7
PR9199.3.M3485S36 2003

BRITISH
COLUMBIA
ARTS COUNCIL
Supported by the Province of British Columbia

Canadä

The Canada Council | Le Conseil des Arts
for the Arts | du Canada

We gratefully acknowledge the support of the Canada Council for the Arts, the British Columbia Arts Council through the BC Ministry of Tourism, Small Business and Culture, and the Government of Canada through the Book Publishing Industry Development Program for their financial support.

Published by
Oolichan Books
P.O. Box 10, Lantzville
British Columbia, Canada
V0R 2H0

Printed in Canada

"We are so made that we can only derive intense enjoyment from a contrast, and only very little from the state of things."

—Sigmund Freud

For Teresa

ACKNOWLEDGEMENTS:

Charlie Foran suggested many structural and stylistic improvements to a much earlier version of this novel. Thank you. I am indebted to the expert editing of Ron Smith and Hiro Boga, who made innumerable refinements large and small to later drafts. Their skill— and especially their patience—were invaluable.

CONTENTS

Dear Liza,

If I had been able to keep my thoughts straight, [...] them all down, I would have something to send you a[...] something to keep. But I have only my own voice in [...] own silence, talking to you as if you were here. Wh[...] I'm alone, all the things I brood about—stories of y[...] and me together, of Daniel and *La Californie*, of the bal[...] on the mountain, of the medieval school at Chartres—[...] all seem as though they could help put us right; tha[...] sharing them somehow would bind us. Now I repea[...] them simply to conjure you closer, make the listener rea[...] in the telling.

Start again, John.

After your departure, *La Californie* became a second home to me. Of course, no one needs a second home if they are fully possessed by a first. In the very beginning I was satisfied by its vestibule. I could step in out of the pummeled, sand-coloured snow of a Montreal January sidewalk and see whether it was sufficiently un-crowded inside, without having made myself so conspicuous—still outside the innermost door—that I would feel awkward about retreating, which would require some sort of explanation, if only to myself. This was an important feature if I was inclined to come regularly, and crucial in a second home.

The café-bar was on a not-too-busy, not-too-quiet street corner near the northern edge of the Plateau district. It was a neighbourhood of moderately run-down three-storey row houses with outdoor walk-ups

and surprisingly ornate interiors, which offered whiffs of plummy Outremont to placate turn of the century up-and-comers: high ceilings with plaster moldings swirling vegetatively; ornamental fireplaces of rich veneers and gold paint in the long front rooms; even the occasional pair of more-or-less Ionic columns to lend symmetry to the salons, as if someone had whispered to the draughtsmen that, even here, without the graces of mathematics, the cosmos would return to chaos.

On the other hand, Liza, I can hear you adding with your lopsided smile, *there is no beauty that hath not some strangeness in it.* After this winter without you I would put it a little differently. The beauties of symmetry are real. The formulae are built into creation. And yet, parallel lines, as seen with the human eye, eventually meet.

When are you coming back? It's time to forgive and write to me, or call, or ring the door bell downstairs. I never thought you would draw it out so long. Liza, I explain as best I can. I try to understand myself through explaining to you, as I always have. It is my only starting place. I worry, though, that I will end up reciting only to myself. Maybe soliloquy is the universal genre. It makes artists of us all, whether we want it or not.

The flat I decided to rent while waiting to hear from you was only a block away from *La Californie.* In your absence, I kept half-turning to ask your opinion of everything from where the bookcases would look best to whether we had a boot mat somewhere. After I flew back alone from France last August and gathered my suitcases as they lumbered around the carousel—stuffed as they

1

Plateau

were with what notes and file cards I couldn't bring myself to consign to sea freight—I sublet a second floor five-and-a-half on Jeanne-Mance. Too much space for one person of course. You know the neighbourhood: not far north of your old place. I suppose this had something to do with my choosing it. I'm sure you can readily picture the baroque map of its make-up. The streets nearby are primarily occupied by the Hasidic component of this alchemical district's half francophone, half Greek-Italian-Jewish-Anglo-Chinese makeup. But that's forgetting the Chileans (1970s), and the El Salvadorans and Guatemalans (early '80s), and the Sri Lankans and Pakistanis, who, as the newest of the newcomers, are taking over the corner *dépanneurs* from the Vietnamese, who inherited them from the Chinese, who had bought them from retiring Italians. My subsector of the area is symbolized by the best combination pool hall-café I know, a place where you can sip espresso or café-au-lait (coarse cocoa grains in the foam) and tear and chew the golden apostrophes of fresh croissants lugged in on trays from the patisserie next door. Between bouts of table-soccer or snooker, all this is served at dainty tables with heart-shaped back-rests of white wrought iron. The espresso machine hisses all day and the balls clack their clean lovely clacks into the late evening and everything seems almost right with the world.

Twenty steps east of the pool hall, at avenue Churchill, I came upon *La Californie*'s front door, set at forty-five degrees to the intersection and opaque with posters announcing both Friday jazz sessions and an *écran géant* for Canadiens' games. It faced, on the other three corners, a *dépanneur* run by an extended family of

13

leather-jacketed Tamils; an Italian restaurant recently closed and now being renovated into a *créperie*; and a *fruiterie* owned by a middle-aged Québecoise and her Haitian-Canadian husband. Two Russian brothers— who, given their beginner's English and French and the cut of their felt coats, had surely just hopped off a jet refuelling in Gander—took turns stocking the fruit and vegetable bins and stepping outside for a smoke.

But about *La Californie*. One of its many appeals was the neon script in the bar's window announcing forty varieties of beer. It was no more than a hundred metres from my kitchen. So I started slipping in from time to time, most often around five when the flat's silences could no longer be exorcised by my work in the scriptorium, or by Bach alternating with the Tragically Hip, or by pots of tea and tumblers of neat Scotch. Each day, by supper time, emptiness became like an extra tenant haunting the flat, someone glimpsed in rooms you knew were uninhabited. By then I would be walking through the afternoon darkness, the whole neighbourhood quickening as the light seeped away. Commuters let down from the city buses, and on their way to pick up bagels or baguettes or Kraft Dinner for their suppers, were illuminated beneath the delicate necks of the streetlights. By now I had stopped taking odd jobs from any of the architectural and engineering firms in town. Or did I mention this in an earlier note, Liza? I grow forgetful in my preoccupation. Even my drafting table went untouched on its spindly legs, holding up a few fading blueprints of doorways and window openings for a co-op housing project from my final, interrupted assignment. My research in the scriptorium was taking all my energy, and my savings seemed sufficient for the time required to complete my investigations.

Dear Liza, dear Liza—there's a hole in my mind and the straw is too long, the knife is too dull, the stone is too dry. What on earth have I been trying to do in these ceaseless internal talks sent your way? And in those spasmodic letters sent to someone I love but who, on my worst days, I worry might not return. My thoughts feel as though they've been reduced to the lowest common denominator: but it is the senses that grieve most. I want nothing but to see, touch, hear, smell, taste—may I tuck those unruly strands behind your ear? No doubt we are both attempting to redirect the past a little, hoping to nudge it into line, thereby leaving a more perceptible path where motivations are plain and simple and we have just selected what to do next. Or is this wishful thinking?

So I find myself telling you about the bar, about Daniel. The incident at *La Californie* last week refuses to leave me, so, for reasons it is no doubt far too late to examine, I find myself telling you Daniel's story during my quiet hours. His story has a persistent form. I was forced to listen. In a way, *La Californie* and my work on Chartres, those two so very different stories, can provide an explanation of what happened between us.

The Plateau district itself became somehow a cause of the effect Daniel had on me. Why, I don't know. Perhaps because it was a part of a place where you had once lived. I'm not pretending that somewhere else I would have "gotten better," been tougher, let Daniel's story roll off me. But if I inhale *this* air every two seconds, breathe dust from spring sidewalks after the snow has been spirited away, take in the scent of the faint vinegar of butcher shops with blind sacks of goats hanging head-down in their windows, or smell the delicate odours of fluted yellow cucumber flowers or of green tomatoes from tiny front gardens on Esplanade, or of the bagels and dill and fetta, the garlic and thyme and *garam masala* from kitchens; if my eyes accept these faces and balconies and bricks and particular litter, accept tallis and saris and shalwar kameez, the black uniforms of Hassidic men and UQAM students and Greek widows; if my ears are open to the sounds of so many different voices, or hear children slapping at street hockey and prancing at aki, swatting shuttlecocks over the fences between paved yards, or I listen to the Portuguese men arguing football in their clubs, to the accordion of the blind man playing for coins on Fairmount, to the titters and secrets and echoes floating through the specific girders of the district's hard-to-pin-down but impossible-to-ignore structure—then how can I doubt that you'll return?

Maybe it was the same for Daniel. If he didn't have this neighbourhood to come to, he might have drunk himself toward freedom and forgiveness at home, slumped in front of the TV, instead of coming to *La Californie*. Instead, here, he took his table farthest from the door each evening a few minutes after five—having finished work, I assumed—and asked Roger or Céline for a beer.

I first noticed him in late September, on my third or fourth visit. I peered through the inner doors and assured myself the bar was quiet. That evening he came in through the side door from the *terrasse extérieur*— three tables with chairs tucked along the side street—as it grew too chilly for drinking beer outside. The leaves

16

were already turning on the mountain. Earlier that day, according to my research log, I had been reading Baltrusartis's *L'Image du monde céleste du IXe au XIIe siècle*, in Jeanne-Mance park. It's a rather celestial part of the world when tinged by fall sunlight. The colours were more fiery near the summit, varieties of umber and scarlet and lemon against a deeper blue than summer offers; the lower slopes were still muted, and near me in the park some of the oaks and other hardwoods were unturned. Strangely, the carnival of colour seemed to flatten the contours of Mount Royal. Sometimes our eyes deceive us in the simultaneous presence of texture and shape. The laws of perspective are there to be broken.

I didn't talk to Daniel O'Brien that first day, though I found myself watching him for a time. He would turn out to be a confusing man to encounter. My immediate impression was that he craved friendship, but his own demeanour betrayed the desire; one of fate's crueler tricks. About five-ten, and slender, he moved in an agitated manner, pausing, checking his watch without noticing the time, unfolding a newspaper without seeing the print, adjusting a collar that was already straight, ritually smoothing his short beard from cheek toward chin with one closing hand, then tugging fitfully with thumb and forefinger. His hair was a bit long for the era. His face was narrow. Beneath the beard his chin was weak.

Above the bar were mounted chalked slates with the menu and specials carefully printed by hand and Daniel studied them, as if to reassure an imagined audience that he was thinking about having a meal. So far as I know he never ordered any of the cheesecakes and quiches, croissants, salads, or pastas of the day. He wore dress pants—black—and dress shirt—white—with no tie, slinging his suit coat over the next stool. The tie was tucked in his jacket, dangling from an inside pocket.

Roger was in back, so Daniel leaned toward the single waitress, who was wiping a nearby table.

—*Une autre?* Pointing at his glass.

—Export, she confirmed without asking him. She wore black shoes, black tights, and an oversized black T-shirt. I had decided, wrongly it would turn out, that she was permanently surly.

—*Et j'viens de boire quoi?* Francophone, I thought.

—Molson Export, she answered.

—Keep them guessing, he added, apparently to himself.

No, anglophone, I concluded, unable to detect an accent.

—*Bien, je prens un Miller.*

The room was otherwise empty. The bar had a hardwood floor, well varnished, and a dozen wooden tables. Behind the bar there was one wall of exposed red brick. Given the decor, the name was out of synch. Had a new owner changed the name but not the interior design, or vice versa? The video screen was in the front, near the windows facing rue Bernard, and I chose a table there, setting down the bound library copy of *Gazette des Beaux Arts*, Volume 20, 1938, and pulled a *Globe and Mail* from my satchel. For a half hour, as twilight approached, I watched the people walking past, the slats of the blind lending them an insubstantial air. I sipped a café-au-lait. I do remember Daniel draining a glass once, maybe twice, when I happened to look around, and I recall noticing that his tilted chin revealed a badly scarred neck that his beard only partially hid. He had clearly been in a fire, years ago.

I turned back to Baltrusaitis, alert for clues in his pages to the fate of Chartres—I sought references, from all angles. I ordered another coffee, and stayed a while longer. A long time in fact. Nothing awaited me anywhere.

As she stood by my table with the coffee, Céline interrupted her languorous chill by jerking her head to one side as if about to look back over her shoulder toward Daniel, but then thought better of it. She gathered my first bowl and saucer. A few minutes later I saw her hurry from the back room and speak with unexpected animation to Daniel, one hand resting on his forearm. I couldn't extract her words from those of the TV announcers—someone turned the Expos on the big screen next to me in the corner, too close for comfort. From where I sat the jade field and glittering uniforms looked like computer simulations. Daniel stood up, put on his jacket as if it were ancient and fragile, and walked past me to the door. Roger leaned out over his bar and craned his neck to read the clock that hung directly above him. Outside, faces swam into the bright lights along *La Californie's* facade and sank away without a trace. I didn't actually meet Daniel until a week or so later, the day after they found the baby on the mountain.

2

Liza, perhaps your interest in my work on the history of the school at Chartres was only kindness all along. I once assumed people were either honest or deceitful about such things, but it's hardly so simple is it? Not so black and white, since, as you suggested, we can to some extent choose what we are—enforce a will, trick ourselves into evolving. Within limits, you would add. Nurture, nature, et cetera. But once you showed me this, I was always at least convinced that if your interest in Chartres, in my Chartres, was a role, it was one you could play without difficulty, maybe even with pleasure.

The days go by like this. Last night I went to sit in the living room, on my futon between the pseudo-Ionian pillars, and put on Bach's *Passion According to Saint John*. I hoped to be lulled enough to try sleeping. I have decided I prefer the St. John to the more famous *Passion According to St. Matthew*. Certainly there's no one to talk to about such things anymore. Our simple breakfast table easefullness together was an immeasurable blessing.

I was feeling irritated by commentators who deem the *Passion*'s symmetrical architecture, its dense polyphony, "archaic". Primitive, antiquated, no longer in normal use. During the first chorale, I grew restless, far from soothed. *O grosse Lieb, o Lieb.* I stood up with a cup of lukewarm tea in one hand, listening to the brief recitative until the second chorale began, *Dein Will gesheh, Herr Gott.* I gave up and headed back along the hallway to my study, where the drawers of file cards awaited me, muttering *O Lieb, Dein Will?* From the back alley the whine and thump of a garbage truck slowly receded. You will be thinking that my preference has nothing to do with Bach's polyphony and has everything to do with John's station as the evangelist of light, as muse of the Pseudo-Dionysius and thus, obliquely, as patron of the School at Chartres. You will think my preference a response to content. But can't we take Bach's musical architecture seriously? He wasn't a dabbler. Can his structures have had nothing to do with the vision he found in John's gospel? A merging of form and content?

The classic Montreal flat is deep and narrow, receding with surprising persistence. A long corridor gives off onto a front bedroom and living room, a second bedroom, then dining area. Behind this is another, shorter hallway, with a door to the bathroom, then at last the kitchen— but not *finally*, as behind this there is one more room (nursery? laundry? storage?) before an ultimate rear exit disappears into the back shed and a tight spiral fire-escape to the *ruelle*. It is in this unanticipated intimate chamber, tucked amid the scents and gurglings and murmurs of gas pipes and plumbing fixtures, that I assemble my writings on Chartres, in the company of telephone, plants, a washing machine of horrid green enamel, and a dusty set of barbells. The hardwood here is desiccated and warping.

The material I have assembled is still growing, though now more slowly until I can fund another trip to France. In the meantime I make do as best I can with the libraries here, and with weekend dowsings at the University of Toronto, particularly in the stacks of the Pontifical Institute of Medieval Studies, where I sneeze dust off the flaking leather bindings. Liza, in my thoughts I often give you a tour of my current collection. I show you the tiny drawers, now over forty of them, each containing about three hundred four-by-six file cards covered by my scrawlings. There are four cabinets, the first two reserved for the photographs, over two thousand, arrayed in labelled file folders—*Celestory, East; Ambulatory: Sculptural Detail; Narthex; South Porch; Jesse Window; Royal Portal Statuary, First Ring*. Various folders fan out on the scarred desk, slips of paper drift across an adjoining table. To find order requires a brave wade through chaos, I suppose. Or *vice versa?* I ask you such questions. I have to make up your answers.

Laden bookshelves cover two walls from floor to ceiling, charts and chronologies paper another. My wooden armchair rests on its casters in the centre of the storm. Since I have no intention of beginning to type until the work is much more advanced, all the notations are still hand written, so that when things go badly the cramped quarters look like a scriptorium after a violent argument amongst the monks. I've lost track of the number of individual items my catalogues contain, but increasingly there isn't much space left for the reputed author. As I may have mentioned before, some friends are beginning to doubt my sanity. Even our old friends David and Claire don't come by much anymore.

The scale of the project disturbs them even more than it does me. It seems to them clear evidence of an unwillingness to live in my own century, to search out the currents and momentum of our culture. They see evidence of a lack of balance. David even accused me of having an almost totalitarian mentality, of refusing to accept the individual's field of vision—one person's scope of labour—as the basis of *what can be done*.

But in searching for the boundaries of what needed to be covered to make both the context and the story of the school complete, I had trouble finding a place to start and a place to end. Edges, like horizons, have a way of tricking us, of shifting in space. Should I invent them? Wouldn't that be far more arrogant? The only edge life appears to have is death. This winter without you, Liza, I have seen what needs to be done by one individual to repair one human gulf, and I have seen that it is a vast task. So I expanded my scope. A medievalist's nostalgia, perhaps, for the unifying temperament, the world in a grain of sand. Isn't there a paradox at the heart of this enterprise? David's criticism surely doesn't take into account *my* particular desire to explain, without artificial boundaries, what Chartres is, what it does, *how it feels*. Chartres as my field of vision as much as the sum of what it embodies. People like to remind me that I was trained—and incompletely at that—as an architect, not an historian. Who would take my work seriously? But I can write in the absence of readers. Even if there is no one listening I can invent what is needed.

So call me crazy. Someone, at some point, must do justice to Chartres. Egotism, sure. I realize the literature on Notre Dame de Chartres is considerable, since I've personally ploughed through much of it, but it is tentative, fragmentary. Chartres is at once a Christian house of worship, a temple of Our Lady and storehouse of her relics—the building can be thought of as a jewelled reliquary on a grand scale, an extended treatise of theology, a triumphant experiment in mathematics

23

and engineering, the assertion of a *mystical architecture*, as well as a secular study of the contemporary culture, the current political scene. Liza, it is a system of thought as elaborate as Kant's *Critique of Pure Reason*, and also, in the commentary hidden in the thus far anonymous faces of its statuary, a work of the medieval synthesizing imagination as intricate as Dante's.

Eventually I hope to explain all of its formulae, speak the mute chronicles of its two hundred windows, lay bare its mathematical and geometrical conundrum, identify the vulgar models of all its saints and gargoyles, explicate its proportions, paraphrase its masonry.

So: I am beginning by researching biographies of the members of the great Neoplatonic Cathedral School of Chartres, starting with those bishops who served a full hundred years before the terrible conflagration during the night of July 10th, 1194. This, like the Fortunate Fall, ruined all but the crypt and towers of Saint Fulbert's Romanesque edifice (itself at least the fourth church on the site, each in their turn engulfed phoenix-like in fire) and in turn led to the decision to rebuild. The bishops include: Guilbert of Nugent, who, although skeptical about the cults of relics, looked reverently on the Sacred Tunic that survived the flames; Fulbert, originator of the humanist curriculum, and our era's favourite scapegoat; Geoffrey of Lèves, son of the ancient house of Beauce, who was a statesman, papal legate, intimate of Louis VI and St. Bernard and who presided as Bishop during the School's most fertile epoch when its influence extended from Scotland to Jerusalem; Allen of Lille; the great Englishman John of Salisbury, author of *Policratus*, the first political treatise of note since Augustine's *City of*

God; and Gosselin of Musy, associated with the west facade of the mid-twelfth century. Others. There are many others. We must know the lives that shaped the minds that formed the thoughts of the Master himself, whose conceptions created a fertilizing context (rather than a set of instructions) for the craftsmen.

There are so many—some great names, as I say, while others remain almost invisible through the haze of centuries.

Last night I almost finished the first draft on my present subject, a too-little-remembered man, Peter, Abbot of Celle, Bishop of Chartres in the decade before the fire, successor of John of Salisbury. He is a fascinating figure. I've gathered most of the information about him that has survived—who knows what other documents might have existed and further illuminated the twelfth century renaissance but regrettably have been lost in the parade of floods and wars and fires of seven hundred years. Perhaps the Germans cindered a few more when they torched the libraries of Belgium in 1914. Fisquet and Leclerc were helpful (remember when you found me Leclerc, as unexpected as coconut palms in the Laurentians, on a window ledge of fifty-cent paperbacks outside a second hand shop in Toronto?).

But I'm excited about Peter, Abbot of Celle. Peter's web of aristocratic connections has led to clues here and there. I found what I think was new information detailing the remarkable number of violent deaths among his siblings and aunts and uncles and cousins, notable even given the relentless butchery of those decades. But what is significant is the extent to which he attempted to communicate his religious experience in architecture. He was a mystic of stone and glass, a pietist of engineering. Churches were not symbols then: they were imitation, mimesis. I am still ploughing through a dry history—written in terrible Latin—of the ecclesiastical foundations at Celle, hoping Peter will put in an appearance.

Hesitating, procrastinating, I have resolved to begin plundering my notes toward assembling the life of Cardinal Melior of Pisa—Papal legate, renowned canonist, teacher, diplomat and administrator—*and*, it appears, present the night the fire danced up through the town to consume the cathedral. Most important, Melior was also the inspiration and turning point, the pivot calling the despairing townspeople into assembly, first casting them into even deeper gloom with the fiery eloquence with which he berated their lack of faith, then standing aside in a paused, breath-strangled moment to give way to a solemn procession of robed and mitred bishops, followed by the Chapter, bearing the miraculously preserved Sacred Tunic, discovered unharmed in the ninth century crypt. A murmur of confoundment, a shush of disbelief, a clamour of piety inseparable from terror sparked through the slowly comprehending crowd, and the Cardinal, timing being everything, harangued them with the now unanswerable truth that far from abandoning them in the night, the Virgin and Mother of God, the Lady of Chartres, had conceded the old and inadequate church to the flames only to clear the space—both physically and conceptually—for a basilica worthy of her, a womb of miracles, a temple without equal in Christendom. Was this an act of inspirational leadership and faith, or simply playing the hand he had been dealt? So it all began, the legend and lure of Chartres—and began even for us, Liza, the beginning of our folly. Not our catastrophe. Because we can still be reunited.

3

The day before I first got to know Daniel, there was a story in the papers about a baby, found dead in her carriage on the mountain. She was found at sunrise on the summit of Mount Royal by a passing jogger who had decided—on a whim, he told the police and then reporters, he could not remember having a reason—to stray from his regular route and swing down across the plaza that stretches in front of the wood and fieldstone pavilion. Normally he headed straight toward Beaver Pond and the exit onto Côte-des-Neiges near his home. The divergence troubled the investigating sergeant, who had been trained to believe coincidence did not exist.

This belvedere faces south over the green copper roofs of McGill University to the downtown and the St. Lawrence river beyond, which at six a.m. of an unseasonably warm October morning was a dark band through the blue quiet of the city, with three necklaces of faint light—the bridges to the south shore—flung across it. Later, on the fair day that followed, the extinct volcano of Mount St-Hilaire fifty miles southeast would be a clearly visible interruption of the plain, and the low mountains of the Townships and upstate New York would blur along the horizon. In spite of the encircling metropolis, it was quiet, excellently quiet.

A sidewalk follows the semi-circular waist-high balustrade of the lookout, and it was there that the jogger found her, lying peacefully on her back at the foot of one of the twenty-five cents-per-view telescopes. We read the details in *La Presse* the next evening in *La*

Californie. Daniel interrupted some convoluted story he was telling, half to a neighbouring table and half to himself, to read the article over Roger's shoulder. Holy fuck, he swore, and, glancing at his half-empty Fosters, asked Roger for a Lowenbrau.

An abandoned baby. An uncommon but far from unheard of event in a city of three million. Someone had lived with her just long enough to decipher the particular plot of *her* fussy periods, to learn her particular scent and keep it as a memory; to learn by heart the crinkles in her accidental expressions; to master the art of tending to midnight feedings without waking up; to realize she had been unique since before birth and to be struck with the uncanny sensation that there was another person, a familiar, living in the house. Long enough for the child's eyes to focus.

But common enough. The demographers could give the data. There is no denying it was something else that made her front-page news. I wanted to tell you about her, Liza, wished you were somewhere near. Her significance lay in the details. She was the unintended victim: the victim of acts freely committed but directed toward other ends; victim not of another's sin even, not so exact, but of a lack of omniscience, an absence of God, if you will, of an inability to plan for all possible outcomes. So we would eventually learn.

After reading the report, I thought my way through it. The jogger would have stopped abruptly and looked about, oddly panicked, as if caught out. There had to be some rational explanation. A film crew perhaps, in spite of the hour. Finally, feeling a sudden courage and release, he bent down and touched the baby's cheek. Taking two quick steps to one side, he groped at the railing of the lookout for support. The cement was as cold as her face.

The details came out later. You'll understand then why he half expected cameras, sound techs, their comforting disbelief. She was wearing a baptismal gown. Someone tried to make her a model for their own cold, dislocated universe, a symbol of their own emptiness. A baby, Liza.

The jogger was a well-known executive—at least, the media implied we should have heard of him—who lived in a stone mansion just down the hill. He told the police (who tried to prevent him from talking with reporters, but there were leaks anyway, so he ended up calling a press conference)—that the initial vision was so strange, or at least that this commonplace sight was so unexpected in this setting, that he stood in a suspended state for a period of time he was unable to estimate. After his first touch, he approached again. He moved forward, trying to be silent. Surprisingly, he said in his statement, he did not hesitate when he turned back to the baby carriage: he picked her up immediately. The coroner's inquiry worried about this action at some length.

The city spread cinematically below him like a superb offering, very blue, blue under blue water. There was a line of solder glowing on the horizon.

Poor man. Honest enough to want to tell the detectives his first unanticipated and even (to him) revelatory thoughts, he was later obliged to read them in four local dailies in two languages.

—First thing I thought is that she wasn't real, she wasn't anything but a bit of weight, all dressed up.

—Yes sir. And do you remember anything else?

—Only one other thing. I remember saying to myself—wondering now at his own bantering words—well, she's not ticking.

4

—*Puis-je?*

Startled, I looked up. I had been gazing into rue Bernard, carefully inspecting approaching faces until they drew close enough to be confirmed as unfamiliar. Early October. Heavy sweaters, autumn jackets.

Daniel stood beside my chair, his eyes glassy. He gestured with a full glass of beer at the empty seat across from me, sloshing the first half-inch across the tabletop.

—*Merde*, he said mildly, and sat down.

I glanced around. Without my noticing, *La Californie* had filled. I had lost track of time. Or, if I might blame the Furies, time had temporarily lost track of me.

He was dressed as before: a white-collar job, but nothing too formal. And the tie off.

—*Fait froid, non?*

Perhaps the chill from the *terrasse*, which the management, in deference to the stubbornness of the city's café patrons, would not pack up until the snow came to stay, had forced him inside.

—*Bien sûr.*

—Course. What's October in Montreal without a bloody blizzard? he ruminated to his glass, switching into English.

I looked sharply back out the window, using the streetlight—where any flakes would flare clearly into view—to confirm that it certainly was *not* snowing. I managed a noncommittal nod.

His brown hair was thinning, though he was likely only in his thirties. In an otherwise handsome face his teeth were yellowed and gapped, and a bit too small for his mouth. He gazed at me for a moment as if at a closed door; then his eyes floated past my head to the big screen. He shrugged.

Céline veered past with an impressive tray of gold-filled glasses. When she hurried by us again on the way back, Daniel stopped her.

—*Aurais-tu un Black Label?*

—*Mais*, Daniel. She looked harried: She'd had little peace tonight to do her usual studying behind the bar. She indicated his almost full glass.

He grinned, or grimaced, and emptied it with startling speed.

—*Alors?*

She sighed and headed for the counter, collecting more orders along the way.

—What's the difference, he said, talking perhaps to me, perhaps to himself, between the Nuremberg defense and the House of Commons?

I looked behind me. On the screen, a parliamentarian was gesticulating.

It was difficult to begin to think that one through.

—Daniel, he said, Daniel O'Brien.

—Nice to meet you, I said. John. We shook hands across the table.

He looked at me quizzically, then, abruptly, with a dull languor. His expressions changed utterly and instantly, like manically edited TV.

—Was your question meant for me? I asked, trying to sound pleasant.

Unexpectedly he leaned forward with an expression of unalloyed delight.

33

—Yeah, sure, why not you? I'm tired of rhetorical questions, aren't you? Damn, there's another one. The curse of our century. Even if you're aware of them, you can't escape. Mind you, that's another shibboleth of the dead century: self awareness shall save you. As long as you know what's wrong with your marriage you can fix it in eight easy steps. Started with Freud and ended with *Reader's Digest.* Anyway, everybody asks rhetorical questions because questions actually implying answers are politically incorrect. Answers are nasty. Still, they're my greatest failing. Questions, I mean. Well, not my greatest. I could hardly know my *greatest* failing, could I? I'd be blind to it. You see the problem.

I couldn't extinguish the smile from my face, Liza. A phrase or two of his even reminded me of you. I seemed, inadvertently, to have struck a chord in him, satisfied some symmetry.

—Mirrors on facing walls, sure, I said. They'll ruin the best mind. Proof of infinity though.

—Tell me about it.

—But: I don't follow. How *is* Question Period like a Nazi at Nuremberg?

Céline delivered the beer. She pulled the cuff back from Daniel's watch and showed it to him. He nodded, and swallowed half of the pint.

—My wife teaches. Isabelle. Psych. At Concordia. Has a class at 8:30, has to leave the house at dawn. So we turn in early. None of your business, right? But here you are, sitting at my table. Anyway, the last train out to Pointe-Claire leaves Gare Centrale at 9:05 weekday evenings. If I'm not out the door—he examined his watch again—two minutes ago, the odds are slender,

34

and it's a damned expensive cab ride. In other words, love is not always a happy thing.

He stood, opened his wallet, wavered slightly, put a twenty down, and seemed to contemplate it.

—Minister of the Environment. Nothing personal. It's just parli-parliament. Deputized decision making. They decide. Leaves us free as birds. It's better than the forgiveness of sins; means we don't have to act in the first place.

—Well that's a . . . an extreme comparison.

He drained his glass and stood it upside down beside my empty tumbler. He fished in his trouser pockets for a moment as if looking for keys, or matches, but didn't seem to find anything.

—Thank you. I'll compliment that as a take.

And so Daniel and I met, Liza. Unexpectedly. An encounter of little consequence. Hardly worth mentioning.

5

Looking back, I can't find the beginning—where did your hollow-eyed request for some time apart begin? For each defining moment I can now, in retrospect, find the flaw, the stupid words, the lack of attention, the underlying currents. But for each of those, turning them over in my too-quiet flat, I can find an earlier cause. A turning point leading to each turning point.

Pick one. Pick the sun. Look, Liza, my love. Outside the sun was still dazzling in a clear sky, and the grain fields of the Ile-de-France showed gold, as if the earth's globe were illuminated from within. It was still July, after all, a whole year gone by. But inside Chartres the stones were cool and the air was like the stones. That exterior blaze of light, from where we stood in the north transept, was a chalking of pink and blue against the coal-coloured elevation of the upper celestory. I said to you, or at least I think I remember saying to you, as we stood before the iron-bound wood of the ancient door to the north tower—the last thing I said before we entered that narrow, harrowing space and began our ascent was—

—Liza, I think I've figured out (figured out again, I guess I should say) what annoys me and enchants me about this place. Chartres was given ornamentation where no one would ever see it. I've gone to extreme lengths. So have others, no doubt. You can wriggle your way out onto a ledge reachable by clambering across a balustrade from the lookout platform of this tower, a flying buttress scything the clouds in half over your head, until you can see under the little stone canopy of the miniature classical temples which cap each buttress—two Ionic columns with pediments—and there, carefully executed a mere eight hundred years ago, is a carved sheaf of barley, intricately chiselled in stone, grain by grain. There are gargoyles visible only from aircraft, unphotographed until the advent of telephoto lenses. You know what that reminds me of?

—Your father.

—Oh sure, Dad. He varnished the outside bottoms of dresser drawers, just because he liked things done right. Fair enough. But why do them right? Okay. Father. But it reminds me of the human conscience. It reminds me of confession. Better still, it reminds me of a conscience in the absence of confession, nursing guilt over something no one else need ever know about. Whispering to the grill cloth after the priest has left. Or trying to keep your thoughts pure. People still do such things. We used to know why. God. Now we still do them but don't know why. Why bother? Faith? Morality? That's one explanation. But were they all believers? As we mean it? I'm not so sure. That's one thing that's so bewildering.

So we stepped inside the door, to the stairs, not knowing any better, to go up and gaze over the cathedral's copper roofs and the thicket of the town clustered at its base and at the white lines of the country roads running across the shining plain, stretching north toward Paris. We looked for the detailing on the chins of weather worn gargoyles invisible from the ground, at the curl of their tongues, the fury and mockery in their eyes, spiralling up around a central column of stone via the twining cord of the stairs. Half way up you said John, John? I couldn't respond. You started to cry.

A few days afterward, the train slid smoothly out of a dream into the low sunshine, the woman in the seat next to me pulling off her gloves one fingertip at a time, as we rode transfixed and separate through the evening into the city.

6

It grows cool abruptly in the back well between apartments when the sun drops. I sit with water boiling for more tea as the kitchen dims. The Greek widow is out there, taking her time at the clothesline. I think: with her son and his wife noisily home from work, assorted arguments volleying off the walls, she can come onto the balcony alone and linger, calming her nerves. The swinging clothes swim slowly into her basket; the pegs click rhythmically into a bucket at her feet.

My work on Cardinal Melior crawls in fits and starts. Having completed his reform of the diocese's administration, he now approaches the great fire that lies unseen in his path, just as the town seems to wait, in my mind, for its unknown future. It is harder and harder to push the story forward. Each step is taken from a small pool of light into surrounding darkness. A vacuum seems to surround the event itself, a barrier of silence. It is a sort of absolute value, that moment of ignition; and absolute values, the scientists remind us, can be approached but never attained.

While the biographies of the members of the great school take up most of my time, Liza, my thoughts wander more and more to the approaching fire that would lay waste the old cathedral and make way for the masterpiece. From a great distance, from a crowd of vague faces and hard-to-pin-down lives, the figure of Cardinal Melior becomes increasingly vivid.

A hundred miles from Chartres and three decades

39

after the event, Guillaume le Breton would interpret the fire that destroyed the centre of the Virgin's cult in France as a fortunate fall, a beneficent disaster. "At this time," he penned in gnarled Latin verse, "the Virgin and Mother of God, who is called and indeed shown to be the Lady of Chartres, wanted the sanctuary that is so especially hers to be more worthy of her. She therefore permitted the old and inadequate Church to become the victim of the flames, thus making room for the present basilica, which has no equal throughout the entire world." No architect could desire a more illustrious patron than the Virgin—and clearly the Queen of Heaven blessed the newest style: out with Romanesque, in with Gothic.

I may be going to Toronto next week. I need to read the obituary of the Cardinal of Champagne (he wrote it himself!), who had begun the administrative reforms of the Chapter at Chartres that his successor Renaud—with Melior's guiding hand—brought to fruition. These reforms were crucial, and crucially timed. To produce an architectural masterpiece, as the twelfth century closed, required the right instruments in place. Whatever inspiration kept the Ile-de-France humming with the construction of gigantic stone edifices, it could not continue to flow indefinitely. I've never thought it a coincidence that at the height of the fervour, Melior arrived from northern Italy into the heart of the French countryside, bringing with him faint foreshadowings of the Renaissance. Forty years later the creative passion was already starting to ebb. By the mid-thirteenth century the vital spirit had returned to Italy, drawn along trade routes opened by the last Crusaders and spurred by the heady mix of

Byzantine, Arab, Latin, and Oriental money, tongues, spices, ideas.

*

In the immediate aftermath of the fire, Cardinal Melior convinced the prelates to consecrate at least half of all their revenues for a *decade* to the reconstruction of the temple of the Virgin. This in part explains the astonishing speed with which the new cathedral was constructed and the unparalleled coherence of its architecture. You understand now, Liza, why I focus on Melior, and why I feel compelled to trace all the paths that lead to him. And, he was there, Liza, on the night of the fire.

The Cardinal left Tuscany's hill towns at the behest of Pope Celestine III, probably in 1192, to serve as papal legate in France. I've been able to trace parts of his six-month-long odyssey. In the twelfth century it was both a dangerous and monotonous journey, even for Rome's envoy—in some places *especially* for Rome's envoy. Bandits and mountain passes aside, most of southern France was under the sway of the Albigensians, and even if the bloody repressions were still a decade in the future, papal legates were not exactly popular in the strongholds of Manicheaism. And Melior held no truck for their conviction that all matter was evil. Chartres is, among other things, a hymn to the possibilities of *stuff*.

Melior met with the Bishop of Turin in September, and was in Vélzelay by early November, no doubt to see the relics of Mary Magdelene. He was definitely in Paris sometime in early 1193, though it's probably untrue that he briefly held a chair at the university there. Sometime in that year he began work with Cardinal Mouçon on the reorganization of the diocesan finances. Melior's comings and goings through early 1194 cannot be pinned down, but one thing is certain: In June he was in Chartres, lodged at the Chapter House, sleeping, eating, praying, studying, within sight and earshot of the cathedral. As I imagine Melior moving through his day, I often repeat out loud what I write, as if reading to you.

Living back in Italy, Cardinal Melior of Pisa was pleased with Guillaume's poem; was delighted that his beliefs and vision had become conventional wisdom. But all of that lay in the future as Melior's little entourage approached the city gate in April 1194. After a brief chat and a swap of souvenir ducats for francs with the city warden—a doddering but still upright old fellow named Chaton, whom Bishop Renaud had sent out to await his arrival—Melior's party climbed the steep slope through a nasty end-of-season sleet that iced the cobblestones so that the horses slipped; up toward the cathedral and the impressive chapter house and bishopric palace that loomed against a sky the colour of cold solder. A messenger boy scrambled on ahead, his tattered leather jerkin flapping as he ran to warn the Bishop of his illustrious guest's approach. From under his drawn hood, Melior caught glimpses of the streets: Tucked under the canvas, stretched over a butcher's stall, behind a curtain of water, a neat row of goats' heads lay on a bench. Further on he saw the small smudgepot fires and great bubbling vessels of the dyers, and the dyers themselves, their hands blue.

Melior rather dreaded the meeting with Renaud,

and was doubtless saying so to Auxerre, who rode beside him. He had learned with pleasure that Auxerre's discretion was absolute; silence was his metier. Nothing but ill: that was all Melior had heard of Renaud, who by all accounts was as convinced as half his prebends that because Melior was a legendary administrator—that is, money generator, good enough to have drawn an assignment in the Vatican—he was *really* here at Louis' request to put the diocese books in order and to show them modern means of revenue enhancement to reflect the new economic order. But there was no way around it: Melior would have to put up with Renaud if he wanted to pass a few months praying, listening, and thinking at the School and before the holy chemise.

Melior was a small man, whose cautious but always elegant speech and manners and thick, peppered beard made everyone remember him as taller. All of his actions, from walking to talking to the celebration of mass, were at once stately and understated, or so wrote William of Newbridge, who had met him in Paris. As they rode side by side, he had to look up at Auxerre, who, at over six feet, was a giant of a man. Auxerre's tangled grey hair lay on his shoulders. His unshaven face might have been handsome were it not for a badly mangled nose with a bridge as broad as a man's thumb that resembled, forty years after being mauled by a wild dog, a dried and lumpy potato. But his patience and energy, and a measuredness in all actions, more than compensated for an uncivil mien.

William of Auxerre, five years younger than Melior's fifty, had now accompanied the Cardinal for over a year. The French court had sent him to meet Melior in the south, in order to accompany him to Paris. And perhaps to keep an eye on him. The court may have presumed he would thus arrive already imbued with the Ile-de-France perspective on the issues of the day. To a certain extent this took place: Melior arrived knowing what Louis *wanted* him to think. Much more profoundly, he was daily, if subtly, exposed to the rigor and severe simplicity of a true follower of Bernard. Although philosophically the big Cistercian was hardly an easy fit for Melior (Auxerre had spent three years at Clairvaux itself, under the master), he had gradually come to find Auxerre's blend of fierce piety and sturdy practicality in all matters—from picking the best inn to ham-smoking techniques to Latin gerunds—absolutely indispensable. Melior had talked the French king into loaning him Auxerre as a sort of ecclesiastical aide-de-camp. How he had ever gotten along *without* Auxerre all these years, he had no idea.

In fact, Melior *did* fully intend to resuscitate the lamentable finances of poor Renaud—he was, after all, here at the direction of the Holy Father, who had been unable to avoid noticing that the economic boom sweeping northern France for a generation under the stability of the Capets and the steady growth in agriculture and trade had somehow failed to touch the key diocese of Chartres. Blessed with not only the most venerable school in Christiandom (and one now successfully feeling its way along the tightrope between mysticism and the new scholasticism, between poles of love and reason, contemplation and logic, between Bernard and Abelard) but also with a fine old cathedral housing a major relic and drawing thousands of pilgrims every

44

year long before the pilgrimage vogue—well, Chartres was too important for Celestine to allow it to remain incompetently administered. So Melior would have to look at the books. Supremely confident of his genius for administration (if a bit concerned that administrative abilities *alone* had brought him to within an eyelash of the papacy), he intended to spend most of his time at two far worthier tasks: praying before the sacred tunic of Our Lady in the hope of taking on some trace of its holiness; and reading, talking, preaching, debating, listening, sparring with the masters of the School at Chartres.

—Imagine, Auxerre. The lineage of this place.

The rain was spattering directly in their faces. They had to pull the horses hard to the right to avoid two ox carts rattling downhill at unnerving speed. Urchins craned their necks from the back of one as it passed. Even if Melior refused to don miter and chasuble in this weather for the sake of a dramatic entrance, the rich cloaks and fine horses of the little procession alerted the townspeople that these were visitors of consequence. Although the driver of the lead cart, Melior couldn't help noticing with irritation, had merely squinted at him, leaving his head firmly covered.

—Lineage, your grace? Of course, I know the chronicles. Charles the Bald himself donated the chemise, many centuries ago. It defeated the Normans— mind you, Normans are infinitely defeatable, it seems to me—when Bishop Gaucelinus displayed it at the city gate. Then, again, in the time of Louis the Sixth.

—Is there anything you don't know Auxerre? I keep hoping there's something. Smithing, perhaps? Herb lore?

Weaving? Arabic? How to compound elixirs? Anyway, you speak of the *sancta camisa*. And you are right to. But I meant the school.

—Ah. A grunt.

—In fact, if Renaud's letter did not lie, the School is housed *there*, no? That must be the palace, surely, built by Yves?

The imposing stone mass of the Episcopal seat, rising to the left of the cathedral's bulk as they approached the warren of streets crowding up against the walls of the "bishop's city," was black with age. The weather grew fouler by the minute. It felt about to snow.

—He exaggerates, my grace. I believe the master has a room in the palace, from what I've heard, but the rest of the school is in an outbuilding.

—Oh well. As I say, the lineage! Over a century ago it was already ancient. Then Fulbert (a pupil of Gerbert of Aurillac! No mean pupil of no mean master). Later Bernard of Chartres, the great teacher. Thierry. And then, as if to overflow the chalice of riches, John of Salisbury. *He* learned from Bernard—economy, grammar, precision of diction: and so, clarity of thought, and so clarity of soul. Not surprising. Clarity of soul.

Auxerre brushed water off his wild eyebrows, and tweaked his great raw beak. He was amused.

—If you'll forgive me, your grace, you sound like a boy presented with his first vellum.

—Auxerre, I'll accept the compliment. Like all youths I am impatient of imperfection. Surely that is no sin. So I've come to Chartres to cure the world—the one within me that is too much inundated by the world without. Cure it of its limits, its limitless limits.

*

As you can see, Liza, the narrative of Melior is inextricably woven into the very fabric, the very stone of Chartres.

*

Twenty years after the events of that Chartres spring, Melior gave his final confession. Even in the early thirteenth century the tradition lingered in many monasteries, powered by the insistent influence of Cluny, that no one should die alone. The transition between worlds was a collective ritual. The last confession needed the most ears. Thus Melior, who never did become a Benedictine but retired, as illness and weariness circled him, to a house of the Cluniacs in the country near Verona, gave his hoarse summation within the hearing of Guillaume of Druand. And Guillaume, in the middle years of that century, by then old himself at Audenarde with the English Black Prince ravaging the French countryside all too close by, wrote his *Soliloquiorum*, telling the story of the confession and final departure of a "great Prince of the Church and intimate of the Holy Father," who had been present at the fire of Chartres "which sent a trembling through the entire world, him seeing the very flames as the timbers dashed to the earth."

The death of a monk—even an honorary member of the order—was much like the weddings of the secular world. The deathbed was a festival. The time having come, Melior, in a white robe meant to invoke the habit of a novice, was carried by two brothers from the infirmary

47

into the capitulary, where the entire community was gathered. The abbot and monks came forward in turn to exchange the kiss of peace. Crosses and candles were placed at the head of the bed, novices posted at the cloister gate with cudgels to announce with great blows on the wooden door when the death agony had begun. Melior methodically gave away each of his possessions. In fact, a sinful number of very valuable books and robes and tapestries had somehow adhered over the years. He then begged pardon in a thin, wavering voice of all he had wronged. At last, his voice steadying somewhat, he began his confession. First, he told them that the gates of heaven stood open, but only by God's limitless grace. (The abbot nodded to two young monks also clad in white, who took up guard, as it were, on either side of the bed.) From somewhere he found the strength to speak for some time. He told them of his great lie during the climactic days at Chartres, the merciful lie required by true faith. The story done, eyes livid with fever, the monks drawn forward to hear a voice become a whisper become a hushing of air, he said: I pledge you to God. I am no more. I can defend myself against death no longer.

Moved as I am by Melior, I've been distracted by the recent events at *La Californie* that I must tell you about, Liza. My work is deflected by this no-doubt unwise . . . what? Shout in your direction. Which is taking much of my time, getting in the last word. It's what drives me out of here, heading toward California's call. I suppose my mind refuses to stop working on that perfect scene, imagined by everyone who has gone through what we've endured, the *good long talk* during which the other finally understands and forgives, where the motives are all straightforward, where the hidden agendas are open, where the revelation is taken at face value rather than as a more sophisticated form of attack. It is not a question of honesty, of good faith. We weren't lying. The fissure lies much deeper. Here I am, pretending you might listen to the long story you already know, like a therapist barred from saying, "Thank you Mr. Wilson, your hour is up." I'm binding you for the duration.

In the end, unavoidably, you'll know me. So I must believe. Why else would I go on writing to you? You will find what you consider lies, self-deceptions, perverse interpretations, selective memory, invalid emblems. But, you see, these too reveal me. I will even tell you what you were thinking, because by knowing *that* you will slip behind another of my defences, which is where I want you. Sad. Perhaps pathetic. But I still fantasize that if you know everything, you will come back.

As for the me who existed before I met you, little is needed. We had our years together; most of what I know, you learned long ago.

7

"December 8th," I would eventually confess to Daniel at *La Californie*, "I met Liza during my first year in the city. On December 8th."

I told him I had been in Montreal for over three months by then; still new enough to the city to be frustrated by the revelation that five years of Ontario high school French and bouts of undergraduate French Lit at Laurentian University could not convince any Montreal francophone over the age of six to endure a conversation with me. My stellar marks in the subject had half convinced me my Québécois blood was proving of assistance. No such luck. I consoled myself with the thought I had chosen Montreal for the sake of the McGill architecture program, not for excavating cultural roots, and because it would be close enough for my long time girlfriend Lee and me to visit back and forth (once a month, we told each other optimistically). Boarding the train for the ten hour ride, suitcase and nonchalance well in hand, I paused, not to take a last breath of pure northern air, but to tell Lee I loved her in a voice that would simultaneously reassure her and confirm the finality of this decision to have our nine months "semi-apart" while she finished her BA (absence to make the heart grow fonder, to confirm the solidity of our relationship). People claimed high school romances never last—Lee and I had proved and would continue to prove them wrong, right?

As I headed east, the train followed the flow of the Ottawa, meeting the St. Lawrence as it crossed the long bridge at Lac de Deux Montagnes—the low hills to the north already dabbed here and there with yellow—and crawled toward the hunchbacked city, St. Joseph's massive oratory visible ahead, white against the green hump of Mount Royal.

I was three months into my program, living alone in a basement flat in the student ghetto for two hundred dollars a month. I was twenty-four; the years seemed to be zipping past. While I really needed only two years of undergraduate work to qualify for an architectural degree program, I had finished my BA in Sudbury to be near Lee. An extra degree would never be wasted, I reassured myself.

Still, it was time to move on, move out. As I saw it, by the time Lee joined me later in the spring, I would know the city; we would finance ourselves somehow; we would be at home. Since my phone bills were almost as large as the rent—this separation from Lee was proving sound only in theory—I was advertising for a roommate. This was an unpleasant idea. Some people, without effort, end up with twenty close friends and many acquaintances before the first semester is over. I still had to force myself to initiate conversations, to go to parties rather than go to films by myself. I flirted with impossible notions: Lee would come in January and move in. Some complex arrangement of correspondence-and-summer-courses would allow her to finish her degree. Or a teacher's college in Montreal would be convinced to accept her as is. This was not likely.

At the time I was writing my first real essay for my Overview of the History of Architecture course—I have it still somewhere (this archival life of mine)—called

"Interior Space in Pre-Gothic France," full of strained undergraduate grandiosities, I'm sure. I may well have been working on it, Liza, on the evening we met.

I shouldn't say "the evening we met," although we often spoke of it that way. This wasn't love at first sight by any stretch. I knew you, while pretending I didn't. My mind played games between its own layers. We had fallen into the habit of sitting in adjacent chairs in the Introduction to Medieval Philosophy course I was auditing, and had ended up side by side at the scarred wooden table crowding a seminar room in the campus's old central building. But we knew little more than each other's first name, and I wasn't giving you a second thought. I couldn't have cared less; yet I felt an odd contentment when you would find an empty chair next to me. After all, I was always there first, so this wasn't my doing; I needed feel no compunction—although taking a seat midway down the less-crowded side of the room did increase the odds. But this was only a habit—classes always end up with semi-regular seating arrangements. It's the human way. Pattern. Variation. New pattern. Besides, it was pleasant to see a familiar face. So there was no intent, or so I tell myself. We spoke only occasionally. I wonder if we were both aware, somehow, that there was something to be afraid of.

The first day you loaned me a pen—I tend to mislay about one a week—and that was the first understanding between us, one that would endure: I would lose things— gloves, scarves, keys, hats, favourite books, crucial tax receipts, theatre tickets, umbrellas, fine fountain pens— and you would replace those that could be replaced on birthdays or at Christmas, and find those that could be found. My knack was considerable, a veritable magic, a sort of conjuring played backward. A document could be carefully placed in a folder until needed, when it would prove to have been downloaded into another dimension. Perhaps we both felt a little apart from the others. Most of the students were in first or second year. I had already done a BA, and I hadn't begun that until I was twenty. The opportunity to extend a summer job as a brakeman for the CN was too good to pass up after high school. I took on all combinations of shifts and overtime and on-call offered and socked away enough money to see me through the best part of my degree. So we were both twenty-four that fall. You, too, had been set back by two lost years, something you would explain later.

We sat elbow to elbow, a small electric space between us. With a fifteen-foot ceiling, the small room was shaped like a chute. Tall windows looked over the lawns toward the parentheses of the Roddick Gates and the clash of greystones and office towers on Sherbrooke. The windows suspended a hypotenuse of illuminated dust. Professor Father O'Donnell, a Dominican priest, spoke his lovely sentences on Aquinas, Duns Scotus, the Pseudo-Dionysius Areopagite, William of Ockham. His favourite was his fellow Dominican Alberto Magnus, teacher of the young Aquinas in Paris. Ironically, though, O'Donnell was a bit bemused by Aquinas's great project of proving the concurrence of reason and dogma. Reasonable dogma, you whispered? Dogs might be reasonable, but surely not Ma. Your first horrible pun in my presence. That I was delighted rather than appalled was a first step.

We liked being in that seminar room together, nodding

politely as the other arrived, jotting down a date from the other's notes, a shoulder touching for an instant as one of us pressed over to make room for another student at the crowded table. But I would always leave abruptly after class. I was, after all, in love with Lee. We didn't know a door was opening beyond ourselves. That's the simple truth of what came about.

I was brought to the party at Claire and David's by an acquaintance from Sudbury who knew Claire—Claire Howes: a cynical, self-described Marxist immersed in things European, with a paradoxically sunny disposition. I stopped at a corner dépanneur for a six-pack and walked the four blocks through the student ghetto to Ste. Famille, where Claire and David and a constantly mutating cast of housemates had rented the top two floors of a massive greystone. It was a great place, where a fluent combination of partying and intellectual banter after class combined with red wine into the small hours of the morning. Rundown rather than decayed, it had a formerly grand entryway stacked with bikes and books and rackets, a staircase with regal newel posts now bearing their twentieth coat of paint. Upstairs, a sprawling fifty-foot living room ran the length of the top floor with bedrooms and kitchen off back corners. A narrow staircase led to more bedrooms and a rooftop garden, where in summer you could barbecue, drink beer, and gaze over the ruelles and mansard roofs. The bedrooms were stocked with unmade futons and rickety shelving stuffed with well-thumbed books from second-hand shops and the occasional shiny textbook. In the kitchen were innumerable glass jars filled with spices, a score of pastas, a dozen varieties of beans and nuts, and a handful of granolas. A teetering stack of beer cartons stood in one corner. The living room was large enough to contain two or three groupings of couch and chairs, an old piano, a few guitars, assorted prints from museum exhibits, sagging shelves bearing the readings of a half dozen BAs and MAs in diverse fields, a few hundred records in plastic milk cases, arrays of cushions.

There were nine or ten people already sipping wine in the kitchen and preparing guacamole for the nachos. With a pleasant feel-free-to-say-hello expression fastened on my face, I found a glass of wine and retreated to a corner to read the titles on the nearest bookshelf. After a few minutes I saw what I was looking for—a free chair next to, but not obviously *within*, a group chatting by the far end of the room. The group included Claire, whom I'd met before. I wandered vaguely over to look out the window, and then sat down.

I'm not sure who was part of that conversation; five or six people I guess. But there you were. You wore blue jeans and a fisherman's sweater, steel grey, with your fine blonde hair—*thin*, you would say—shining against it. There were one or two small lamps lit, a couple of candles burning. From where I sat, I could study you unnoticed: a slightly round face belying your otherwise slight frame; a soft chin; a pale, somewhat long and sensual neck; slender shoulders and hips; small breasts. Your complexion was almost sallow, slightly freckled; and your eyes, pale blue. You didn't look toward me, at least not when I looked at you.

—Jesus, glad you're here John, said Claire. As was her manner, the others must have gotten the impression

I had raced over in answer to an urgent call. She also betrayed no evidence of the fact we had spoken to each other at best twice in our lives, and then only briefly. To know Claire Howes was to be an intimate. It was hard to take your eyes off her—not because she was lovely, but because of what might happen next.

—We're split down the middle, she went on. Arguing. Christ, the things we tangle about. How did it start?

—Claire, the point! someone laughed.

—The point. What do you think is the greatest force, what shapes history the most: economics or ideology?

Claire was not one for small queries. Articles on textual variants in *Troilus and Cressida* would never be her style. She turned and looked at me.

—Well, I said. I'm not sure it's always easy to tell which is which.

—Bingo! said a man from the depths of the couch, swigging wine from a mug, his face already reddened. Put that in your pipe, Claire! Of course economics is the pivotal force if everything you're studying turns out to be really, at essence, economics! There are always people in the world who will try to explain *Hamlet* on the basis of currency speculation in September 1598. She's been trying to tell us—John. Pleased to meet you. Adrian— that Nazism was the inevitable outgrowth of German hyperinflation and under-industrialization in the 20s. Nothing like a little under-industrialization to perk up a party. Inevitable, I believe that was your word? And I suppose Auschwitz was no more than the printout of a bad run of GNP figures?

—I didn't say inevitable. Your word, Adrian. I said *compounded by* for Christ's sake. I'm not a Heideggerian or anything. Inevitable? I'll leave inevitable to you NDPers. Let the dollar fall, cut interest rates, spend tax money like drunken sailors and Canadians will inevitably end up as rich those living in Cape Cod but as modest as those in Manitoba. Rich, happy, and fully employed.

Claire spoke with genuine viciousness, but she then stood, seized three or four empty glasses, and asked her sparring partner if he needed wine, which he did. She disappeared toward the kitchen, the curling ends of her dark brown hair—bluntly cut—bouncing against her shoulders. That year, Claire was finishing her BA, which she had started at seventeen. Being Claire, she had already selected a professor at Université de Montréal to supervise her MA thesis—on Marcuse, I believe, and the production of literary texts during the industrial revolution. She loathed Western capitalism with great sincerity; neither was she a hypocrite in any simple way. She lived very modestly on very little money. It is true of course, as you often pointed out, that she had the habit, common in McGill circles, of buying secondhand clothes to both save on expense and confound the textile factories transplanted to low-wage, non-union corners of the globe, but then flying to Cambridge for a two week not-to-be-missed seminar Foucault was due to attend. Needless to say, Mom and Dad had money, which she refused to touch except when absolutely necessary.

The room was filling. With the animator absent, our little group fell silent. A fellow next to me offered me a cigarette and we talked amiably; I didn't look at you. The stereo, reloaded by various hands, played old-time punk like the Clash; Celtic traditional pieces; thrash and metal; segues of jazz. I watched the crowd; a few couples started to dance.

—I'd say the Family Romance, how about you? you said.

You had moved to the chair beside me. I felt sudden nerves, which subsided as I happily realized there was no harm in it. I loved Lee. Since that was *there*, like an extra ID card, there was no problem. But the timing: the previous week I had given Lee a small diamond. Not a public engagement, just an "I'll wait for you " promise ring. But that was fine. I would wait.

—Hi. Pardon? I sipped the wine, calm now, casual.

—I'd say the Family Romance is the greatest force shaping history. Okay if I sit here? Is he coming back?

—Beats me. Sure. Do you know Claire Howes?

—No. I've only just met her.

—Me neither, except to say hi. So, the Family Romance. I doubt you mean Father, Son, and Holy Spirit, which I guess Claire would call economics anyway.

—No. More Oedipus, Electra, Agamemnon.

—The strongest force in history? I don't know. The whole *question* sounds pretty ideological to me.

—And you're not an ideologue, right?

—No. Ideology needs some willing suspension of disbelief. I haven't the will, it appears. So far at any rate. I'd be tempted to guess geography and climate. Good seeds for cultivation, animals handy to domesticate. I'll be content when I can suspend ceilings with a bit of flair.

You laughed. You knew what I meant. A yearning crept upward in me.

*

I don't know what it was that made me tell Daniel so much about us and our first meeting. Mostly, he talked to me, on and on. But from time to time he demanded some *quid pro quo*, as if it were part of an obscure deal. When I got to this part of our story, Daniel became unexpectedly intense, leaning forward with his elbows on the table.

Claire did come back, forcing a rearrangement of the chairs. The earlier conversation seemed to have dissipated however; the debate turned to literary theory, and was conducted in dense jargon. Not knowing the lingo, you and I ended up seated side by side near the wall in two director's chairs, talking easily, watching more and more people join the dancing. I learned you were majoring in psychology, which you described as a highly institutionalized way of avoiding Freud. I suggested you were probably a heretic, and an old fashioned one at that. You laughed again, because you knew I meant it as a compliment. You said you already knew I was in architecture, and I tried to remember if I had ever mentioned it during the philosophy classes, but I doubted it. I learned you had grown up in a small town in southern Ontario, in a family of five children, your father a high school science teacher and lay minister at the local United Church, your mother an English teacher and a painter who never painted. We watched people dancing in the dim light to the throbbing music, but they seemed far from us. The room turned in great slow circles.

I was thinking: she thinks I like her, and although certainly I *do*, she misunderstands, because I don't find her attractive in that sort of way; I mean she's just not the type I have to worry about; my emotional equilibrium isn't disturbed by her. Of course she might not be interested. No, she is. But this is okay. Safe, and because it's safe it isn't disloyal. If I were struggling against a strong attraction, the decent thing to do would be to go look for my coat.

My mind works that way sometimes, more or less of its own accord, like a snooker player clearing the table; ridding the terrain of these intricately arranged coloured balls by applying a convincing combination of logical forces.

The rest of the room stayed remote, in spite of my snooker skills. I clipped my answers a bit short, to regain our original pretence that we weren't sitting *together*, only in adjacent chairs. It would be too bad if you got the wrong idea. And you were thinking (I thought), he's *sane*, he's *complicated*, he's halfway nice looking, he's interested and interesting. I felt you were finding quietness with me. The quiet was in me, but hadn't been part of me until now. How I came to such a conclusion, I'll never know, but I was quite confident your longing was for a *studied passion*, one that you look at and look at until its force consumes you.

There came a point where convention touched us: this was when, having both sensed our compatibility (tangentially, because we had barely glanced at each other, both of us talking to the space past the corners of our eyes) that I was supposed to say, "Seems we're left out—want to dance?"

The moment induced paralysis, because I had absolutely no intention of dancing with you. I was not paralyzed by indecision. Oddly I was *not* tempted. I should have been, in the classic scene of the type. I was frozen by confusion, but the confusion came from an unexpected urge to *explain* all of this to you. And this urge, of itself, seemed much more problematical than the minor betrayal of a dance, or not, after three or four drinks.

As I told it to Daniel, Liza, this was the moment when I should have explained why I wasn't going to ask you to dance. This had several potential repercussions. Severe embarrassment if it turned out you weren't in fact the least bit interested in dancing with me. It's one thing to be turned down for a dance. It's something else to launch a frank disquisition on why, unfortunately, in spite of how we might feel about each other, I couldn't ask you to . . . only to learn that . . . . But the other possible outcome, it seemed to me, was that you would appreciate my honesty, be pleased at how we had read each other's thoughts and at how naturally we could talk about the situation, and that this would create far more intimacy.

Lend me your thoughts on this bit of rationalization, I asked Daniel last month, while signalling for another round. Daniel my man, surely you can muster a few nasty barbs about how I deluded myself. Don't hold back.

*

But, Liza, at such moments I am unable to turn away

61

from dramas of revelation. I guess that is a virtue. But if the craving to be understood (to be noticed?) trumps loyalty to someone else, then what? Some loyalties need, at times, a retreat into solitude, into waiting.

I am getting to this, Liza: the story of Cardinal Melior, finding himself through blind chance in a bishopric guest room next door to the ancient cathedral the night Chartres burned.

For a moment I felt mute.

Looking straight ahead, we were two spectators.

—Maybe—you might be wondering why, Liza . . . I was thinking about asking you to dance but I'm . . . I don't want you to feel insulted because I haven't asked you . . . but of course you may not want to dance anyway.

There was an understandable silence as you unravelled this speech and assessed possible interpretations. There wasn't a convention to guide the moment.

Perhaps he's just uninterested, you thought. But if so, he wouldn't have mentioned wanting to ask for a dance at all; he would just go for another beer and not come back.

—No, I wasn't wondering . . . . But sure.

—I meant, I don't want to dance.

—Oh. That's fine, really.

—No, no. I mean I want to, or I would want to. But I have a girlfriend. Lee. A serious girlfriend. That sounds kind of solemn, doesn't it? But we are more or less informally engaged. I just wanted you to know that. Okay, I'm not making sense. Let me start over. Lee and I had to be apart this year while she finished her degree.

We accepted that and agreed . . . . Well, I'm sure you really don't want to hear all this.

—It's okay. Don't worry about it.

But my attempt to avoid *connecting* hadn't worked. We were now on entirely new and closer terms.

—But no, I really want you to understand. If I *didn't* like you so much, everything would be fine. A little dance, no harm done. Not nice, of course, and I'm not saying I would anyway. But this is more . . . well . . . it would have been a lousy thing to do.

—Yes, I think so.

—Sorry, I just feel awkward.

—I'm sorry. Me too.

We still weren't looking at each other, although we were allowing our glances to meet. I was breathless, and unexpectedly exhilarated (by my own virtue?). A greater temptation than I had recognized had been resisted. To dance with this intriguing woman, this inexplicably disturbing woman, would have been disloyal to Lee. You were feeling a mixture of embarrassment and bitter disappointment, I thought. Was it arrogant of me to think so? Perhaps. But we were destined for each other—there is no ego in that. *Destined*. What a word. But true.

—Really, it's fine, you said softly. I'm too messed up right now anyway.

Inexplicably disappointed, I stood up. You were calm.

I was not calm. I was excited; I was happy at having resisted you; I was already feeling nostalgic for our impossible future together.

There was a long pause. Neither of us moved. Then I walked away.

*

The kitchen was packed. Candles burned in the mouths of wine bottles marbled with wax. I caught snatches of conversation about student loans, bad profs, Jacques Derrida, Irish folk music. Jesus, I said to myself, then repeated aloud: Jesus. I needed to bolt out of the house, sprint home, call Lee.

Your familiarity and strangeness had completely unnerved me.

Better still, I should run straight to the bus station, get money from the ATM, and climb onto the overnight to Sudbury. Romantic, but impractical—for starters there *was* no overnight bus to Sudbury. Through the maze of shoulders and shouting faces I fought my way to a table crowded with wine bottles. I pushed hard against a couple with their hands under each other's shirts and found Claire and David O'Shea.

—John, right? asked David.

I nodded.

—I'm David. He had an elongated jaw, a longish neck, a wide smile. We were just talking about you. Economics and ideology. Which is which? Claire was quoting you. Good point. Economics is the effect of ideology, I'd say. Ideology says, lower taxes. The result is X, Y, and Z. Economically. Lower revenue for the government, social safety net with bigger holes. Et cetera.

—Stick to the subconscious, David, said Claire. Isn't that *delightfully* simplistic, John? Why do you think American Republicans want to lower taxes?

—I have no idea, I said. I'm hoping to be an architect.

—Oh heavens. Economics will be *inescapable; it'll* haunt your every vision.

Claire could charm you and your worst enemy at the same time. Still, there was something else to her—she wasn't easy to pin down.

—Cheerful thought. You're probably right.

This was the beginning of a long friendship with both David and Claire, which lasted through their series of passionate unions and equally passionate disintegrations. By now they appear to me positively mythological. But at this point they were newly acquainted, bickering platonically and having a great time. As it turned out, Liza, you knew David slightly—he was a PhD student in psychology, and was teaching a seminar you were taking. So he was a strand in the weft of coincidence and fortune that drew us to those two chairs beside the dance floor of the upper room on rue Ste. Famille. David, for example, was the only one from his huge family of eleven to go to university. That's one link on the chain. Then, after he left his home in BC, he dropped out of Notre Dame in Indiana. That's two. He wanted to get into York's MA program, but McGill offered a better fellowship. He stayed on to do his PhD rather than accept a superb offer from Berkeley because a woman he was interested in at the time was doing a teaching degree in Montreal. A handwritten note on a campus bulletin board caught his attention: *Wanted, extra housemate for large 9 1/2 in Ghetto.* That's five. You ended up in his seminar, out of the twelve in Psych 101. Six. You wanted to borrow a book the evening there was going to be a party. And so we met.

I picked up several bottles. They were all empty.

65

—Sorry, said Claire. I have no idea where all these people *came* from. I'm pretty sure there's still beer in the bathroom.

I sat on the john feeling I had escaped a trap of my own making. The tub was within easy reach, and I managed to pry open a bottle on the faucet. The cold beer sent a lovely charge through my body. That icy alert is a factor to be considered in the night's outcome, a minor weight on the balance.

On my way back into the sound-saturated, densely populated living room in search of my coat and gloves, I veered right and headed down the stairs, having decided that fresh air would do me a world of good. At the bottom step I drained the bottle and stood it solemnly on the lintel.

—Archivolt, I declaimed aloud. Pinnacle, splay, formeret, tympanum.

With a sensation of absolution and exuberance, I pushed open the door into the night.

You were alone, huddled on the top step. You half turned your head, did not even seem surprised, and then looked down the street to the south where a half-moon sat on top of a building. I had stepped into a role from an old movie, hard to exit despite its taste of cliché. Fate? Coincidence? Like-minds?

You turned a bit. I saw you were crying, silently. I suppose it was then that I was lost, but I held out, wielding my self-image of loyalty against a surge of romance washing through me—romance, love's great adversary.

My hand was only inches from your head. I looked at

66

your hair, and at my hand, and could foresee my fingertip touching it, a light tracing. It moved forward, my hand, as I watched.

—I should get going, I said. You must be cold out here.

You grinned a bit, sadly, looking no higher than my feet, then shrugged. But I knew, somehow knew, you were split in two, Liza; you were struggling with a second inhabitant.

Rudely, I yanked open the door and fled up the stairs.

I forced my way through the crowded room in search of my coat. I felt exhausted. The way seemed continually blocked; the music manically loud. I stopped, baffled, in the middle of the dancers. Why was I there? I pushed someone out of my way, and stumbled toward a heap of coats in a corner of the hallway. I dug out a coat and put both arms into it before realizing it wasn't mine. As I threw it down and bent to rummage further I looked straight into the bathroom through the half-open door. A woman sat on the toilet, panties binding her ankles, eyes closed and head swimming to the music. I was irrationally furious. Pulling out my coat I charged down the stairs, the crowd and noise disappearing behind me. I stopped for a moment, hyperventilating. Through the round window in the outer door were trees etched by streetlights; shadows; a flash of snow.

I opened the door and almost stepped into you as you were coming in. I looked directly into your eyes that were, finally, looking directly into mine.

Afterwards, I thought the events of my life seemed to have been unwitting preparation for that moment.

I'm not sure how long we stood there, poised on the threshold, trying to untangle our feet. I experienced a disturbing revelation as your eyes gazed into mine. The eternal round; the vicious circle; the mandala of perfect harmony; all existed in that moment we had avoided by positioning ourselves at angles. Yet I had seen your eyes before, I had known them all my life. Somehow I had forgotten and only now remembered. This didn't seem possible, but it was true.

Then you kissed me, or I kissed you. A rough, inexpert meeting of our mouths. I don't know who decided.

Closing in, we kissed again, slowly. More like fingers; a way of touching. We were astonished and filled with dread. We knew each other, but we couldn't possibly .... The wonder and fear were like moving to a foreign country. I had intimations of interior zones I had not known existed, physical sensations of the metaphysical. Everything became possible, and would always remain possible.

For a long time after that, we didn't touch. We were trying to absorb a new belief, afraid of its sheer scale, wondering about our capacities to respond to it. From time to time people brushed past us, leaving the party, and disappeared up the street. At one point David O'Shea poked his head out the door, looking for someone. He glanced at us, bowed slightly, and withdrew.

We stood there, still sensing the kiss. I think minutes passed, five minutes, before we spoke.

—This is terrible, I said.

—I know. I'm not at all ...

—No, I didn't mean it's terrible. I mean it's wonderful.

—It is.

That finished any remaining resistance.

—What should I do?

—How long have you and Lee been together?

—Three years.

—Oh, God. I'm not up to this. I don't know. Don't do anything.

—Liza, I . . . .

—You've never said my name before.

There was a long silence.

—But I like the sound of it, you whispered. This is impossible, John. Don't do anything.

—You've never said my name before.

—John.

I spoke quietly.

—Somehow I think in the end I'm going to have to tell Lee I've met you. That's crazy, isn't it?

—Wait. You looked away. You must wait, you said.

—I won't pretend I don't love her. I do.

—One thing, John. I will never ask you to pretend. As soon as either of us has to pretend, our love means nothing. We mean nothing.

—I will never pretend.

You leaned towards me although I could feel your hand trembling when you placed it on my arm. Your eyes were shadowed.

—I love Lee. I can tell you that. It would be dishonest to use some other word.

—Should you tell her? Already? Do you know what to tell her?

—I don't know. You mean, because nothing's happened?

—Of course something has happened.

—But Liza, I don't *love* you. I can't, because I don't know you. Yet it seems inevitable, just a question of time. Of when.

—Yes.

—In movies people fall in love with someone else because there is something wrong with the first relationship. You know: that didn't work, or this part of them wasn't satisfied, they were being stifled, mistreated. But that's not *true* for Lee and me. Nothing was wrong between us.

—This would be a lousy film.

—We were wonderful together, Lee and I.

—John, maybe I should just go.

—Liza, is there someone you have to tell?

—No, there isn't anyone, but there is something I have to tell you. Soon. But first you need to get away from me and think.

Our relationship was so new, yet within an hour we would be more entangled than we had ever been with anyone else. Revelations were uncomplicated because we weren't yet capable of jealousy, anticipation, mutual expectations, images of each other.

—Where do you live? I asked.

—Off Park Avenue, near Mount Royal.

—I'm closer. Just a couple of blocks.

—Let's go to your place. We can't keep talking in this doorway.

—And you'll tell me what you want to tell me.

But you didn't tell me anything at all that first night. We walked back through the frost, past a school playground,

70

the corner dépanneurs, past the second-hand bookshop window in which your face was reflected. I was trying to take it all in: the beauty, the sacredness of this moment; my own feelings of guilt and betrayal at the pain I was soon to cause Lee. I was giddy and silly. I was in despair. I was tragic. High as a kite. Doomed, blessed. We snuggled into each other waiting for lights to change. We were comfortable with each other. I had no *role* to play.

It was like being alone, together.

Sex is a relatively simple intimacy. On that first walk, we knew how to hold hands; which one of us would step around a puddle starred with first ice; who would jump over. We knew how our elbows might crook together; what the other would find funny (the trickiest intimacy of all). We knew in advance when a new surge of excitement—or distraction—or bewilderment—was about to strike: all without words.

I unlocked the front door and we ducked down three steps into my crooked hallway—some renovation had introduced a jog half way along its length—carpeted with a brilliant green substance derived, I supposed, from Astroturf. I knew you were going to laugh at it, and you did.

—Are you happy?

—Yes. Until I think about it and get scared. I didn't know I could still be happy. I thought that feeling was lost, permanently. But I am. Happy.

I looked at you, at your face, your eyelids, at a little scratch on your cheek. At your irises, the light blue of oceans on maps.

—When I looked at you Liza, I remembered.

71

—I had looked at you before, somewhere, a long time ago.

—I remembered your eyes, but also . . . .

—What?

—What it was like to be you.

I took your coat, noticing your throat, your collarbone, as I did so.

—I know you, I said. It's only the details that are missing.

I touched with one finger the delicate curve of your neck. That you were physically there, that I could touch you, was amazing.

—For example, I went on, what's your middle name?

—Alexandra.

—Elisabeth Alexandra Llewelynn. With a name like that I'm going to have to write you passionate verses.

I put our coats on the rack.

—Damn.

—What?

You had started, as if at a flash of lightning.

—It's nothing. I left my hat at the party.

—Oh, you said, sounding relieved. I'm sure it'll be there in the morning.

—No. It won't be there. When I lose things they never show up again. You'll have to get used to it.

*

As midnight approached, we drank jasmine tea in the kitchen, and ever since, I cannot drink tea in kitchens without your ghost in the chair across the table, haunting the opaque windows of night time, your hands wrapped around the mug, your fine hair a sharp shadow. You gaze into the cup, then look up at me with a little off-kilter smile, reaching up with your right hand to sling the hair behind your ear.

We had tea in the kitchen; we edged around the corners of the table to hold each other again, to touch each other's face with the fingers of the blind, to cry (about exactly what we weren't sure), then back to our tea. Alternately solemn and ebullient. My thoughts of Lee were dark stones that your presence could repeatedly submerge but not dissolve. Still, it was clear in which universe I now moved. Finally, I made a bed for myself on the couch. We hadn't needed to address the question of making love; we knew we wouldn't, that it would be a little while.

In the bathroom, brushing my teeth, you already curled up in my bed, under my blankets, I was surprised to find a towel just where I'd left it, the soap dish sitting there holding my soap, the shower curtain hugging the wall and—as I looked into the mirror, feeling short of breath and terribly unreal—my eyes again, your eyes.

I walked into my own bedroom after switching off the bathroom light and was in total darkness, listening to myself breathe, listening to you breathe. As my eyes adjusted, the light from the small window onto the back alley found you in the bed, sitting up now as if waiting for me, looking smaller, more slender still, in the too-large flannel shirt you had found in the drawer.

As I stepped forward, you reached and lifted my shirt, traced slow arabesques on my stomach.

—What a lovely belly, you said.

—But you can't see.

73

—I'm feeling my way.

There was a sudden flatness to your voice that puzzled me. I sat down on the edge of the bed. Outside, in the lane beneath the greystones, people walked by, an insomniac couple with their dog. I combed my fingers through your hair, kneaded one shoulder gently. We were hovering, lightheaded again. I felt the outside of the heavy flannel, gradually divining the form of your breasts. Barely moving my fingertips, one on each breast, barely touching the cloth, I circled each nipple, then centred my circles, stirring them into stiffness. You reached for the top button. Your hand was white in the moonlight, liquid. I took your hand away, undid the button myself. You pulled yourself up and kissed me with an open mouth as my hands moved quickly over your chest and belly and back.

—I don't have the foggiest who you are.

—But you adore me?

—I adore you.

On the way out, I stopped at the door.

—Are you scared?

—Yes.

—You never told me, Liza. You said you had something to tell me.

—I can't, not until we've . . . you've decided.

—If I will leave Lee? I feel as though it's already been decided for me.

—I know. But it hasn't been, John. Not until you've decided, not had it decided for you. You have to think about her.

—It's too terrible to think about.

—That's my point.

—Why will you only tell me then? What is it, Liza?

—If I give you everything now, before she even knows what is happening, it would be . . . adultery. Like adultery. Wait a bit. You can't rush this.

I waited two weeks, though as the days passed the delay seemed increasingly pointless. I spent the hours when we were not together calling you, or thinking about calling you, or talking to you—often out loud—even when I was by myself. You were determined that I should have time, and space, in which to think, to find distance, to try to reach a resolution that would be meaningful, that would be based on something we could understand. As opposed to blind faith? I would protest. What's wrong with a little blind faith? But we weren't very good at distance. If I had a bit of will power on a given day, and actually tried to keep to a resolution not to see you until the next morning, you would chance a quick phone call to say hi and find me so delighted, so relieved to hear your voice that we would talk for an hour, or meet for coffee, or, increasingly, spend long evenings in my apartment getting some studying done in between delighted attacks, as the Middle Ages would have put it, on the fortress of the beloved's eyes.

I talked to Lee twice. Normally she and I called each other more frequently—every other day or so. I found excuses for not calling. When I did call, I felt irrationally bitter that she detected nothing in my voice. What had we meant to each other if a lie could be so successful? But finally, mid-way through the second week, I called to tell her I was getting on the Friday train, and in the middle of chatting about our course work she asked me if I loved her. I told her I did.

My trip to Vermillion felt barbaric from the start. It was the wayfaring of a hooded man, bearing an axe. And I remember little of it, Liza.

I've never told you before, but you should know, that the phone rang the morning before I left. It was Lee. Of course, I couldn't tell her over the phone. I had no desire, however furtive, to do so. But that day, my mind half in Vermillon already, Lee knew there would be something different about this reunion. Ten seconds of pleasantries elapsed before she asked, uncertainty in her voice, what was wrong. I couldn't answer. By the time I could say something it was pointless to lie. I knew she knew, more or less. So, astounded by my clumsiness, I told her.

In the most extraordinary situations we are left with poor lines, abandoned to the same language we speak every day. She said, No John, don't say that, don't tell me that, it's not true, I know it's not, it's not, it's not. She said: I love you, don't you know that? She asked me if I loved her and I said with utter conviction that I did, just as much as ever, and it was true. She asked me your name. It seemed to matter. But telling her seemed impossible. She insisted. I said your name was Elizabeth. She told me again not to say what I was saying. In desperation, I said I would be on the eleven a.m. train, and that I would be at her place before midnight—and I hung up.

Remembering that conversation, I understand the Furies, the Greeks' Erinyes: why they were needed, why they seemed to have so little to do with guilt as we understand it, or with responsibility, or fairness. Surely, as I stood there, my fault or not, the universe itself

76

demanded vengeance, called for screaming birds flying at my head. I changed then. I lost affection for myself. I think that mattered, in the end.

So she sat and waited for an entire day for me to arrive.

An hour after she called I stopped by your apartment. You were saddened by and understanding about my trip to Vermillion. You said little, hurting with me and preoccupied with suppressing a natural-enough but incommunicable jealousy. The unspoken assumption that we were bound together was still there; the spooky effortless intimacy haunted every gesture, glance, word: but all this was as if on hold.

I walked down to the McGill metro station. I remember only one, stupid moment. Stopping in front of a flower seller in an underground passage, I momentarily considered bringing Lee our private symbol, two yellow roses. To show her I still cared, to soothe. The ability of the mind to construct cruelty out of misplaced romanticism never ceases to amaze me. Luckily this time I caught myself, gawked at the flowers, and turned away. Three stops took me to the train station, where I bought a ticket, intending to return the following day, and waited twenty minutes, kept company by a pack of Craven A's. I hadn't smoked for months but I needed to stake out a new and genuine me.

It took an hour to get off the island—the river was open at Lac de Deux Montagnes—another two hours to Ottawa and a twenty minute station stop, then the long six hour curve up the Ottawa River through the

Shield's low pine and birch hills to a last stop in North Bay a little after dark, where I grabbed a sandwich in the station. Two hours later the train pulled in to Sudbury, under the nickel refinery's superstack, its lights sketching edges of an enormous lavender cloud. I caught the final Northlander bus for Vermillion.

I learned only months later that Lee went from silence into hysterics that afternoon. Her worried parents decided to call a doctor. He prescribed a sedative. I walked to her parent's house from the bus drop-off in front of Carabucci's Shell station. Lee's parents and her sister Valerie had left us to ourselves. Lee cried softly from time to time but was relatively calm. And, not knowing her heartbeat was slowed by the drugs, I took comfort in this. She was badly hurt, but in the end, in the long run, I told myself, she would be all right: it seemed to be that kind of sustainable pain, mourning, not devastation. This later made me wonder if I had completely misunderstood our relationship, or if I was simply capable of unexpected coldness. I felt immense regret for the life Lee and I imagined together and would never have.

I can't remember a single word we said to each other as we sat in the McIvor living room. Later, sitting on Lee's bed, we held each other, silenced by the loss of what had been untrammeled and unconditional. I felt bitter both for hurting Lee and at losing her, yet never considered any other possibility. I kept wondering if I was sane, but never if I was going to give you up. Lee's eyes were soft and much too kind.

Valerie's vicious letter (we had been good friends in an older-brother, younger-sister sort of way) recounted that day and detailed the subsequent months of Lee's depression. She failed some final exams, got counselling, seemed to recover, then abruptly left for Vancouver in the middle of a summer-school attempt to salvage her diploma, taking a part-time job some cousin had found her. Lee, in the phone call and handful of letters that followed, had hidden all of this.

For a long time afterward, especially on trips home, even when you were with me, I would have dreams about long, explanatory meetings, where Lee and I would "talk it out," the pain replaced by old affection, blame dispersed. Now I have memories of those dreams and have to think long and hard to be certain none of them happened. But what I did to her became a permanent part of me, maybe too big a part. Did I accept my ability to ruin a life, accept an inclination to apocalyptic moments, assume that my turn would come and then make that assumption part of my will? Is the human desire for pattern so strong that we prefer shapely tragedy to meaninglessness? At last I stood at the door, and, somehow, broke out of the still life Lee and I formed there and turned, down the steps, down the front walk and away.

In those months I would catch myself half thinking that I had somehow forgotten to tell her about you, that I would have to go through it all again: get to the station, buy a ticket, sit motionless for hours on that train, the moment of breaking the truth approaching again. Then I would snap out of my reverie, and remember with relief that it was over.

I don't know where she is now. I don't know whether someone else now believes in her with a blind faith. I couldn't talk about her much with you of course. I sometimes felt you believed she had disappeared from my inner life, with time. To some extent. But I was changed. Walking away, I gathered with each step the conviction that one half of a symmetry had been cemented into place; an intricate, subtle symmetry, like the archivolts of Chartres' Royal Portal or the great arms of her transepts, but symmetry nonetheless; and that somehow, someday, the pattern would be completed.

8

The same journey in reverse. Ravel, unravel. The train eased into *Gare Centrale* in Montreal around nine in the evening. I bought a paper and sat numbly in an overlit coffee shop at the station, drinking back-to-back double espressos and reading the same paragraph over and over. Sometime after ten I was back in the flat, boiling water for Kraft Dinner, excited and appalled at the prospect of calling you. No, I couldn't, not tonight.

When the buzzer rang, startling me, I knew it was you.

You stood under an umbrella, your hair blonder in the streetlight against a black raincoat. You seemed like my long lost love, returned at last. We both felt quiet and dark, like the pooling rain.

—I'm not coming in, you said. I wanted to know if you were all right.

—All right?

—Stupid question. You're not all right. I just wanted to see you, John. I was worried you weren't real.

—I'm not. If I could do what I just did, what am I?

—I thought when you were there she would be so real you'd wonder if you had imagined me.

—No.

—How is . . . .

—What do you want me to say, Liza?

—And will *I* ever lose you, John?

—I'm giving up words like forever. I said them to Lee. But you know what you are to me. We're part of the same whole. We'll go on together.

We both attempted a smile, stretching a bright fabric over the pain.

—I'm going home. Call me when you're ready.

—How did you know I was back?

—I waited.

—In the rain? You should come in for a minute and get warm.

—No, you said gently.

I did call you on Monday, just after lunch, disoriented but desperate to talk. I needed to be rid of the strangeness that was the unnerving twin to our intimacy. Whatever small light was left drained away into nothingness unless you were there to reflect it, a beginning point for the tracing back. We went for a walk. That's my primary memory of our first weeks—those long walks we took together, becoming part of the weather.

We met in Jeanne-Mance park, half way between the ghetto and the Plateau, and made our way along the gravel path that spirals slowly up the side of the mountain, a gentle two mile slope to Beaver Pond on the summit. Fat snowflakes hung in the air and settled in cinematic slow motion on our faces when we stopped to kiss. Squirrels loped from branch to branch; tree trunks rose naked and stone-like, spreading solemn fan-vaults into the thickening snow. We walked and walked, missing lectures, through the still woods, through the full and moving air. We asked each other strange questions that seemed of grand importance. If you could live any one place for one year, where would it be? Do you have toast or cereal or eggs or nothing for breakfast? How many children should we have? What's the first thing you remember? Are your parents happy? And yes, what is the essence of history? Finally, at four o'clock or so, as the daylight began to fade from the pathways, then from the treetops, then from the sky, we wrapped ourselves in our coats and wove our limbs together on a bench on top of the mountain. You asked me, What is the most important thing about you I need to know? And as if I had the answer prepared (but I was surprised to hear it myself), I told you the story of coming downstairs in the night and discovering Mother in her garden, pruning in pitch darkness and watching her walk past me, weeping. Not "my mother" after all, but a lonely woman, grief stricken and a stranger.

The apartment without you this winter is unbearable. I have found myself reciting to you, more than once (hearing the echo of my slurred words to Daniel when I spoke the story out loud) how, on the downward slope through twilight and then darkness, as we reversed our steps, I asked you the same question: What is the thing about you I really need to know? I was nervous. I sensed we were a part of necessary symmetries that allowed me to know, before you spoke, that I would be given more than I bargained for—but that it would also be your best gift to me, our mystical vessel.

I had already learned some details of your background. Born in Toronto, raised on your parents' hobby farm in the hills of King County north of the city, two years at the local high school in Kleinberg before transferring to a private girls' school in east Toronto, a year at Ryerson Polytechnic studying fine arts, followed by another swerve into McGill's psychology program. A sister, two years older, married and living in Guelph; an eighteen year old brother, mildly handicapped and attending a special school in London, trying to become more independent.

We had no preconceptions about each other. That made the telling possible for you, perhaps? And because finding each other seemed so mysterious—think of the *odds*, we kept repeating—we were perfectly willing to accept all that came with the miracle. We had also not yet accumulated the inevitable sense of ownership that goes with shared lives. I don't just mean "possessiveness" and petty jealousy. It is a mutual haunting, and unavoidable. In a living room with two lamps, is the light divisible? At that point, alone on the mountain, we had no stake in each other's pasts. We could be liberal with understanding.

—Did I tell you my Dad is a high school history teacher, John?

Your voice caught me off guard. Its timbre was altered. I wasn't sure that I would have recognized it over a telephone. It seemed to come from somewhere just behind you. I felt ill. I tried to pretend calm.

—Yes. And your mother's a principal. At a junior high?

—Vice-principal. But at a small school. She teaches half-time. English and theatre arts.

—Great home library, I bet. We have two shelves of books at home. Other than my bedroom. About forty books. My parents are books-for-Christmas-presents types. I think they respect books too much to actually own them. No. Come to think of it, it's a cultural thing. Of course, neither of them finished high school. Dad reads westerns and mysteries steadily. About one a week. But only from the library. Never buys them.

You were walking beside me. You weren't saying anything, you were letting me chatter; but you were drawing inward—as I glanced over I sensed you were resigned, profoundly resigned.

—Liza, I'll shut up.

—Oh, John.

—Please. Tell me about your parents.

—Dad was a failed minister. His words, not mine. Not Mom's. He has a B.A. in Divinity from Emmanuel College at U of T, and worked for a year and a half as an assistant minister at a United Church in Oshawa. At night and on weekends he was finishing his courses for ordination.

—And...

—Six weeks before the ceremony he contacted the diocese and asked to have his name withdrawn.

—What happened? Loss of faith?

—No. Not loss of faith. I only know what Mom told me, since, at least with his children around, Dad usually just joked that he was a smart enough listener to know a lousy preacher when he heard one. Everyone found his sincerity touching. Mom and Dad were dating when it happened. There wasn't any one event that I know of. Apparently he realized he disliked being a pastor. He dreaded trying to make soothing conversation day in and day out to hospitalized elderly people he didn't know; teaching Sunday School classes irritated him; and presiding at church suppers and annual picnics drove him up the wall. Mom says he decided being a minister *would* destroy his faith. So he got out.

—But he came to regret it?

—I'm not sure. Regret? I think he knew it was the

right decision, for him, but he always felt his spiritual longings should have had more visible *results*, that he should have lived a more fundamentally religious life. I remember an argument he had with my uncle about this. I think my uncle was defending the idea of Dad leaving the profession to save his spirituality. How could faith have visible results? It's an invisible thing. Dad was furious. If the spirit exists but has no effect on this life, then it may as well not exist. He always felt the existence of spirit, outside time, was the source of human dignity, the root of meaning for the individual life.

—Surely we can treat each other decently simply out of our knowledge that *we* experience both joy and suffering, and that one's a hell of a lot more pleasant than the other . . .

—Dad and I went through all the defenses of humanism. I've worn out all the buzzwords. In the end he couldn't buy it. He kept saying, over and over, "Sure, but why give a hoot about the other guy? What difference should it make to you if he's just a heap of chemicals?"

—But Liza . . . I remember I was getting unreasonably agitated.

—Of course, I can't possibly know what his "faith" is. But I think he has this unwavering conviction that he can't—*he* can't—do anything with his faith without the practical world muddying the clear water. The clear water is his centre, and he treasures it, but can never be reconciled to its *uselessness*. Even Mother Teresa has a large organization to run. Gradually he concluded that his God had given him a faith he wasn't worthy of. He wanted to sit and think, and try to understand, try to sense, try to glimpse heaven I guess, feel a presence. That seems wonderful enough to me. But for Dad . . .

—Sounds like Saint Bernard against the scholastics to me.

—You'll have to fill me in. But the point is, I had a pretty strict childhood, classic Methodist, slightly updated for the 70s. We weren't forbidden to play cards or anything like that! But alcohol, for example, just wasn't around. My sister, Jennifer, couldn't date at all till she was sixteen, and then Dad, in a kindly sort of way, intimidated the hell out of her boyfriends. But more important . . . there was the continual emphasis on— what should I call it?—our worth; our personal dignity; our "beauty in the eyes of God." As teens, we felt put upon, being stuck with a father who dropped out of the ministry then raised us like minister's kids.

You stopped, and looked at me, both nervously and sadly. Letting go of my hand, you plunged both of yours into your coat pockets. I dusted the snow off your shoulders.

—If we stand still too long, I said softly, the snow will bury us.

—Oh well, we'll be entombed together. You paused, then said, I'm going about this all wrong. I can feel myself laying a groundwork, as if providing an explanation. I know better than that. I'll just say it. The situation with Dad isn't what I want to tell you, after all, although it didn't make what happened any easier.

It? What? I was getting impatient with all of the unidentified references, the prelude that seemed to be getting no closer to its object. But instinct told me not to let you sense this, to let you find your own path.

We had arrived back at the foot of the mountain. Across Parc Jeanne Mance a steady procession of traffic glided up and down avenue du Parc, muted by the thickening snow. Picnic tables—barely sitting above the rising drifts—stood in the clearings. We swept the cuff of snow from one and sat on the tabletop, our feet on the bench.

—In June of the year I finished grade ten—I was fifteen—I went out with a friend to a party thrown by my sister and her friend. It was the week school was ending. Jennifer's friends were graduating. Going off. Splitting up. They were nostalgic and sad—a bit desperate and panicky—and they didn't care about anything. The party was what we called railroading. Somebody who looked old enough or had borrowed ID would buy a few cases of beer at the Brewer's Retail, and we would drive to the end of a dead-end concession road and walk to the railroad tracks. They were old, rural tracks—not used anymore. And we would drink. It wasn't the first time I had gone. I don't want to explain. Cause and effect: they are the demons I've worked hard to get rid of.

Your voice broke, and I thought you would start crying, but you didn't.

—I'd gone railroading before. I used to have dreams that I'd left beer bottles in my underwear drawer and Mom would find them if I didn't manage to wake up and move them. Jennifer and her friends were in a different mood that night. They drank faster than usual, and they *weren't* having a good time. Is there ever, anytime in life, anything more wistful than the last month of high school? I don't remember the earlier parts of the evening well at all, but I think there were some nasty arguments

88

with boyfriends, screaming even. Somehow I ended up alone with my girlfriend. Jennifer had been crying after an argument, and had sat down against a tree a ways off, and then fallen asleep. Four of the boys . . .

I suddenly pinpointed the odd quality of your voice. You weren't talking to me; you were reciting—to yourself, to a mirror.

—I wasn't all that drunk. I'm not seeking reasons, or making excuses. We had another beer with the boys. I don't remember where all the others went, or why. It was warm, and the June air was like soft curtains; it was very dark, no moon.

Your voice was a metal bird.

—And I didn't care either. I understood so well how Jennifer was feeling. She was going to U of T, and none of her friends were. It's easy to laugh now, but the end of high school felt like the end of the world. I slipped into a terrible lethargy. I will always be afraid of it, for the rest of my life. Nothing mattered. Her, me, now, later: what difference did it make? That's what I remember most. There was a crack in the world and it turned out to be empty. I didn't care. My friend was necking with one of the boys, but then she pushed him away and got up and started walking slowly back toward the road through the long grass. One of the boys asked me if I was going anywhere and I said, oh, I don't care, and two of them . . .

—Liza, you don't need to, it's not any of . . .

—It is. It's my business and it is your business. They took turns having sex with me. I was a virgin. It was painful, but not as bad as it's supposed to be. I had sex with all four of them. I knew their names. It took so long. I remember how long it took. One or two of the

89

boys were pretty drunk. When the last one finished they stood there, not looking at me or at each other, pretty shook up too, and walked away. I was sitting up, with my arms around my knees. One boy, as he was leaving, picked up my sweater and wrapped it around my shoulders. It probably seemed to him the sort of thing he should do. I sat there a long time, waiting for something.

For a while I felt detached, breathless. But then I started to cry. I was crying and trying to get my jeans back on when Jennifer came back looking for me. She didn't say anything. She just stood there, looking at me, then she walked away too. So I lay down again on the grass, starting to hurt. In a few minutes the pain was severe. I had to get up and walk all the way home. It was a couple of miles. By the time I got home it was very late and my parents had been trying to get Jennifer to explain why I hadn't come back with her.

You stared up at the snow.

—In August I had an abortion.

—Liza, I love you.

—This will be easier I think. A little bit. Telling you at the start.

—It doesn't matter.

—It matters. And that's the easy part, the easy part for you to deal with. This is the start of the story, my dear, not the end.

—I'm sorry. Of course it matters. That was stupid. I didn't mean it.

I wasn't horrified, or appalled, or angry, Liza. I might have been, I suppose. I'm not pretending any gallantry. But those emotions didn't seem possible at the time, not toward you. I've never been certain you believed that,

90

and now I guess you never will. But you were outside judgment, for me. No, that's not it exactly. I just felt grief, and there wasn't room for anything else. What I *was* was scared. I understood already, before you went on, that you had almost been destroyed; and, at the same time, that the sex and the abortion were part trigger, part cause, part effect. A painful sequel was inevitable, but the eventual consequences were all out of proportion. Why?

—Everyone—my parents, my sister, the doctors—always thought the sex was the trauma. They thought *that* was what had "happened to me." But they were wrong. My John, this will be so difficult, I'm sorry. The worst part wasn't really anything that "happened." That was hard, but more just a change, a loss. Such things happen to people, right? People handle them, grieve, toughen up, and get over it.

You laughed.

—People go on. My parents aren't bad people. They were in shock, confused, they thought they had misunderstood their world, had missed something going on beneath their attention. I could imagine what they felt. How I cursed understanding what it was like for them. They had failed. And I suppose they felt some shame. They're human. But mainly the pain I caused them was the result of my pain. They suffered most because their child was suffering and they couldn't help. They suggested, and I agreed, to change schools. In October I had what doctors call a nervous breakdown, because they don't know what else to call it. I didn't feel that *nerves* were involved. I don't remember this time very well, which is the normal thing apparently. But the breakdown was the worst thing I have ever experienced. Mainly because *I* didn't experience it. I was lost within a relentless pressure that injected anxiety, hour after hour after hour. Now, the breakdown is the thing in the world I am most afraid of. If that force, that pressure takes over again I will not be able to face it. I can't imagine facing it. The breakdown fed on itself. One doctor described it as auto-parasitic. That's what the cause-and-effect model misses. I don't think what happened with the boys in the woods, or the pregnancy, or even the abortion *caused* what I went through. The breakdown was—it took something of me. And that severing caused more breakdowns, which caused . . .

—I know Liza, I whispered, I know.

Your eyes were hungry. For a moment *your* voice returned.

—Maybe. Maybe *you* do.

Do I, I thought? Do I want to? I have to.

You shook your head.

—I'm not trying to explain, you went on at last, as if trying to find your place again in the story. What did I learn? That a mind, that *me*, isn't really there. Okay, I don't quite know what I mean but that was the conviction I came out with. I shouldn't be studying psych. My therapists were against the idea. But I'm okay now. Madness missed me. I didn't go crazy. I didn't go crazy. You'll be happy to know. I used to say over and over to myself: go crazy. I think by the standards of these things my "breakdown" was far from the worst. John, I've never been able to say these words to anyone. My breakdown. You can't imagine what this is for me. Four or five months of hell, a few weeks of real delirium, a few months of zigzaggy recovery—then firm ground, sudden upheavals, firm ground again—and that was that.

You pulled in your shoulders, as if trying to fold into yourself.

—I've always wanted someone to know what I saw in there, John. I want someone to understand, or at least share the attempt to understand. But how can you ask someone to do that for you? I am so tired of being alone. That's what you never seem to read about in the literature. The isolation. The utter isolation. We think we are real, that there is some *thing*, *you*, permanent and firm as bread or a tree or the sea. But in the worst weeks I knew that the self doesn't even dissipate, like fog; or drain away, like water or sand; or get pulled out of shape like an old sweater; or shatter like a vase. Because it's not as tangible as any of those things. A mist is fixed by comparison. We *are* real, aren't we John? You are John, aren't you?

—Now that I've met you.

—A mind, a person, is clear and sharp and even beautiful as long as what? who? looks at it. Going crazy is when the personality appears to be still there, still in place, but suddenly it's out of focus; someone thumbs the dial on the binoculars and everything blurs into smudges of light and shadow. An abstract. Just a little slip—gone. And how could you ever take that blur and refocus it, figure out who this was?

We sat at our icy picnic, our hair filling with snow. I already knew you too well to say very much. We found our arms around each other and rocked in a winter cradle.

*

93

By the time we felt able to venture from the cocoon of our coats and scarves and warm breath, the city was submerged more deeply in silence. We kicked our way through deep fluff, the air charged with more flakes. I was wishing I had worn boots. I had dug through the back of my closet that morning, among old running shoes and unsprung umbrellas, but my winter boots had apparently vaporized over the summer. The previous spring seemed a decade ago. The previous spring I had been in a different life. So had Lee. And you.

We crossed avenue du Parc at the war memorial and plodded the two blocks to your flat on Esplanade in a quiet so complete the outer world seemed to be respecting our wordlessness. What you had told me needed to be voiced, sent out, that was certain. But afterwards, any mere solicitude would have seemed trivial. After all, you had insisted throughout that you were describing, not explaining. So very early on we learned to be silent in the presence of this story. Learned too well, perhaps.

I stopped at the foot of the wrought iron staircase to your third floor walkup, the storm still gathering strength, the snow swirling, the upward spiral of stairs in shadow. The porch light was finally visible a few feet from us. The streetlights stood in a dim receding series, parallel lines which, in the distance, seemed to meet.

You kissed me on the nose.

—I feel like we're starting over.

I can't remember who said that.

—After a whole three weeks together.

—I knew it would be all right, with you.

—With me? It's just all right, if you're all right.

—I'll live. I'll live now.

I listened to your boots clattering up the metal steps, into the snowing dark.

2

La Californie

9

Talking with Daniel, in *La Californie*, I repeat myself.
Alone, I talk to you. I say things like: Liza, spring
progresses, and I try to welcome it. What do people
substitute for spring fever in the jungles of Zaire, or the
deserts of Baluchistan? You remember how it is on the
Plateau: a light wash of green haze in the park, the streets
gritty with the snow gone, the winter's litter—hoarded
for months under discrete snow banks—revealed like an
old vice. Dog dung everywhere. On front balconies and
in back alleys grandmothers bang the dust out of carpets
and slosh grey water over porches and doorsteps, just
as they did a lifetime ago in Greek villages or the rural
Punjab or towns of the Beauce.

This weekend it will be May. Since my brain spends
most of its time wandering the vestibules and transepts
of Our Lady of Chartres, climax of the twelfth century's
installation of the Virgin at the centre of its cult of
incarnation, I suppose a May Day ceremony of some
sort is called for.

Do my letters lie unopened on your doorstep, as
does the mail for the tenant in the third floor flat above
me? Almost every morning, when I find the flyers and
letters and bills below the slot of the door downstairs,
I set one envelope on the little pile I've built outside his
door—yet another letter addressed to Mr. Li. I've never
seen him, or heard footsteps overhead. When I've asked,
Madame Parizeau assures me he is merely on vacation,
that his rent cheques arrive regularly from Arizona.
But I've noticed that most of the letters bear the same

handwriting. Who writes so often, yet hasn't been told where he is? I'm gradually beginning to feel part of the same world, the society of those with no forwarding address.

I go to the scriptorium with bad nerves. My progress on the planned series of biographies of members of the school at Chartres has been slowed by the gradual realization of just how crucial the section on Melior is. A judiciousness in my choice of words, skill in each formulation, a tautness of reasoning (after all, the scholastics believed you could approach the divine on the ladder of reason)—these are necessary every day, and it's exhausting.

But today, I let Melior bide his time. This morning I put in two good hours of work in my cave behind the kitchen, door closed as always. I was sorting the notes I had compiled during those wonderful summer afternoons together in Paris and Lyon. Merely the sight of the stained, crimped covers of my black notebooks— stuffed in knapsacks, clamped onto bike racks—made me short of breath as I pulled them from a bottom drawer, and made me listen carefully for your footstep at the door. Clearly at the time I had been too contented. But with your doctoral fellowship and my part-time teaching we were suddenly solvent, free to load our suitcases with guide books and your autumn reading lists, rent those absurdly tiny flats, linger over coffee, newspapers and fresh croissants from the corner *boulangerie*. Each day we selected a morning outing—museums, little-remarked monuments, unknown chapels, the galleries—and then, after lunch, while you settled onto the fold-out couch with course outlines and texts to inflict on the freshmen in your seminars, I headed off to the libraries, the archives, the diocesan repositories, the registry offices to dig for details of the civic, religious, aristocratic and military figures of the twelfth century Ile-de-France— aldermen and aediles, bishops and provosts, dukes and knights and legates—who were, I was increasingly convinced, one of the subjects of the sustained allegory of Chartres statuary.

By noon I was bleary eyed from working in the scriptorium and needed Montreal spring air. I stepped over to St.-Viateur for my ritual purchase of two bagels just out of the oven, one sesame seed, one poppy. As I headed toward Parc, their warmth and scent wafted from the paper bag. I slipped into the elegant streets of Outremont, to a park where I sat in the sunlight and leafed through a photocopied chapter of Gousett's *Histoire des croisades et du royaume franc de Jérusalem*. Chartres was rebuilt in the heyday of Crusading. It seemed unlikely to me that somehow, somewhere, the influence of such events did not show up in the Cathedral.

The pond in the park was still empty, a great dry washbasin clogged with leaves; but the trees, protected here in the lee of the mountain, were pushing out little furled leaves. I liked this spot. Neighbourhood daycare centres used it often, the children marching brightly along holding onto their rope. The swing sets were still swingless. But the children attacked slides and tunnels, and sand boxes in bad need of a stir, with enthusiasm. So I sat on the bench in the corner of the enclosure by the hedge and read, munched my bagels, and glanced at the playing children.

As their high-pitched laughter and voices faded into

the distance, the tone of the day darkened and left me with the pigeons and the impudent squirrels. Strolling back along Bernard, I remembered the recent night when Daniel's ironies, his rhetorical questions, finally lost their refracting dazzle, and I began to see through them. He actually told me something about himself. Never enough to get a clear picture, mind you.

I must have come in to *La Californie* unusually early that evening, because Daniel wasn't yet on his stool, wasn't yet staring into his glass as if beer foam could be used for divination. And he was as reliable as dusk. As *La Californie* was otherwise empty, and Roger was as usual preoccupied with his books—the texts always anonymous in a leather slipcover, always accompanied by a steno pad—I almost hated to approach the bar. But I ended up chatting with him. I knew Roger's rhythm: at the end of each page he would look up, canvas the room for thirsty customers, then settle back into his study. In spite of my frequent visits, and in spite of the fact I was inclined to like him, I knew nothing about him. When he brought the coffee I had gestured for, some sort of polite comment seemed required. After all, there was no one else around.

—Thanks. Good book?

—*Du rien*. What, that one? Good? No. Dully written, simplistic apologies, sad. Tragic without having earned it. But interesting.

—Okay, I'm curious.

—October crisis. It's named *Pour en finir avec octobre*. By a member of the FLQ: Francis Simard. He was with the cell that killed Laporte.

—Nice light reading.

102

—Yeah. It's for a course.

We ended up chatting over two espressos. After all, we were both amateurs, trying to turn pro, him at Polisci, me at Medieval History. He was writing a Master's thesis on the "Autobiography of the FLQ." It turned out he was thirty. Early on, he had dropped out of college after one term in order to talk about how to improve the world in an assortment of *brasseries*, and to earn some money, drink beer, smoke extraordinary amounts even for a Montrealer, and think about going back to school.

—What finally made you go back?

He laughed.

—Tobacco taxes. And my last job.

—Worse than this one?

—Are you kidding, Jean? This is . . . well, *c'est la Californie, non? Le paradis.*

We were laughing over Roger's description of working the graveyard shift in a warehouse when Daniel came in, looked around in a sort of ferocious daze, and stripped off his tie. He settled a bit imperiously at a nearby table, as if daring us to object.

—Genesee Cream Ale. Roger!

—Hmm. *J'n sais pas.*

—*J'espère, mon vieux.*

—So Roger, I said, as he got up. Does Simard say why they did it? Killed Laporte?

—Ah, well. *C'est la grande question, non?* To create a better society. Of course. For *le peuple.* A just society. But then again, why *at that moment*, did they decide? He says they couldn't stand it any more. They were prisoners now too. Trapped by what they'd trapped. He says something like: you feel the need to end his *captivité*, because it's your *captivité* too.

—And wasn't that kind of them? said Daniel. Graciously freeing Laporte from imprisonment by murdering him?

—Is that a rhetorical question? I asked.

—Not if you're the guy holding the rope.

While Roger went for beer, I sat wishing I were alone. My relationship with Daniel seemed pointless: he was an acquaintance I knew little about. Daniel brooded, tugging at eyelashes, worrying in-grown hairs in his beard, trimming his nails with his incisors. Roger dropped off a bottle and a glass on his way to take an order from some new arrivals. Against my protests, Daniel requested a beer for me as well and gestured for me to join him at his table. He turned the bottle around—indeed, Genesee Cream Ale—and seemed momentarily content.

—Tough day at work?

Daniel stopped pouring.

—Depends on what you call work. Is work a way of distracting your attention from your soul, or lack thereof?

—Only if you're rich enough to ask questions about it, Daniel.

—Aren't we correct this evening.

—Naw. Work is love made visible.

—Jesus, John. Where did you dig that one up?

—Kahlil Gibran. When I was sixteen I thought he was a genius, and a saint to boot.

—Yeah, well I ain't gonna work on Maggie's farm no more.

—Easy to say, unless you need the money to eat.

—Workers of the world unite. He held the bottle

above the glass, upside down, idly watching the last drops fall. Then he studied the bubbles ascending in the amber, scrutinized the composition of the head.

—Anyway, there's no sense sitting here every night, chatting about your fairy tales and my fairy tales until I run off at the last minute to leap onto the train to Pointe-Claire to try and convince my wife Isabelle, Saint Isabelle of Pointe-Claire—not to leave me again. After all, what the hell do you and I know about each other?

So she had already left him once? But the intensity, the mawkish *importance* of it all, I could do without. Not tonight, thanks.

—So, let's talk. Where're you from?

—You really want to know, John? he asked defiantly.

—Sure.

—Is there any sense telling random patrons of café-bars the tale of one's life? Wouldn't I be better off seeing if there's a withered priest propped up in one of the confessionals in the local church? I won't tell you unless you really want to know.

I was getting more than I'd bargained for. I was too tired, too depressed for this enterprise.

—So, Daniel went on. I'm from Ottawa. Don't take fright. The very place. Capital of the Dominion. No, strike that. Vanier actually. So much for that story. Not really the wrong side of the tracks. More like Ottawa's rec-room. Irish da. My grandfather is from the place itself. Nothing fancy though, no westerly sainted isles. Dublin born, left during an economic downturn—don't ask which one—in Ireland. A middle-aged man. Just up and left. 1930s. My father was a child, fourth of six, first one born on this side. My mother's a Quebecer. A

Tremblay even. A secretary at Supply and Services for thirty years. I warned you. What is more boring than the story of another man's life, when there's probably a hockey game on? Especially when the important parts are left out.

—Well, put them in.

He bit off each word.

—You think you could bear them, John? Anyway, I warned you.

No, you didn't, I thought. Warned me about what? Does everyone have a terrible story to tell?

—We had a nice little frame house on a nice little frame house kind of street with a nice little fenced in yard, not twenty minutes on foot from Rockcliffe Park. One sister, that's it. My mother was a Quiet Revolution Catholic before her time. She had been the ninth of nine and knew her *maman* in the Saguenay had resented her—while loving her dearly, mind you—from the moment of conception. She went to mass on major feast days if the weather was fine and she wasn't tired and there wasn't company coming over later. As she put it, this kept the peace and probably didn't actually do her any harm. Dad, on the other hand, had felt guilty from the moment he escaped Ireland. To compensate he kept track of religious obligations the way dentists keep track of tax breaks. For good measure he kept track of them on behalf of my sister and me too. I believe I spent a tenth of my tender life in a pew.

This isn't an excuse, John. Got that? This isn't an excuse. Isn't the era obsessed with excuses? Leave me out of it. You can get on with the era—not me. The idea of personal responsibility is *our* big lie. It's what we've got

106

instead of Father Lenin. He spawned the grandest set of criminals the world has seen since Hitler—here Daniel took a ferocious swig—the Soviet KGB and all their minions (a dozen million butchered, a few dozen million ruined, a hundred million nitpicked into oblivion and brutishness). Not to mention the old folks in Beijing, along with their dear chum Pol Pot.

—Beijing? Pol Pot? I asked.

—The Chinese crowd? Easing their way into Hong Kong stock portfolios and playing quiet rubbers of Retirement Bridge while the pretty daughters of mid-level lackeys serve them tea and snatch and help them put on their socks. Had we given Pol Pot another year or two, CNN would have put him on Larry King. I wish it were a joke. Mind you, Pol Pot was small potatoes. He only killed one and half, two million tops. A failure of the imagination.

I was still trying to see the links between too much Mass as a youth and Pol Pot.

He propped a beer bottle upside down in his glass and waved at Roger with both arms. He went on.

—You were about to bring up the Nuremberg trials, no doubt, John?

—Well, no. But sure.

—Good, don't bother.

He looked over his shoulder at Roger, who successfully lip-read an order for two San Miguels.

—Do you know, he continued, how many people were *actively* involved in operating the machinery of the death camps? Rail lines, train up-keep, requisitioning box cars, gas purchases, earth moving equipment, construction materials, filling in forms to order more bullets, scheduling, uniforms, oven tenders, designs, contracts, delivery and installation, ash removal, a new coat of paint for the earth moving equipment, accounting, payrolls, planning studies, blueprints, commissioned reports, monthly meetings, troop allocations, rations, searchlights, shovels—it was an organizational nightmare from the word go. Lots of stress, I bet. Probably millions. Depends where you draw the circle. So, do you know how many were convicted at Nuremberg? Little known fact of history. Nineteen.

I was gazing through the ribs of the blind into the street. It was almost dark. When I looked back, Daniel's chin was pointing at the ceiling and the slow flick of the fan. This full view of the angry braid of scarring startled me. It had been no minor burn. The San Miguel disappeared down his throat, a last rush of foam, his neck pulsing. He seized the other bottle he had ordered and plunged it into his glass. Apparently, I too had disappeared.

—Daniel?

He did not ignore me. Where he was, he could not hear me. The beer surged over the brim, foam sliding down the sides of the glass. He hefted it, dripping, and began, more slowly this time, to nuzzle the liquid. Simultaneously he waved his left hand in a small circle above his head. I caught Roger's eye, and frowned; but he shrugged, and I had the sensation that there was something here I didn't understand.

—You had a nice frame house and your father was Irish.

Daniel looked at me over the lip of his glass. He rolled his eyes and continued to drink.

—Christ, *don't* tell me then. It's not as if I asked.

In a moment of puzzled insight, though, I realized we were sparring like old friends.

Roger brought a John Bull's English Bitter—how Daniel's orbiting hand had specified this, I don't know—and a clean glass. Daniel fondled the dark bottle approvingly. He poured. I was beginning to partake of his rhythms, and found the thick slide of the liquid down the glass's side soothing.

—Nineteen convictions, John.

—Okay. Nineteen.

—My mother, you know—his words were slurred— she always told me at *bedtime* the story of Goldilocks and the Three Bears. Do I remember? I think I remember. Everybody knows the sh-story, right? Okay. So I've heard it a million. Times. Yes, I am THE WORLD'S LEADING EXPERT ON GOLDILOCKS AND THE THREE GREEDY BEARS. Even told it—told it—a few times myself, John my friend.

—I've never told it.

—Poor bastard. Anyway, stupid asshole of a story. I mean, I've heard it over and over again, and I never figured out what was the goddamned *point*! What is the fucking *point* of the goddamned *story*?

He was shouting.

—So she comes in. She sits in papa's chair, and momma's chair and baby's chair. She busts the . . . *chair*. And then the porridge bit. The bit about the big bowl being too hot and the medium-sized bowl being too cold and the little one just right. Completely against the laws of thermodynamics, that's for sure. So again it's the baby bear's stuff gets wrecked. And upstairs for the beds, and then she falls asleep. Bears come home. Discovery all round. Broken chair. Gobbled porridge. Girl in bed. John! What is the christly *point?*

La Californie was beginning to fill, and bemused patrons were buzzing, craning their heads to get a look. Roger came over.

—I don't know, I said lamely. I never thought about it.

—Jesus Mary Mother of God. You never thought about it. Christ almighty. *Tabernac!*

—Daniel, Roger said. *C'est presque huit heures et demi. Il faut que tu partes. Isabelle va se demander* . . .

The news galvanized Daniel like a quart of black coffee. He set the glass to one side, elbowed his way into his jacket, re-stuffed the dangling tie into the inner pocket, put a twenty on the table, and stood. He hovered for a moment, looked at three walls in turn.

—*Salut*, he said, to Roger, or to me, or to himself. He marched slowly toward the door.

This was too much for me. I was swimming.

—Roger, I insisted. *Peut-il se débrouiller? Trouver son autobus, trouver le train? Et si non—sa femme* . . .

Roger stared at me steadily.

—Don't worry about him John.

It seemed like an order.

The night after Daniel's outburst I was back in *La Californie*, feeling stupidly nervous when I noticed it was past his usual arrival time. Why should I care? I had to laugh—I *had* been wondering about the moral of Goldilocks and the Three Bears.

It was a chilly mid-April evening. Montrealers were watching the sky, their psyches spring-thin, worried about a late dump of snow and slush. Towards seven, he finally came in. The sports report was on the big screen. The *Canadiens* dynasty was past mere waning. A sad humour was creeping in. Yet another new coach was talking about a renewed sense of commitment, about looking after things in our own end. I saw Daniel at the door, and he saw me. He strode straight past my table to the bar without a glance, unbuttoning the throat of his dress shirt. Céline was on duty.

—*Cher, cher, cher,* he said. *Salut, salut, salut.* He leaned on the rail peering at the magnificent bottle array. He pointed.

—Upper Canada Ale, *s'il t'plait. Deux.*

Bottles by their necks in one fist, two glasses in the other hand, he kicked back the chair across from me and rattled down a glass and bottle beside my empty coffee cup. Céline brought over a copy of *La Presse,* and set it down without a word, gesturing at a headline.

We sat and read: long columns of print, boxed features, columnists searching for angles, as well as photos. The story of the baby had caught on; the response was all out of proportion. CNN had even sent up a crew, knowing a sensation when they saw one.

—Long day of work, Daniel said. Then he stopped to clear his throat. A guy tries to relax, fend off stress, have a beer, and *this,* screaming at you like a harpy from the fucking front of the newspaper. Citizenry! they're shouting, Why aren't you weeping? Weep! This is what's left of the public sphere?

—Is that a rhetorical question? I asked.

—Is *that* a rhetorical question?

—Of course not. I wanted an answer.

111

—An answer, John? Jesus.

He swore, reached over and seized the newspaper.

—Céline! he hollered. *As-tu un Guinness? J'ai payé mes bills, non?*

—I hadn't realized *beeels* was French now.

—Get a life, John.

—I wish.

—*Monsieur Politesse ce soir,* Daniel? Céline muttered, heading to the bar.

—*Et non,* she called, *j'en ai pas.*

—*Alors, un Heidelberg.*

—*P't'être.*

Daniel spread the paper before him, ironing it with his palm. He hunched over, reading carefully.

Then he looked up at me, or over me.

—Voltaire, he said. The bastard.

—Come again?

—He wrote someplace— *'bernac,* is this going back to college?—someplace he wrote, "We owe consideration to the living. The dead we owe only truth."

—What do you mean?

Daniel stabbed a finger at the newspaper.

—Today's news tidbit. The baby they found on the mountain last week. She was wearing a baptismal gown.

—That's not news. They wrote that the first day.

—I know, but confirmed now. And she was strangled.

He looked pale.

112

10

Liza, maybe I had to listen to Daniel's rant because I saw the same woundedness, the loss of self, which so frightened me in you. In the months that followed our first meeting we had to find our way back into the real world, with all its loops and coils. We felt off balance at times. On one level, we understood each other intimately, instinctively, gracefully. But on a practical plane we knew hardly anything at all about the other. We found ourselves in a mystery: understanding without knowledge. We spent the ever-longer nights getting to know each other. At times, it was a comical process. Finding, in your record collection, the *Talking Heads* and Lou Reed mixed in with Mahler and Sibelius, I walked over to the window and stared into the night, bewitched by coincidence.

All this was punctuated by letters from Lee that silenced me for hours, spun me backwards into the unreal past where she now lived. My own history felt erased like a chalk drawing. You read her letters. This seemed inevitable at the time, but now, remembering, it seems an invasion of Lee's privacy. Then, it was part of a campaign against distance. Love is a ruthless faith.

For months after we met I would often claw myself out of sleep and sit sickened, heart banging painfully in my chest, certain I had ruined everything. My dreams operated with brutal simplicity: erasing my time with you, letting the present slip my mind. The dreams are hard to describe. I remember a strangeness, a horror of unfamiliarity. My consciousness was thoroughly imprinted with you, but some housekeeping part of my brain lacked all sorts of basic data about the intruder and rebelled, generating phantoms. Chartres is one attempt to make the mind's fragmented kaleidoscope whole, to make it stand still in glory, the colour ordered and soldered together in the great stained glass visions.

In the dreams of these early weeks together you would come into a room where I was sitting and ask my name. I would walk along a woodland path, holding your hand, until at some point I would look over at you and discover in fact you had been someone else all along, often someone I had never met, or someone I knew slightly and hadn't thought about in years. Or I would be sitting quietly in a sunlit yard and an airplane would fly over, unusually low; this would terrify me, and I would begin to scream, bringing someone running from the house, again someone I barely knew and cared nothing about, but she would hold my head in her arms and kiss me and say "I love you, John."

To convince ourselves there is someone in the mirror we build up houses of habit to live in, representations of space and clarity, rib-vaults to hold up a great sky. It starts with sitting on the same side of the breakfast table every morning and ends with the indoor cosmos at Reims and Salisbury and Chartres. Waking up from these nightmares, trying to relocate the mundane me of everyday habit, I thought I glimpsed what it would be like to "lose" one's mind: when your *interior* voice begins to sound unfamiliar, when the comfortable, thoughtless mumble of consciousness squeaks and squeals and snorts at you. You're not listening. You're not speaking. You're not there. This helped me understand, during our first year together, the terror of your past crisis, and deepened my fear when it resurfaced.

Another dream was even tougher to handle, and could not be cleansed away by long morning showers, strong coffee, sprinting off to classes, burying myself in architectural abstracts or the grammar of Old French. This nightmare took a form easier to remember: vivid, coloured, plotted, inevitable. Once it began I was impelled through it to the end; like a torn branch floating down a river, I could only wait to arrive.

This dream was composed out of fragmentary memories from a two-week stretch of one summer spent in Toronto with Lee, visiting my brother Robbie just before he went out west. His apartment was in the eaves of an old, three-storey brick house in the east end, just past the trendier parts of the Beaches. Almost every morning of that trip, Lee and I went walking along the lakefront, alone except for the earliest joggers. In the dream I would walk along the boardwalk, my hand in yours, Liza, happy in a supernatural silence. A stormy night had spattered the sand with leaves and maple keys, with gravel and bits of wood and waterlogged litter. The sand itself was damp and randomly moulded, swept here and there into small piles or low ridges. Our steps thudded dully on the weathered boards. There was nothing beneath. The sky was empty. Although the morning was now calm, waves were still washing ashore; white foam lay in semicircles at their furthest reach. Seagulls swept in with the surf, crying, alighted, leapt upwards, disappeared. Afterwards I could never be sure when you too turned out not to be there, or even turned out not to have been there in the first place—but by the end I was always alone. The sun was up, the sky turning to pearl.

At some point on the walk I would step down off the boardwalk, alerted by some sixth sense, some dread acuity, to the odd geography of a ruff of sand. The half-mound, the sunken shape, showed signs of disturbance. Nervous, I would lean down and brush a little away, but it would cling to my fingers, and I'd pull them back, trying to disentangle them from what became a stringy mixture of the sand and Lee's brown hair. Oh no, don't do that Lee, I would say, oh no Lee. On my hands and knees I would begin to dig, scooping with both hands. An obscured face would appear; heavy head and limbs; I was wailing and trying to get her out of the soil.

Sometimes, in the days that followed those dreams, I would catch myself mourning, and have to remind myself again—thinking hard, *bearing down*—that *that* letter, at least, had never come; that the body in the sand wasn't real.

All of the settings of our early months together now have the wistful clarity of something watched through a doorway, seen through a lighted window. We worked our way through the *Guide to Great Cheap Food in Montreal*—Vietnamese, Thai, Spanish, couscous joints, Greek, Italian, Indian, Mexican. We mapped every pathway on the mountain. We cross-country skied half way around Lake Memphramagog, but didn't see its monster. We haunted the rep-cinemas until they went out of business, waited impatiently until they reopened in a new neighbourhood with new idealism, and began again. We read each other's course texts, as if trading minds—long evenings of getting up only every twenty-five minutes to turn over the record, with me wincing my way through Freud, Jung, Nietzche, Skinner, Piaget, Klein, and you underlining all the psychological metaphors you insisted on finding in everyone from Vetruvius to Vincent Scully. We went to David and Claire's parties (they were now a couple, however improbable that seemed), both in honour of our miracle of finding each other through them, and because they were becoming our friends. But what was most remarkable was the un-self-consciousness, the doing nothing, how we padded around our apartments together, listening to music, fixing a snack: the glory was that from the beginning we did these things without calculation, without adjustment for the quirks of the other, because our quirks were, as the theologians say, consubstantial.

We looked in the windows of the world and felt as though we looked *out* at them, since where we were was *always* inside. We were bemused at how the rest of the world could survive without what we had together.

11

Daniel's gaze roamed to the screen behind me in *La Californie.*

—The Canadian Beer Ad, he mocked.

I turned to see large numbers of beaming people reveling beside a swimming pool.

—This is the age of democracy, right? he continued. And what represents it better than the Canadian Beer Commercial, trillions of dollars spent hawking identical brews produced by two huge companies that probably accidentally bought each other years ago? You too can choose your own destiny. Out of the Blue. Ex says it all. Reminds me of bloody psychiatry—choose your remedy.

He took a long drink from his glass.

—So you want to know what happened next. Why do we always want to know what happened next? Rhetorical question. There's no answer. I went to UQAM. Wanted to study history and speak French.

—Feel free.

—*Pas avec toi.*

—*Pourquoi pas?*

—You're the English part of my brain. Christ, how should I know? French is my mother tongue. I prefer to translate this story. In French it might sound true.

He tore roughly at his eyelashes for a second, then held his pinched forefinger and thumb up to the light, peering.

—Happening place then. The loud part of the Quiet Revolution. Met lots of nice ladies and laddies, read till my eyes fell out—Second Punic War to the War in Vietnam and every war in between. Minor in French Literature of all things. Want to hear some Racine? Bit of Diderot? And finally, just when diploma time came, I conveniently met Isabelle.

—*Ta femme.*

—My wife. Isabelle Lafontaine was a psych major.

—Oh God. The fate of the late century. We're all doomed to be married to psychologists. Wedded to the insides of our brains. Unable to stand back and have a look at things.

—You too?

I didn't have the energy to explain.

—I'm divorced, I lied.

—I'm working on it, he fired back.

—Not funny.

—No.

He sipped at the beer with an unusually contemplative air, pulled gently at his moustache.

—Sorry. So we got jobs. We fell in love. The world got rosy, we fucked each other until the angels sang, we got new jobs, we got married, we got better jobs, we got half a duplex in lower Outremont.

I whistled.

—Glorious, eh? We got half a duplex in lower Outremont, Isabelle got pregnant, I bought a baby carriage at Eaton's and practiced pushing it around the pond in the park on Bernard with the groceries in it, Isabelle got plump and extraordinarily juicy. Superfluously desirable. Delicious. Nutritious. Roundish. Heavy. Breasts like whichever goddess it is who kick-starts spring.

—Or you could leave out the good parts.

119

—Without the good parts, can there be real tragedy?
Ha!

He seemed pleased with himself. He waved at Céline.
She held up a bottle in query and he shrugged, nodded.

—Looked like a Belgian bock from here, he said. This
place is amazing. What a selection. Anyway, it was a nice
little duplex. I know you, John . . .

—No, you don't.

—I know you, and you would have liked it. Proper. In
spite of yourself, but you would have liked it. Pleasant
white porch, half for us and half for an orthodontist and
her lovers. Hardwood floors. White walls with a few
nice oils, some prints, a weaving from our honeymoon
in Guatemala.

—Guatemala?

—Of course Guatemala. Did you think Niagara
Falls? We were grand. Two floors. Designer kitchen
with an exposed brick wall, study good and full of heavy
tomes. A little paving stone drive along the side for our
Renault, a little half yard for the bouncing baby. Nice
dinner parties—I do some lovely pastas, and Isabelle was
heavily into Thai, a decade ahead of her time. Brilliant
lady. You'd adore her.

Céline arrived with two squat bottles. We poured the
beer; it was the colour of bourbon.

—And you were still working.

—As a matter of fact, I think Isabelle is your type.
Thick black hair—good Québecoise—cut kind of
short—blunt, perky hair. Pale skin. Drove me wild. So
there I am, happy as a clam, prancing around that little
pond with a baby carriage full of pâté and quiche from

Cinq Saisons when—well, when a little crack opened in the bloody fucking universe.

I took a drink.

—Did you think about the universe when you were a kid, John me bud, trying to get a grip on the idea that there was no end to it? I always thought there *had* to be a place where it stopped. But then of course what was *there?* When I tried to think about it the best I could do was an immense black wall, a bit curved, concave, not very rough but not very smooth, high enough so you couldn't quite reach the top, extending in both directions for, well, forever. That goddamned wall still seems real to me. I know it doesn't solve the problem. But you can lean up against it, run your hands over it, push on it. Of course, what's beyond that, and so on. And then you find a seam in it, a little rift. Chink in the mortar. Shall I go on, John?

—If you want to. I never asked.

—If I want to? Lovely thought. So that morning, when I was pushing the baby carriage around the pond, I met a most interesting young fellow. Not a day over twenty. He wondered why I had a baby carriage full of groceries and struck up a chat. Maybe he just liked my jeans. Anyway, to her most wondrous and extraordinary and everlasting shock, Isabelle came home from work at midday—back pain, couldn't take another minute at her desk—one fine spring midday, big as a tent, and . . .

—And . . .

—Shall I?

—*Daniel.*

—And discovered her husband standing by the kitchen sink with a rather appalled expression on his face, normal enough given that his pants were around his knees and a handsome U. of M. student was sucking his enthusiastic cock.

Daniel smirked.

—Shocked, John? Appalled?

—Don't be stupid. Drink your bock.

We sat. Cars went past on Bernard, filling up the quiet. The after work crowd was beginning to thin, leaving Céline busy wiping up tables before the evening customers arrived. I half turned my chair so I could pretend to watch the screen. The all-sport channel was on. Motorcycle racing. Riders dressed like Darth Vader were hugging streamlined cycles orbiting a track, tilted continuously at impossible angles. The spectacle seemed a perfect opening for one of Daniel's soliloquies of sarcasm—"What is the meaning of the sacrifice of left knees in motorcycle racing?" or "Does the scientific establishment *realize* their models of the atom, and the solar system, are subconsciously derived from motor sports?"—but he merely consumed his beer in measured draughts, until it was gone. One of the riders dipped too low. He and his machine catapulted lightly into the air and bounced across the track. It didn't look very convincing. I beat Daniel to the punch and ordered two Blues in honour of Canadian beer commercials.

When she brought them, Céline asked whether we were engaged in transcendental meditation. Daniel answered that no, on the contrary, he was contemplating the art of professional motorcycling and thinking of a career change. Céline took a pack from the breast pocket of her black shirt and lit herself a cigarette.

—*C'est sérieux, ça.*

She glanced at me, in an exploratory way. A little less guarded. I shrugged, and she went back to the bar and her textbooks.

—She leave you?

—Céline? Never. She's the loyal type. No one needs loyal friends more than a traitor. Trust me.

—Fine. I looked at the screen.

—Ah. You meant Isabelle. Why do you think I worry about the bloody 9:05 to Pointe-Claire?

He looked at his watch. It was seven-thirty. He didn't have to leave *La Californie* for almost an hour.

—No. That's the simple version. He barked. Man betrays woman (pregnant woman no less), betrays her with another man no less, no less, woman staggers about the apartment, weeps, is hurt (actually, she didn't stagger, scratch that), is hurt, he gathers up his things, she is irredeemably hurt, or she gathers up her things and goes to live with her sister or her best friend who attends bravely at the birth, confirming the unbreakable sisterhood. No. Not like that. Except maybe the irredeemably hurt part. Is that not, he said, in mock grandeur, the very pith and pit of truth.

—Yeah.

—A comical scene, don't you think? I mean, in the kitchen, for God's sake.

—Funny in a sitcom. But not if it actually happened.

—No. Not funny.

He looked me straight in the eyes, searching. For once his gaze wasn't muddied, or blank, or squinting with bitterness. For a moment. Then he smiled, beatifically.

—Mind you, fellatio's rare in sitcoms.

123

We started to giggle. Céline, coming back after taking an order, gave us puzzled glances on the way past.

—I don't know how, said Daniel, but we kept going. I survived. She survived. We went all through it. My sex life, I mean. It would have been simple enough—terrible, but simple—if I could have just told her: look, my big secret's out, I was trying to live a lie, stupid me, I'm gay. But I'm not. I wasn't. I mean, not mainly. It was stupid. Man or woman it was world class idiotic. It was vicious. But that's me. Dan Vicious. Isn't that a British punk rocker? I did it. No ifs-ands-or-buts. Bring on the judge. But anyway we talked and talked and she asked how often. First time since we were together, third time in my life. She asked what I wanted to do now. I told her I loved her. She spent a week visiting her family in Sherbrooke solo, and then she came back. Even you, St. John of the Cross, don't want all the hideous details, do you?

—I'm not asking.

—Why not? Fire away. Little inquisition never hurt anybody. It's all this tolerance that's killing us. Pry. Analyze. Pick me apart. Hold me up to the light of day. Turn over the rock and let the vermin sprint for cover. Let it all hang out and we'll be okay. I'm okay, you're okay. *Céline! You okay?* She's okay. That's our motto kids (his voice rising): come out of the closet, fess up, hop on the couch, go on a talk show and *ev*-erybody will be *okay!* Give me a break.

He stopped. Every muscle in his face relaxed at once.

—So. Where was I?

The rapidity of the change was breathtaking, theatre magic.

—She came back from Sherbrooke.

—Oh goody.

He was beyond me again, Liza, the light from the screen on his becalmed face.

—Yes?

—Cliff diving. Anyway, Isabelle returned from Sherbrooke. We put it back together. But of course there were parts missing. Bridges had been bombed. Entrances had been bricked up for eternity. The sincere sincerity had been torched. We were left with *wanting* to be sincere. We had to work at it. Know what I mean? You do. I know. Willed love. An admirable thing indeed. Human. Accomplishment. I saw it on TV. Like the decision to have faith. To decide, more or less rationally, that whatever the hell is left after the slash and burn routine is still better than anything else the planet is likely to offer, given the state of things, and to make it your own personal goddamned saint, scar tissue or not. Just as good as love maybe. But different. No, not as good. I guess we don't believe that. Even *Reader's Digest* doesn't believe it, not really. Muddled. But what's left. A worthy remnant, that's us John-boy. Can you get used to perfection being gone? No, you can't. It's hell.

—Hell of an ending.

—You jest. I'm just beginning.

He waved to Céline like an outfielder calling for the ball.

—Two months later, he went on, I was there when Kate was born, our daughter. The only miracle there is, really.

—I'm afraid I wouldn't know.

—It's . . . John, it's the main thing. His voice seemed to split into two octaves. Mary Mother of God.

I thought, suddenly, he was going to break down before my eyes. But he came back, re-found his tone.

—And we went on. I loved it. I took leave from work. Isabelle went back to the clinic after her maternity leave was up, and for six wondrous months (oh, plenty of claustrophobia from time to time, but a little claustrophobia is good for us damned moles), for six great months I looked after Kate. Seems great now. Cleaned her bum.   Spooned the Pablum. Warmed bottles. Sluiced the smushed carrots out of her hair. Came running when she woke up in the night, to bring her to Isabelle's breast. Trooped through parks without incident. Was the first to spot the first tooth.

—Sounds nice. Really.

He stared at me intently.

—Baggage, John? Aren't we the gloomy one. Nice? Not really. Wait until the end of the tale.

Get on with it, then, I thought. Two beers appeared on the table. We gratefully dumped their necks into our glasses. It was such a quiet evening—only one other table was taken—that Céline had been immersed in her management theory textbook.

—Céline, he said vibrantly, *qu'est ce que tu voudrais gerer, exactement?*

—*La Californie, naturellement.*

—Ah. Hmm. Is it over before it's over, he mused. No, it ain't over till it's over. Yogi Bear.

—Berra. What's not over?

—The story. At that point it seems to me it could have gone either way.

126

—So which way did it go?

—California.

—You got that right. Cheers.

—No, I mean it. It went to California.

I looked at Céline's retreating figure, thinking *Céline?*

—The *state* John. It went to L.A. Like lots of good little Québécois who want to be big. Without the church, it's Carson or nothing. All the tiny pivots on which it all turns. Amazing. Before my six wonder months, even before Kate was born, Isabelle did a career U-turn. It was because she was home for a month on maternity leave before the birth. If she hadn't been freed from work with time on her hands waiting for the big day she would never have gotten the urge to do a thorough cleaning. Even the closets.

—Serious.

—Probably a mother thing. The shrinks could fill us in. So if she hadn't been in a purge-the-place-till-it's-pure mood she would never have been rummaging through old boxes, and if she hadn't been rummaging through old boxes she would never have lifted out, opened up, and sat down and read right on the spot her half-done doctoral thesis. Clinical psychology. The woman was in a fragile mood. A new life flailing away inside her. Crisis with yours truly. It hit her like a Montreal cabby running a red. Three wasted years of her life. (Her words.) Two days later she was ploughing through her research notes. Before Kate was even born she had herself re-enrolled, had talked her old supervisor into a meeting, and was pricing word processors.

In the interim, Céline had cleared away our bottles.

Daniel held up his glass to the light, squinting at the colour like a wine taster.

—What is this stuff?

—Amstel.

—Tolerable. If she hadn't got a computer she probably wouldn't have gotten so much work done during her maternity leave. Isabelle was a woman possessed. I have asked any number of women since and they all assure me a new mother is completely exhausted, not to mention maternally preoccupied, during the first months. The world's ambitions, they insist, seem remote and juvenile, shallow and materialistic. One is dreamy, cocooned, psychically fulfilled. Isabelle, on the other hand, was a perfectly attentive and affectionate—and nutritious—mom until the moment Kate laid down for her naps, at which point she switched into a driven grad student.

—Good for her. And she didn't burn out?

—Better than rusting. Neil Young? Sure, she was wiped. Except when she was working. Which she never missed. Tidy chunks. One hour in the morning, one hour in the afternoon. Click click click. Sounded like a bird at the window. Then she made up for it by sleeping ten hours each night, dead to the universe. I ferried Kate in twice during the small hours and Isabelle would move from deep oblivion to dozy just long enough to roll onto her side, flip Kate into position, give her ten minutes on each, then slide back into dreamland while I padded around the kitchen in my slippers pat-pat-patting for the burps, expertly changing the *couche-couche* in twenty seconds flat, and putting her down. Putting my Kate down. This was 1999. The year my Kate was born.

—And, he went on, if Isabelle hadn't gotten so much

work done during her maternity leave (her research had been more or less complete—it was writing, organizing work, so the two hours meant another page in the can each day), she might not have seen the end in view and been able to keep at it evenings after she went back to work. But Jesus. How can this mean anything to you? It doesn't. How can it drill its way into your damned near impervious cranium if you don't know Isabelle? That's where the big gap lies. Chasm.

He banged the table between us, making my glass jump.

—And how can I explain Isabelle to *you*, John, my priestly bugger? Dear Isabelle, how can I tell John here what it is about you? God knows you loathed me at times in those days. On the common human principle that I gave you several excruciating wounds. And for a moment—here and there, no longer than that—you even returned the favour.

Ah. One handy feature about Isabelle, John. She looks the way she is. Extremely rare attribute, actually. You grant the point? Good. Damned near epistemological, Isabelle. Look. Isabelle is a beautiful woman. That's not the important thing, though.

I didn't doubt it. Daniel was a handsome man in his way.

—Isabelle has the classic Québécois features: black hair, and thick, hair with weight, cut blunt on her shoulders. I told you this. Brown eyes, with bits of green, quick, burning. Fair skin. A few pale freckles. She wears black T-shirts, often with a very dark vest or dark tweed jacket—almost black, but with a bit of texture, threads of different tones. And old silver; a bit tar-tarnished, not too much. Antique brooches. Heavy but intricately worked bracelets. Large earrings, with a dull gleam— she usually picks them up in second-hand shops. Someone's eccentric great-aunt. No makeup. No nail polish. Black, and old silver, some rich dark wool, a bit of leather. That's Isabelle. And that is exactly what she's like. I can't find any better way of trying to express her personality. I could repeat generalities I guess—muted but burnished intensity, somber passion that longs to be free of somberness, death-conscious but loving every damned minute better than me. Far better than me.

His voice was starting to ascend a scale.

We were silent, for some time. The cliff divers had given way to whining motocrossers, windmilling through mud. I pushed my chair around a bit when Daniel carefully negotiated a path to the men's room, and tried to watch it. Through the haze of my fourth beer the sport had a certain epic appeal. Well, you couldn't wear armour any more, I philosophized drunkenly; there were no tourneys, no lances, no maidens putting you to serious twelfth century tests, like lying next to them in their curtained bed having been advised they would be utterly naked and proving your mettle by never touching once, never looking once . . . . So we charge about on motorbikes. If I hadn't had so much beer I might have sensed the damn-the-torpedoes bitterness on Daniel's face when he came back, having secured two John Smith's Specials on the way. Instead I was merely appalled at the thought of yet another beer, and yet another type at that. Wasn't the modern man supposed to have his own brand? What was he looking for? All we needed was a heavy stout to finish us off. And it was just after eight.

In fifteen or twenty minutes Daniel had to be out the door.

He dropped the bottles onto the table from about six inches up. One tipped with a thunk and rolled, slow and fat, toward the edge. Ignoring it, Daniel jerked back his chair like someone opening a sticky drawer and aimed himself into it. For a second I resolved to let the bottle smash—then grabbed it and stood it up in front of him. He twisted off the caps and slid me one bottle. I slid it back.

I'm full as a biblical whale, I said. I couldn't possibly.

—So much for the blinding contract, he crowed.

He was drunk at last.

—*Binding.*

—Binding contract.

—What binding contract? I just don't need another beer.

—What sadder thing there stands than unloved beer. Shakespeare.

—It'll get over it.

—No, I'll save it from loneliness.

He seized a bottle in each fist and dumped the contents into two glasses, pulling the necks of the bottles out as foam surged over the rims. Céline appeared at his side, glaring at me.

—John! *Prends-en-une!*

—*Pourquoi moi? Je ne les ai pas commandées!*

But I knew what she meant. Still, I had limits. She rolled her eyes again at the situation, glanced at the two empties, sighed, and departed. Daniel drank as if newly arrived from the Sahara. He refilled.

His voice was icy now, and low, a monotone.

—Isabelle looks like she is. I told you. You weren't
listening. I know that. You've got your own life. Listening
is hard. Really hard. Isabelle looks like she is. When she
dresses, she is simply arranging the presentation of what
she already is. When she smiles, she's happy. She doesn't
represent. She—does—not—represent, I meant. Anything.
So you can see, it was unbearable.

I couldn't see, exactly, but I was convinced. Or at least
convinced he believed it.

—If Isabelle hadn't gotten so much done during her
maternity leave—he paused, as if aware he had heard
these words recently, then rolled on—she would never
have kept at it even after she went back to work. If she
hadn't pecked on and on at her computer night after
night after night after night after . . . . Oh Jesus, John.
Oh Jesus Christ.

He looked at me hopelessly. I thought he was about to
weep. Maybe he already was, Liza, in his way. But then
the edge came back. *Our* tone, I decided, our very own
tone. He drank, clenched his jaw, chewed the side of a
finger. A minute passed, two. The bitter tone that saved
him from falling silent.

—And so it went. So it goes. Kurt baby. Tappity tap
tap. Summary of analysis. Concluding remarks. Annex
one. And two. Bibliography. All the rituals in place,
bound in the requisite number of copies, lugged in a big
armload to the thesis office, duly deposited. If she hadn't
held it all together, like Superlady herself, she wouldn't
have been Isabelle, smoldering like a well-banked fire—
mommy, full time wage-earner, lover—my lover—and
prep prep prep for the orals, the panel of supposed
experts, an hour of pretending to consider the merits of

the work (they had decided weeks ago she would pass), celebratory bottle in the department chairman's office. I loved how she soldiered through it all, just getting it done and behind her, seeing what she wanted—the chance to do research, write, fling her fiery thoughts at the phenomenon of the human brain. If she hadn't juggled all the balls so calmly she would never have found the energy for docs, docs, and then post-docs. Yes! Post-docs! Grant applications thick enough to choke a filing cabinet. Submission deadlines. Nominators hounded for letters. Fat envelopes flying off in all directions. It was—Daniel stood up—it was a sight to behold! And if she hadn't!

Though his words were slurred, nothing could clip the wings of his sentences. He poured the last of the beer, and, hovering beside the table, drained the glass.

—And if she hadn't?

—Pardon?

—If she hadn't?

—If she *hadn't*, we wouldn't have loaded up the truck and moved to Bever-lee. Post-doc! UCLA of all places. Great psych program. Basketball team not what it once was, but hell. Off to California!

And he was off to the bar. California, he seemed to be saying, Liza, was the root cause. Of something. I put my head in my hands. I felt sick. Night had fallen. Behind me, I heard Céline saying no. But Daniel came back, with more stout.

—Ye'd have to be completely jarred, not to say Saxon, he lilted in his best second-generation Irish, to drink the Guinness itself out of a bleedin' *bottle*.

It was quarter past. To be on the safe side he should

133

have been out on Bernard already, straggling toward Parc and his number 80 bus. Five more minutes at an absolute maximum.

But now he was fastidiously pouring his Guinness down the side of a tilted glass, having apparently already forgotten his declaration about the savageness of Irish stout once bottled and determined to conjure a perfect head. His methodical air must have been too much for poor Céline, who finally burst out from behind the bar to whisper ferociously in his ear before again retreating.

California, I kept thinking. Weird. Just coincidence? Daniel was calm again; nothing up.

—No mansion with a *see*-ment pond, though. Not on Isabelle's posht-doc. Doc. The local equivalent of a four and a—four and a half, in a four storey box in a funny sort of neighbourhood about a twenty minute walk from the campus. If Isabelle hadn't been superwoman we would never have stuffed the Renault full and driven a big hypotenuse across America itself, found the apartment, and settled into paradise. Inter-zone between the Latinos and the Blacks. Whites sprinkled in. Nice enough. Oceancrest Boulevard, except you couldn't see the ocean and there wasn't any crest. But hell, that's America, no? What the hell.

—So, I said lightly. Did you go to California in honour of *La Californie*, or do you drink at *La Californie* in honour of your time in the real thing?

Half the Guinness was gone. And abruptly he seemed to be losing control again. I was struck, Liza, not for the first time, by how haphazard alcohol's hold on Daniel was: an on-off switch. The room was again at three removes, and he approached it vaguely, with half-phrases, impulses—whatever came to mind.

—Well, *sand*. Calves always ached like hell. Tired shoulders too. Pushing that damned stroller along the beach. Kate was starting to. Of course. No John. She was starting to walk. *La Californie?* Until otherwise some— until somebody *informs* me otherwise, I'm assuming it's a coincidence.

He filled with old emotion. It was the closest I ever saw Daniel stray to the sentimental. He sat with his chin just above the dark pool of his Guinness, gazing into that great middle distance where the drunk searches for lost things.

—Her hair was just the same as her mother's, he whimpered. Just the same. Same black. Felt the same. I can still feel it—his hand explored the air above the table. It's almost there. John?

—Yes, Daniel.

—You know what her first words were? Spring? Yeah. Spring of our California year.

After a bit I sensed he thought he had already told me.

—Her first words were . . . I prodded.

—Sitting on the apartment floor. Held up her short fat arms and said, clear as a bell, "Daddy-yup!"

—Great, I said vaguely, puzzled at his morosity.

—This will be the hardest . . . part. You'll listen. You'll *listen*. I know you will. You'll probably even pretend you care. That's all right. Kind decep-deception is the closest to honesty you can hope for these days. Well. Let me start. Again.

Abruptly he swept up the glass and downed the rest

of the beer. Céline had heard his last words and arrived by Daniel's side with an expression I had never seen before on her normally languid face. *Feroce*.

—*Non*, Daniel. *Tu ne recommences pas. Pas ce soir. C'est tard.*

—*Céline, franchement, va-te-faire foutre.*

—*Je le ferai. Mais plus tard.*

I stood up, afraid to help, afraid to do nothing. Céline, pushing Daniel's torso forward, was tugging his suit jacket off the back of his chair, hauling him to his unsteady feet, and loading him into the coat. A customer at a nearby table made a wisecrack in French I didn't catch, but Céline paused long enough to spit a terse *idiot!* in his direction. Daniel stood up straight and pulled his lapels into place as if it had been his idea all along. Completely unnerving me, he formally shook my hand and declaimed:

—*Pour faire partie du petit noyau, du petite group, du petit clan.*

In response to my puzzled air, he added: Proust. *Un Amour d'O'Brien. Ou Un Amour de Swann.* What da 'ell, heh?

Céline seized his arm, roughly, his head whiplashing, and steered him toward the door. On the way through he nearly fell twice.

I sat down, spent.

—*Mais, peut-il se débrouiller?* I asked Céline, as I had a night earlier. I pictured him veering into an alley and mistaking a garbage can for his bus. But she turned away.

She seemed to know he would manage.

And I could see him, an hour or two from now,

descending from the train into the cool suburban quiet, wandering slowly through its night circles and crescents and courts toward a house, perhaps near Lac St-Louis, near its glittering dark body. One more corner, one last sidewalk, and the gradual approach of the porch, the house lit from within. Him outside, standing a moment on the bare lawn, swaying gently in the spring breeze off the lake. His grief there was unbearable to me. I had watched his face through too many evenings, and had come to know it, Liza, better than I know my own. I have only ever looked at myself in a mirror; I have never seen myself from where someone else watches. Who knows what they see? His preparing to go on; the latch key already in his hand in his trouser pocket; knowing the perfect sadness of damaged love that can never be restored to what it was; but willing to go on through, willing to live with the cruelty done—the harm inflicted—present like a third partner to the union. Oh of course you can always say *I'm sorry.*

Still, there was a sort of hope in his very persistence. But whether such hope was a beautiful thing, or a kind of horror, wasn't clear. So was this why I feared him?

He found his way up the steps and stopped before the front door. I saw a glint as, laboriously, his key was guided into the lock and he let himself in. The entryway—and the living room and kitchen beyond—were quiet, one lamp left on by a reading chair. Perhaps she was up in the bath. Perhaps, after a hard day and facing an early morning commute, she had turned in early. He stood by the coat rack, listening.

Outside *La Californie,* I cursed. It was snowing hard, a

swirl of outsized flakes appearing out of the darkness and waltzing down, a million feather pillows shaken out. As each flake touched the sidewalk, it disappeared. Small mercies, I thought, looking at my sneakers. I turned up my jacket collar and crossed the street. My streets, though I was not "from here." My own middle distance. The shopkeepers from Sri Lanka were hurrying to get boxes of fruits and vegetables off the sidewalk, in out of the snow. They wore dark brown leather jackets. A delivery bike leaned against the wall by the entryway, its dark metal beaded from the wet snow. I passed a pair of empty storefronts. Inside the first store, cardboard boxes were scattered here and there, like an art installation. The next held two step-ladders, with buckets of paint at their feet. Two doors further along was the Polish cobbler's. His name was Henryk, I think. He'd fixed a sole for me. Now as always he sat behind his table sewing at his old machine, surrounded by tongues and hands of leather, never looking up.

I angled across Bernard in mid-block then turned along Jeanne-Mance, my hair beginning to feel wet. There were lights in most of the flats, yellow windows, curtains drawn, turned inward. I clattered up my steps. I read once about the wife of one of the Russian dissidents. After he had been taken away to the camps, she had to live wherever she could find someone to take her in. She wasn't about to be given work—not the widow of a traitor. To thank those who sheltered her, she used to search the surrounding woods for wild berries to bring them. She wrote that after spending most of the day in the woods, she used to slow down as she came back to the house in the evening, wanting to delay her arrival.

She kept thinking that her husband might have been let out of prison, and would come out to meet her. Going more slowly, she could hope longer.

The door was locked, the rooms dark. Inside, a copy of the *Gazette* lay on the floor. I picked it up, and laid it on a small table in the entryway while I sat on the stool to untie my shoes. You weren't there. On the front page, another story—another leak from the hospital, or the ambulance crew—about the baby who had been found on the mountain. It was front-page stuff. Lying there in her carriage in the little white gown, facing up at the sky, she had been surrounded by small, framed photographs, family shots of weddings, births, baptism day, with all of the adult faces carefully cut out.

3

Chartres

12

Our first spring together approached, the snow lifted, the school year wound down. We kept our two apartments: one of them was usually empty. The snow turned into rivers and disappeared down the sewer grates.

We were passionate. We weren't lovers. The snow, in little sparkling streams, found its way into the St. Lawrence and the sea.

Heading back to Vermillion to find a job mending rails on the long curves north toward Hornepayne or Folliet was out of the question. Other than a brief visit home after exams, you were staying in Montreal. David O'Shea had helped you land a summer job compiling bibliographies and indices for a research project at one of the institutes. All April I followed leads, mailed CVs, scoured bulletin boards, with my heart slowly sinking in tandem with my bank account. Riveting asbestos brake pads at $5.50 an hour seemed noble, but crazy. An advertised warehouse position, moving goods from Point A to Point B on dollies, would have been clean and quiet, but it would last only six weeks. Not enough dough. I got lucky in the end. But then, the fates were on our side. I was on my hands and knees trying to read the titles on the poorly lit bottom shelf of the philosophy section in my favorite second-hand shop, Wordsworth, when I heard one of the shop's two employees explaining to the owner that due to summer courses he wouldn't be able to sign on full time as he had the previous year. I stood up, a bit dizzy from having my head upside-down. Desperate at the thought of not seeing you daily made me bold.

—Hire me.

I knew the owner—Allan, a wiry marathoner with a magnificent sixties beard and gentle eyes—enough to say hello, but only as a customer. He seemed pleased by my spontaneity.

—I could give you thirty hours a week... eight dollars an hour. Six hour shifts. You can read when we're not busy. What were you looking for down there?

—A guy in one of my classes claims he saw a translation of Nicholas of Cusa.

—Dark red binding. Under "M." It's the last part of a mystical theology compendium. See it?

—Yes.

—Dusty, I bet. I bought it in '91 or '92.

—Not so marketable?

—You never know. Nice book to have in the shop.

—John. John Wilson.

—John. Any ideas for the store?

—You've got more D.H. Lawrence than you know what to do with.

—Used to sell like crazy. Until about 1985. And I've got boxes more in the storeroom. Twenty-five copies of *The Rainbow*, never mind *Lady Chatterley*. People were getting it off their hands. It'll come back. Buy low, sell high. How about Nicholas of Cusa as a signing bonus?

Eight times thirty, times sixteen or so weeks. Enough.

—I'd be delighted.

I recite it to you this way . . . my take on things. We had both been reluctant to take trips home that winter, to go through the introduction-to-families ritual. We knew we were going to spend our lives together, that was obvious. It wasn't that we thought of those trips as coming ordeals. We kept meaning to go to Toronto or Vermillion, some weekend soon. I was certainly curious to see what kind of people had produced you: not merely perfect for me and somehow foreknown, but also the kindest person I knew. Was I idealizing you? But I have never stopped believing that, not even now.

I had been straightforward with Mom. But neither she nor Dad were the types to talk about important things other than by extreme indirection, so what you meant to me was present only by its absence during her weekly phone calls. Repression, as you would have it.

But after using the excuse preparations for midterms to cancel a trip over Easter, by May a visit to Vermillion was more or less inevitable.

We had luck with the weather. A late spring hot spell had the leaves out in full force even on the hills north of Ottawa, their light, lime green richly interrupted by the dark scattering of fir. Do you remember? The sun polished the lakes beyond the train windows; the river itself, often invisible behind the slopes, was always there, a silver border, a thread of light. I was trying not to think about Lee, trying to quell the sensations of her that the old Via Rail car itself seemed to stimulate. I was distracted on the ride north and west, morning wearing into afternoon and eventually into a long purple twilight. It was nobody's fault that I was unable to sit beside you, your hand on my knee, your head on my shoulder when you dozed, without thinking about Lee—the human brain refuses to have a singular relationship with the world around it, much less with the will of its master (servant?). So much for anagogy. The seats, the window views, the colour of the conductor's cap, the accents of the conversations around me: each time I relaxed, my thoughts swerved to her. I would find myself telling her something, relating some anecdote, then remembering again that even the voice-in-my-head that talked to Lee, and scripted her replies, had been betrayed.

Dad met the Northlander bus. It all went well enough. He busied himself with the bags, and trunk key, and seat belts, and queries about the weather in Montreal. Seeing him, seeing the outline of Sacred Heart's steeple and the ancient worn hills, jolted me hard into the entire torn, burning world I had walked out of (leaving Lee locked inside), but I was brought back by your quip, asking me to point out all the major tourist attractions. Now I had to try to see Vermillion through unfamiliar eyes. That too was my new world.

Similar to the way I must now, with unfamiliar eyes, try to plod along the path of Melior approaching the Chartres of eight centuries ago: first having to enter his foreign universe, then pass with him into the new-to-him Capetian realms, into the Ile-de-France, the already ancient towns; then step by step to the porch of the radical School within the ninth-century diocesan palace walls adjoining the old, doomed cathedral—and try to re-experience his slow immersion in its renowned curriculum, its great fusing of science and faith, Mary enthroned as Wisdom, unknowingly preparing himself for the catastrophe to follow, and for his great test.

Dad, who looked at ease around you from the start, noted from the front seat that he would be happy to give a guided tour of the Wilson domain, including two

146

floors—up and down—three bedrooms and a bath, front veranda, Claire's garden—she's tilling up a storm, John, wait'll you see it—and one basement workshop.

—The highlight saved for last, I said.

Once we were inside the door, Mom too was kind, if less relaxed. She would try to be fair, no matter how much she worried that you were—given the suddenness of it all—in the process of ruining my life. She knew Lee, and knew me, and knew what Lee and I had meant to each other. She and Linda—in about grade eleven then—took you and your overnight bag off to the back bedroom where a bed was always kept ready for me or my brother Robbie to land in. I was fixed up on the veranda. Mom and Dad served us a three-course meal, followed by huge slices of blueberry pie—my picking, your Mother's preserving, Dad announced—served with dollops of ice cream. Everybody was suddenly tired and off to bed, leaving us with our pie at the kitchen table, grinning insanely, utterly happy.

I lay on the verandah cot in the absolute dark unknown in Montreal, listening to the whirr of the space heater and the haunting boom of trains shunting in the rail yard, harmlessly dreaming, as I always did on these trips, of coming back here to stay someday, settling into the rhythms and gestures and faces of home, in a known light—yet knowing that I never would. The door creaked. I heard you pad across the floor, and I tried to find your dark shape against the deeper gulf. You slipped in beside me, wearing a T-shirt and panties, lay in my arms with your ear tucked against my shoulder.

—It's dark. Cool. Silent. Now that the trains have stopped. It's lovely here, John.

—You're lovely, I said. You're the loveliest thing in the world. When I hear the trains I always feel immense, but hollow. With you here, I can embrace it.

—I love you. At last I don't feel like I need to ask anyone to forgive me.

—That's because you don't.

—I know. There is nothing more unacceptable to a modern therapist than guilt. I've been told and told. But part of me keeps pretending I feel guilty. I don't like the word "pretending," though. If you can't help it, is it pretense?

—No.

—I like your mom and dad.

—Me too. But they're so settled. I can only take it in short stints.

—Our kids will say the same thing someday.

In the sheer, Precambrian distance, steel wheels shrieked against a flange of rail. A pair of dogs barked at each other down by the river. I leaned out and turned off the heater. We sank one layer deeper into quiet. You rolled against me and on top, then sat up. Reaching down, you touched my face and my hair. You leaned forward and kissed me, and then you left.

Alone in Montreal, I often rehearse such scenes in my thoughts, though I long to set them away for good. After breakfast, and its round of polite questions, we set out. First down, into what Mom always referred to as "your dad's basement." We had lived in the house since the summer I was born. You ducked cobwebs and ceiling studs. Before us we saw old skates and soccer cleats with knotted laces, preserving jars saving dust, a torn and oily cardboard box full of bolts and nuts and unidentifiable widgets, a defunct washer and dryer, relaxed mousetraps, gummy buckets of paint, a helter-skelter of rakes and hoes in a corner, red clay flowerpots, a cheerless Eazy-bake oven, a floppy baseball glove, wire, cord, string, chain.

—But only to fool you, I said, coming to the door that led into the back basement. Look at this.

We stepped through. I flicked the switch.

Dad's shop was spotless. The long workbench standing against one wall was clear of tools; each hung on its nail against the plywood backboard within its own white painted outline. Shelves bore one of Dad's innovations: long lines of old baby food jars hung like tidy bats, blue lids nailed to the underside of the board, each holding a different size of nail or different calibre of screw, or a one-thirty-second-inch longer bolt, all easily accessed by simply unscrewing the jar from its lid. Another board, against another wall, held power tools, their cords wrapped around them with the plugs tucked in. The smooth cement floor, resurfaced yearly in grey paint, had just been swept. The new, yellow-handled broom stood by the garbage can next to the dustpan—inside, if we'd looked, we'd have seen a fluffy heap of sawdust and wood shavings. Dad's array of machines—assembled using the CN's buy-out package—gleamed: table saw, lathe, scroll saw, router, grinder, press, and power jigsaw. A simple, cleanly built dresser, still lacking drawers, sat near the small window overlooking the back yard. The drawers, still without handles, were near by on a drying rack of Dad's design. I took you over to check. Yes, the underside of the drawer bottoms had received a coat. You were suitably impressed.

—It's pristine. It's . . .

—Japanese.

—Yeah.

—It's the Ontario farmer-railwayman's indoor working version of a Japanese garden. If you move a stool, like that one, Dad will get a headache because the Taoist harmonies are out of whack. These things are genetic, so I'm probably doomed.

—He does beautiful work.

—He's a perfectionist. Here, anyway.

We headed up the back steps and out into the yard. Only the tulips and crocuses were in full bloom, but Mom's ambitious plans for the summer were already clear. The rock garden that now occupied the back half of the yard—opening out from a narrow bower created by the latticed rose bushes in the front half—was richer, more complex than the previous year. Flourishing, the grasses, sedges and wildflowers emerged from lower levels of groundcover and small shrubs—mint, blue-flowering rosemary—framed the rear lawn, which grew wilder each year; or wilder within Mother's original design. Some of the first roses were just beginning to unfold. Just as Mom had no business getting rosemary to flourish north of Sudbury, her roses were impossibly successful. The large blooms to come would be well-formed, deep velvet reds and clear yellows common enough in Sussex and the Loire valley but startling in Northern Ontario. The fruit trees in one corner of the garden were now mature; the aspen and maple that helped separate the sunny front half from the shady rear refuge—planted about the time I was born—were now twenty-five feet high. The winding gravel path tied the two halves together. A gazebo in the front was perfect for summer evenings; a bench half hidden on the edge of lawn and rock under the fullest shade tree was ideal for reading a book on a hot day. Or for secret assignations on mild spring nights, you pointed out.

I marvelled again. Skilful planning and complex texture made the modest yard seem twice its actual size.

We exited through the back gate—now almost buried in the dense hedge that formed a final border—into the lane, and out onto the main street to see the landmarks: Steadman's, the Wing Café, the Legion with its dusty windows, the pool hall, the Bank of Commerce and Home Hardware, the gift shop and Sears catalogue outlet, IGA, the pizza takeout, Allen's Men's and Ladies' Wear. And the outsized bulk of the CN building plugging the end of the street. Only the tracks and the bush lay beyond. That was all. We stopped in front of the conspicuous gap between Steadman's and the hardware.

—What's so funny?

—You'll never believe this one, I said. This was where the fire station used to be.

—And?

—Burned down.

—No.

—Yes. Why not? How can you fight a fire if it's at the fire station? They had to call in trucks all the way from the valley. Got here far too late.

—Psychotic town, Vermillion.

—Psychotic?

—Sure. The mind attacking its own defenses.

We took Albert Street down to the river. Climbing the flood berm, our backs to the row of bungalows and split levels, I pointed across the water—which slowed here, and fanned out to form the basin where the town kids swam—to the smooth shoulders of rock topped by stunted firs and white stripes of birch. You could, I said, walk in that direction for a hundred miles before bumping into the next town—if you were lucky.

—Nothing but forest?

—Nobody here calls it forest. Thin trees, thick underbrush, rocks, lakes, bogs, rivers. We call it "the bush."

We walked the crest of the berm until we came to the spot I had wanted to show you. Two masses of black rock erupted out of the turf, each about twenty feet high, smooth, rounded—like sleeping beasts. They framed a flat, grassy refuge. The rocks angled toward each other, so that the far end of the space was narrower, a doorway to the river and hills beyond. A few birch trees stood in the confines, speckling the ground with shade. I liked the way this space combined ancient, irreducible rocks— another few million years would leave them unaltered to the eye—with a sense of shelter that nevertheless opened toward the great distance. Not unlike the vista at Chartres.

We worked down the flank of the rock to stand in the centre of the grass. A couple of pickups passed on the street behind us; the white river glared in the sunshine in front of us.

—John?
—Liza?
—I hereby pronounce us husband and wife.
—For as long as we both shall live.
—Can we go into the bush? you asked.

As if determined to conform to stereotype, Mother had spent the morning boiling a hambone. The previous night she had set the peas to soak. When we came back in after the town tour the smell of pea soup hit me at the back door. I groaned.

—She only makes it twice a year, I whispered. Mind you, she didn't even decide to do it. Trust me. With "company" due in on the train, she filled a pot with peas and put it on the stove Friday after supper as unconsciously as she ran the dishwater.

—So? I like bean soup.

—And you love Chicken Guy Ding, Liza, I said. But that's good, because every time you come home you'll be company, and out'll come the pot.

If you really wanted to go to the bush, I knew where in the bush I really wanted to take you. I found Dad in the back basement, inspecting his varnish for bubbles, and asked to borrow the pickup.

—Liza wants to see the bush, I explained.

—I thought she seemed a reasonable woman, he said, his first and last judgment.

—I was thinking Mill Vant might be nice, and maybe on out to Old Tim's Lake.

—That might take some wading, Dad guessed. Keep an eye out for bears.

—But it's the end of May!

—Snow came off late this spring. There might still be the odd ornery one about.

We turned left at the post office and rumbled over the tracks into what was officially West Vermillion but which all the locals still called Simpson, after some otherwise long forgotten settler. It was a suburb of tiny houses with tiny yards, homes little bigger than shacks, thrown up by the CN in the twenties to house the (mainly French) brakemen and roundhouse crews. Simpson was still vaguely thought of as the "wrong" side of the tracks, though a burst of half unsold subdivisions—split levels with chain link fences and trees on sticks—was changing that, adding Sudbury commuters to the town mix. Two minutes later, past the curling club, we were out of town, and, with the exception of the thread of tarmac giving way to crushed stone, out of civilization.

The spring day was growing unseasonably hot. In the cab of the truck we pulled off our sweaters. I loved this landscape, though it made me melancholy—all the more for its harshness, its lack of the picturesque—and was hoping against hope that you would understand this, even feel its pull yourself; I was hoping you'd see something more than extremely modest rock-faced hills and short, scrubby pine, small lakes inclined to be muddy, and no vistas. Off the road, on the right, there was the cove of Brown's Lake. The gravel shoulder tapered to a gravel beach, where someone's four-by-four was parked, the owner fishing somewhere out of sight, the dark blue water thrown into shadow by a cloud sweeping over; and beyond it again the low iron hills, the silvery aspen, the spring-green birch, the emerald pine. On our left, exposed rock faces were streaked with rust. One lower outcropping, a split off cube like a ten-ton die, bore a message in white paint: Rose Loves Steve. Does Steve love Rose, you asked? We sped past, around a bend.

The scenes repeated themselves with slight variations. Ten miles later as the truck slowed and I put on the right turn signal (as if there were anyone else on the road), you touched my cheek.

—Yes?

—It's beautiful, John. But it's sad. Sweet sorrow.

How could I have doubted? I rolled down the window, threw you a glance, and yelled at the bush: JOHN LOVES LIZA!

As we bumped slowly down the mining road—the ore had been exhausted a decade ago, and the track was no longer maintained—I explained that the turnoff was called Mill Vant. No one was sure why, but Mom's assertion—a corruption of the French for "Mile Twenty"—seemed possible. The road, reasonably enough, was called Copper Mine Road. And this path, I said, pulling the truck over, climbing out, and pointing to a faint seam in the sumac, has no name.

Only the lure of prime blueberry picking terrain kept visible the traces of what had once been a dual track churned out by mine trucks hauling ore. One track was now an unusually straight footpath—though we seemed to be the first to trample down this year's twitch grass and six-inch aspens—the other trail was distinguishable only by the absence of larger trees. Where truck undercarriages had once decapitated saplings, the young trees were now higher than our heads. We walked single file. Even from here, Liza, I can see your worn leather backpack slung over a green T-shirt, your hair bright with sunshine, jouncing on your shoulders. Once you stopped suddenly and turned around and took my face between your hands and kissed me.

I recite as if to you, but I suppose I recite for my own ends, how the bush gradually grew denser; we had to push our way through encroaching jack pine branches that scratched at our foreheads and thickening spring underbrush that was swallowing the path. At least it was too early in the season for black flies. The deerflies were vicious, but few. After about fifteen minutes, we paused. I pointed to the left, where an outcropping of Precambrian rock rose out of the forest floor to a thirty foot jagged height capped by birch and aspen. The pathway, barely visible here, swung to meet the rock. The mine mouth was boarded up, though near the top there was a black gap a foot wide. A slack barbed-wire fence ineffectually surrounded it. Mining company signs warned of danger, forbade trespassing. On the rock face above the weathered timber a comic with a spray can had painted in large white letters: TUNNEL OF LOVE.

—For chthonic lovers, you remarked.

—Primeval, I agreed.

—Orpheus clambers out through the hole there once a year, cursing himself for looking back, for not quite believing, not quite trusting.

—The forever-contemporary man.

—Icon for our times.

—Liza, you have a genuinely morbid Northern Ontario imagination.

—Thank you.

—And poor Euridyce, heading back down to the

156

copper shafts, thinking if only the bastard had trusted me we could have dined on ambrosia forever.

—But he had to *look* for her fault. Typical male.

—Touché. Not much ambrosia in Sudbury anyway. So Euridyce is still down there somewhere? Want to have a peek?

—Let's not, and say we did.

—When we were kids there was some story . . . . Now that I think about it, it couldn't have been true. If it had been, somebody would have known the names. Anyway, there was a story about two kids—they were always kids from the Valley—a lot of people around here use that as a synonym for "generally irresponsible Frenchmen"— kids who got lost in the woods. One of the search parties found a jacket or something, and footprints, and followed the footprints right up to the entrance of the mine. Supposedly they never found any bodies. We kids always figured they were still in there, wandering up and down side shafts, trying to find their way back out. Even now, when I know it's nonsense, the place gives me the shivers. Endlessly walking in the dark.

—So surely this isn't the place you wanted me to see so badly.

—No, but stopping at the mine to tell scary stories is a crucial part of the package tour. We have to go further. There's still a bit of a path, see? I wanted you to see the great blueberry grounds, a little past where we'll stop. A stretch of woods burnt out there six or seven years ago. The berries are fantastic, come July.

The path began to rise, wriggling over boulders with trees emerging from splits in their sides, winding along the chasm of an old streambed, dodging impenetrable

157

copses of bushes and trees and stone. A mile past the mine, we emerged onto a ridge of moss-covered rock. Below us, an elegant surprise appeared—an unexpected valley, boxed in by burnt hills. Its bottom was flat and sunlit, bare stone and low bushes. On the far side, where a jumble of giant rocks disappeared into greater depths, a glitter of water pounded into unseen pools below. I could see Old Tim's lake in the distance. We needn't get there today. Birch etched the scene with white. Firs provided darkness, undertones. I pointed to where the waterfalls succumbed to shadow. There, deeper than we could see from here, was a tranquil pond, with gravel shores and rocks that arranged themselves perfectly to serve as picnic tables.

—It's wild, and peaceful; confined.

—Like domestic bliss. Shall we?

—John, do you think you'll want children someday?

I tried to get you to look at me. I even took your chin and gently attempted to turn your face toward mine. But you were looking across the valley, or at the sky. I understood. I'm not sure I had ever considered the question, consciously, before that moment.

—Of course. Your children.

—Good.

The sun beat down on the backs of our necks out of a high sky where blue glared into white. It felt like July. I stripped off my shirt as we picked our way down the rocky slope. The ridge was perhaps a hundred feet above the level floor of the valley. I took your backpack—camera, snacks—and slung it over my shoulder. Where it had hung, sweat darkened your T-shirt. At the far side of the valley, where the stream cut out the lower ravine, the rocks were slippery with moss and lichen, so we climbed down by stages, often helping each other at waist-high ledges. At the bottom the scene was superb, just as I had remembered. Black rock extended, slightly tilted, toward a stone-hewn pool twenty feet in diameter. Water poured into it from a four-foot drop, a narrow chute of white water that the basin absorbed, stilled. At the other end, the pool fanned slowly over a curb of granite until it dropped by degrees onto a series of low ridges, before gathering again into another, larger pool with gravel shores. From there it disappeared underground into crannies and sluices, to emerge, I knew, hundreds of yards away in the marshy approaches to Old Tim's Lake, two or three hills to the south. Small trees grew out of the sides of the rocks just above us, laying branches of shadow over the water. Larger trees lined the rocks that topped the ravine on all sides. It was cooler there than it had been above—a watery, shady side-chapel.

We found a spot near the water-drop where we could sit on a flat ledge and dangle our bare feet in the black pool. The water was icy, and we soon pulled out our toes to let them warm on the rocks. We sat and ate apples and chocolate bars. Exploring further down, by the lowest pool, we discovered that the gravel shore gave way, near a rock face, to a grassy verge. Magically, when you wrapped your arms around me from behind, and ran your hands slowly over my bare chest, you too were shirtless. Your breasts were cooler than my sun-warmed back. Standing on tiptoe, you slowly stroked my belly as you kissed my neck, and then caressed my nipples with two fingertips. I tried to turn around, wanting your mouth, but you wouldn't let me. Briefly you darted your tongue between my reaching lips and slid your hands down over my pants, scratching at my jeans in an almost absent-minded way where my hardness stretched the material. Unbuttoning my pants with one quick jerk, unzipping them more slowly, you turned me around, pulling my hands down over your breasts. A moment later I was kissing them while you were trying to get my jeans over my hips. I found the opening of yours already undone as we slowly lowered ourselves onto the grass, your fingers grasping—hard, quick. We had been there all along, for years and years, and were now reawakening at last, finding our way again.

But as you lay back I felt a change. Rather than moving with abandon, your hands, now on my back, seemed to be holding on. I was searching, unfolding your folds, and you were gasping, but in short, hard intakes of breath that seemed more concentration than pleasure. I slowed my movements, and raised my mouth from your collarbone. Your eyes were open. They seemed focused somewhere behind me. You said neither yes nor no, but I understood and eased to one side, curled against you, leaned your head against my chest. I felt that we needed to talk about this. But the stillness seemed safer, and had its own beauty. So I thought at the time.

We lay side by side on the rough grass, gradually becoming aware of the itching, tickling. We didn't move for a long time.

—Beautiful clouds, I whispered at last.

—Do you think it's possible, John, that we've had other lives?

I was abruptly chilled.

—John?

—Yes, darling. Because I've heard you ask that before, somewhere. A long time ago.

We turned our heads, looked searchingly at each other, scared. We waited, and as if a shadow passed, the present recaptured us.

—Is this a popular spot?

I reached over and flicked away my shirt, which you had laid across your stomach.

—Worried about being a public spectacle?

—Well . . .

—Bet you didn't know the Old Italian word for bedroom was camera.

You sat up with your arms stretched wide, the sunshine on your breasts. You scanned the rocks above us.

—No, I said. I've almost never seen anyone down here. You might want to be careful in berry season. But even then, the best patches aren't that close by. They're up top, where there's more sun.

We got our jeans, pulled them on, lay again on the grass. Lying propped up on one elbow, I watched your face.

—Oops. Let me get that.

I flicked away a tiny spider sprinting across your brow.

On Sunday, in honour of the dead British monarch's birthday, we indulged in the full array of Vermillion culture. I walked to Mass with Mother, while you watched Dad in his wood shop awhile and then curled up in the easy chair on the verandah with the *Sunday*

161

Star. In the afternoon, following a stroll along the river, we walked up to Centennial Park where the season's first slow-pitch tournament was under way. We sat in the bleachers while the Lions Club Royals trounced Ted's Esso. I tried not to think about Lee. Two of her friends spotted us but didn't come over; two others did, and watched me closely through the introductions. They were trying to figure out, I assumed and explained to you later, whether I was the victim of a tragic error or merely the incarnation of evil. Then we stopped by the beer tent just beyond the outfield fence, and sat in its shade at picnic tables drinking beer from plastic cups, listening to the chink of aluminum bats. A few old high school classmates were there, home after a season in Muskegon playing minor pro hockey, or a semester at Laurentian, or on an off day from the railroad.

After an hour of baseball, and then supper, we settled in to keep Dad company in front of the Stanley Cup finals. I wandered out between the first and second periods to chat with Mom while she worked in the garden. You flipped through the years' worth of *National Geographics* in the den and tried to get dad to talk about himself. He likes you, I told you, a lot. So keep trying. In five or ten years he might give something away. Then you can tell me.

On Monday we convinced them both we were perfectly capable of walking up to the bus depot. A few minutes before we left, Mom found me alone in the kitchen.

—You're okay, John?

I felt tears welling. Unable to really share with you, Liza, the pain of that night in Vermillion with Lee, I instantly became a child, wanting Mother to make it all better.

—Yeah. I am, Mom.

—You don't seem yourself. You're not working too hard at school?

—Really, no, I'm fine.

—Have a good trip. Here.

She handed me an envelope.

—It's from Lee, she added. I didn't send it, with you coming home. She maybe thought you'd be here for the summer.

—Probably. Thanks.

I slipped the letter into my back pocket. On the veranda, getting my things together, I took out the crumpled envelope and smoothed it. The household garbage was on the porch waiting to be taken to the curb, so I unwound the twist tie, set the letter inside, and re-closed the plastic. Picking up my suitcase I walked to the door, put the suitcase down, reopened the garbage bag, and took the letter back out. I heard two sparrows squabbling in the eaves. In the back bedroom I found a box full of my old stuff on a top shelf and laid the envelope there, unopened.

The train trip back from Vermillion was quieter, muted, as though we were back on familiar ground. The weather, too, closed us into the gentle sway and click and lurch of the train car—low clouds pressing the dark hills, curtains of rain and fog drawn over the vistas. Sudbury, North Bay, Mattawa, Renfrew. I dozed with my book on my lap. Already I was reading medieval history, centred on France as most medieval history is; it was beginning to steal time from my architecture courses. What to make of the notion of the "self," when you, Liza, noticed and pointed out to me that I was beginning to read in this new area systematically, obsessively, whereas *I* thought I was coming home with this additional reading a little more often merely because my new study carrel in the university library happened to be near the history shelving.

This didn't wash: you pointed out that the history nearest my desk was American Civil War, which I didn't know a thing about and still don't.

And okay, so I *did* sign up for a summer course in Latin. But I had always wanted to have a bit of Latin, a vague sense of obligation, and it wasn't offered at St. Jude's in Vermillion at the time I was a student there.

So I dozed and read. You mostly slept. A good idea, I was thinking, watching the rivulets of rain running diagonally up the window beside me, the glass cool when I laid my forehead against it to stare at the metal coloured lakes. We were meeting David and Claire for Thai food that evening. Claire was just back from a semiotics conference at Cornell, and would no doubt be banging out ideas like a pinball junky. Best to be rested.

But you slept so long—unconscious through the North Bay stop, and still fitfully searching for more comfortable positions without quite awaking long past the turn south at Mattawa—that I began to wonder if you weren't feeling well. I remember trying to get at your backpack's front pocket—tucked under your seat near the aisle—without disturbing you. I needed to make a note, and had lost my pen, the beautiful black lacquer fountain pen you had given me at Christmas. Then I found myself somewhat hoping you were a bit ill rather than upset about the previous day. I sensed that at times, at certain unpredictable moments, parts of you were paper lanterns—lovely, easily torn, easily destroyed by an idiot with a match.

Somewhere north of Renfrew you curled up against me, head on my shoulder, arm limply across my lap. After a moment you kissed my cheek and sat up gingerly. You smiled, but didn't see me; you seemed distant; I couldn't quite find where your eyes focused.

Dinner with David and Claire was exhausting, and David seemed sympathetic to our fatigue and your evident struggle to be civil when we begged out of traipsing over to St. Denis for coffee and the famous pecan pie in the trellised back garden of Ce Truc Là, Claire's newest *brilliant* café. Claire herself was on a high, so that we had to extricate ourselves by force on the sidewalk outside the restaurant. But there would be other dinners, other theatre nights and concerts in the next few years—either the four of us, when they were together; or with Claire and whoever, or with David as a threesome, when they weren't.

13

After another long day of reading and fiddling with my notes, of trying out a sentence or two, I make my way again to the park, where, in the afternoons, a different local day care brings the children to play. The change of venue might make my thoughts less preoccupied with you, Liza. Cardinal Melior, as I follow him in my research and thoughts, moves closer and closer to the School and the fire.

An hour after passing the gates of Chartres, Melior was in the apartment Renaud had reserved for him in the west wing of the palace, stripping off the damp inner layers beneath the sodden outer ones. He had successfully left the vidame Roger at the threshold: Renaud had seemed determined to attach this official to his suite, but even Melior, no stranger to arrogance, thought the vidame of a cathedral chapter rather underemployed as a butler. In truth, Renaud had been tiresome, but less so than feared. When Melior had explained that while he would be happy to take a glance at what were no doubt the already expert administrative procedures of the diocese—and even suggest an emendation of technique, of bylaw, of tariff here and there—the focal points of his visit would be the School and the chapel holding the chemise, Renauld had raised no objections. Of course he had smirked knowingly at Melior, implying he knew—just between us senior princes of the church—what sorts of speeches were required in an audience chamber with no end of clerks and seneschals and summoners about. Ass, thought Melior, tossing his shirt onto the bed. Well, at least he had a bed of his own; a mark of honour indeed, in France.

It wasn't a bad room, though the fire burning fitfully in the grate made precious little headway against a fierce draft, and he was a little miffed that the window gave onto an odd narrow courtyard rather than affording a view of the church. The floor was covered in checkerboard tiles and the high, narrow bed—uncurtained—fitted cozily into an alcove outfitted with oak cupboards. The armchair sat on a small platform, one step up, and was as uncomfortable as granite, but beside it, mounted on a marble octagonal plinth, was a circular, two-level reading stand, the bottom holder the right height if seated, the upper if standing. Ingenious!

A scraping in the corridor announced the arrival of his trunks. Dry clothes, a bite to eat, then first to the School to meet the acting master, Robert of Aulnay—or rather maybe first to the cathedral, goal of so many other weary pilgrims? His heart yearned. Of course, he would first visit Our Lady—all the more certainly because chatting with Robert and scanning the renowned library's nearly five hundred volumes sounded all too appealing. Whatever he wanted, he needed silence first: calm, a measuring out of himself. Eliminating Renaud from his thoughts . . . . Now where had they put Auxerre? He hardly wanted to eat alone.

An hour later, a modest meal completed, he did want solitude. The light was almost gone but, after a dull day, a clearing in the west washed the air with a gold-tinged clarity as he made his way up a shadowed alleyway that ran along the east side of the cathedral to at last reach the yard before the church. Here he could see the already famous new west front straight on. Hooded, in a plain cloak, Melior leaned his back against a stand where a fishmonger was busy shoveling his unsold wares into a barrel strapped to the back of a rude cart.

Only the top of the new south tower shone in the last of heaven's light. Much higher than its northern counterpart—which had been capped with lead after the second storey had been finished and the money ran out—the tower, crowned with light, was breathtaking, both in its soaring height—thirty times that of the hovels abutting the outside wall of the Episcopal enclave—and in its exquisite proportions. Finished a mere twenty years earlier, its fame had only recently reached northern Italy. Melior had seen a sketch in the notebook of a travelling friar: but he now understood the man had had more enthusiasm than talent. The tower's broad, square base, clad in the fine, light grey stone quarried, he was told, at nearby Berchères, was penetrated by three elevations of deep twin bays, the point of the lower bays' spade-shaped arches transformed yet continued by slender columns scaling the spandrel and culminating in rounded arches curving solidly under the firm division beneath the third storey—which was hollowed, lightened, by broader and deeper round arches in preparation for the amazing fourth level. Here, the square, through an intricate combination of steeply pointed crockets, columns, and openings that Melior could for now only begin to analyze, was transformed into an octagon whose eight panels sloped elegantly upward and inward to meet at a point that seemed not really a point, its terminus from the ground so infinitely slender that it appeared to continue, invisibly, ever finer and more immaterial, into the empyrean.

Behind him, startling his reveries, he was distracted by another loud slap of fish against wooden staves.

It was disconcerting, he had to admit, to turn his attention away from the south tower to its decidedly stubby northern neighbour and the now undeniably *low* nave of Saint Fulbert's early-eleventh-century church. Its overall scale was impressive enough. He had counted over a hundred strides on his way from the palace, immediately behind the cathedral, to the front. And he knew that Fulbert's genius and piety—and connections—had enabled him to fill the interior with wonderful ornaments: gifts of candelabra and altars and statuary from half the sovereigns of Europe—King Robert and King Canute among them. And he knew that, wisely, after the fire of 1020, Fulbert had preserved the still more ancient crypt beneath as a home for the relic of Our Lady. Yet . . . . It was a muddle. The wonderful tower, bittersweet, showed you, taught you, that geometry and its subtleties were God's beauty, that this was how the spirit of humanity—here, now—could be structured through rays pouring in at its eyes into a likeness more closely approximating that of creation itself. The *principate* of number. It was clear. He understood it better now. And it made the virtues of the old church—he was walking forward to take a look at another wonder, the new portal, an unparalleled cavalcade of men and women and angeldom recently brought to completion in the opening left by a fire fifty years earlier—it made these graceless in the company of the hunched roof of the nave; the crippled north tower;

the dull, barely ornamented exteriors of the transepts; the blind, windowless wall of the front above the door. Now in darkness, he felt the need to hurry inside. Giving the dim splendours of the portal a quick glance, saving them for daylight, he pulled open the heavy centre door and let himself into the vestibule.

People. And darkness; darker than outside. Many people. He heard rustling, whispers, a cough into an echoing space, what sounded like the mew of a cat; he could sense many bodies, both nearby and receding into the distance. Catching something out of the corner of his eye he turned abruptly, his heart racing. An old man, six inches from his face, stared fiercely into his eyes. The fellow was ancient, his face an estuary. He pulled his lips back like an animal preparing to snarl, to bite, but his jaw was empty of all but two lonely black stumps. Yellow: as Melior's vision began to adjust to the dimness (a ghost of light still touched the Norman nave's narrow windows, and somewhere far ahead a candle flickered) he realized the man's eyes were yellow, the whites ruined with jaundice. Could he see at all? His left ear was gone, probably in some fight, and his hair but a few webs on a mottled skull. A bent hand came up slowly. Melior stepped back, ridiculously proffering his bishop's cross like a password. The man did not notice it, if he could see; and anyway, Melior now realized, the hand was slowly crossing the air, indicating the axis of the world.

—The Lord and Our Lady be with you, Melior managed to whisper.

But the man was already staggering past him, seeking out someone else to bless. Someone more worthy, Melior

170

thought, and for once this thought had no trace of the formulaic self-abasement drilled into him as a novice.

The nave was full of people, bedding down for the night on its sloping pavement. Pilgrims. The poorest pilgrims. Merchants would put up at the town's dozen flourishing inns, Barons and Dukes at nearby castles of liege lords, cardinals at the bishop's palace. These were the people who had walked: single droplets gathering into rivulets for safety—that is, if a mere dozen together, a couple of the stronger with cudgels, could be called safe in most parts of Christendom. A week's walk for the locals, a month's for the hardy from remote corners of France, a year or more of plodding for fanatics of the Virgin from Sicily, Ethiope, Armenia, Rus. He could smell them now, even if it was too dark to glimpse more than shadows—urine and mildew, feces and sweat, the dung of their dogs. Most were already sleeping, rows of dark forms on the floor. It reminded him eerily of the dead brought back from battle, lying in shrouds like so many overturned boats along a strand where the bishop had been brought out to bless them, laid out away from the town so sea breezes could lift away their rot from the nostrils of the saved.

Auxerre was beside him, a shadow turned substantial.

—My grace, will you see the crypt? They keep Our Lady there for the night, locked in an ironbound cupboard.

—Auxerre. Not sleepy even after that hellish trek today? Are they afraid of thieves?

Had he detected sarcasm in the monk's flat tones?

But he must follow, or be lost again. He strained to pluck movement out of the night pressing in on him.

They felt their way to the left, sandals shushing against

the flagstones. In the aisle, near the heavyset, tree-trunk column at the beginning of the Norman arcade, Auxerre stopped. A candle appeared in his hand, lit. The flame flared, finding oxygen in the draughty church. Firelight showed the respond, caked with soot, wavering and disappearing above them as if sinking away into dark water, and illuminated the brown cowl of Auxerre, with a glint of eyes in his shadowed face. At his feet, a narrow set of stone steps descended into a gulf beneath the old floor. Auxerre reached into the folds of his cloak. He handed Melior a warm iron key, the length of a finger, and the candle.

—Compliments of the sacrist. I met him near the high altar. He's as old as it is. Hertogenbosch, he is called, if you need to find him again. Odd name. I'll tell him you have the key. He guards it jealously. He assures me it is the only one, but then, that's the way of sextons, isn't it? Sorry, sacrist. He assures me he is not a sexton.

—You're not coming down?

—Two minds together are never pure, my grace.

The crypt, according to the chronicles, was already venerable with age when, in the year of Our Lord 911, Gantelme showed the holy tunic at the New Gate and Rollon's besieging Normans fled in terror. Was it excavated for the building of the church, destined to be burned by the Danes in 858? Or was it the foundation of a yet deeper history, of the edifice torched by Aquitaine in 743?

Melior cupped the flickering flame. His hand glowed pink. Auxerre seemed to have already withdrawn. He descended.

*

I whisper to myself: listen, Liza. As he went down, the steps surfaced out of darkness one at a time, each as unreal and incorporeal as a face in a dream. Carefully, each footstep made them real, sure. Sounds from the nave shut away behind him. What business had fear, here? He tried to banish it. But he had no doubt, no doubt that God approached. Melior did not consider himself a mystic. He did not scorn the *via negativa*—for others. But he distrusted sensations targeted, yearned after, meditated upon, and then "miraculously" found. He worried it was the devil of self that was discovered, or that God became nothing more than the search itself, the faith of the church a reassuring solipsism. That was not his church. If there was nothing truly found, the search became, well, optional. So he preferred to wait, and not to presuppose—as far as he was able—what, exactly, he was waiting for. Auxerre would no doubt consider this attitude only another byway of arrogance, the calm patience of the Italian prelature. So be it.

Another step. No, not a mystic. But twice or thrice before, God had come to him, always through Our Lady, and then there had been no doubt—as there was none now. It was happening again, after so long. The world about was shuttered and muffled; the sky itself above the lamentably earthbound arches of the old church had disappeared; a circle had drawn tight around him. But why this terror? His blood was in his mouth—he had bitten hard on his tongue. As he reached the bottom step, and his sandals again shuffled across the grit of old stones, he tried to shore himself up with a passage

173

of Richard of St. Victor he couldn't quite remember, not word for word. The soul must use every one of its capacities, Richard had written, particularly reason—that was what Sugar of St. Denis, busily knocking walls out of his old priory to pour light and geometry in, had assured him he would find in the School at Chartres, the *soul* using reason. The soul, he tried again to recite, must use every one of its capacities, particularly reason; and humans could approach God by that means. I approach! he almost called aloud, instantly ashamed at his presumption. Stepping around an abutment, he saw the low, rock altar before him: One could approach God by that means. But only approach. Only through love was it possible to reach the plenitude.

I'm an old man and a child and a fool, he said to himself. Do you know me? A low, barreled ceiling peaked only eight feet above the floor. The chamber's stones were damp, and covered here and there with patches of moss. He turned his head sharply, but it was only the black bird of his shadow on the walls and ceiling behind and above him. Somewhere, nearby, water was slowly dripping. The small altar was stripped. An age-stained oak cupboard stood nearby; a kneeler was set before it. On his knees, Melior reached forward and inserted the key. The act of withdrawing it pulled one door slowly open with a small creak. That was enough. He set the taper in a small holder bolted to the wall beside the kneeler. He waited for the next drop of water, wherever it was, but it did not come.

Inside the chest stood a T-shaped bar of blackened wood, about a foot high. Draped over it, and under and over again, was a cloth—not blue, he thought, not that anyone had said it would be, but an off-white grey, about a yard long and a foot wide. Its ends were loose threads, as if it had been cut roughly and with haste from a larger garment. There were a few small stains—but then who would dare wash it? A single splash of water, then silence again. In the shadow of the cupboard, with just the one candle burning, flame tugged against its wick now as some small movement of air found its way even here. The cloth was palely suspended in darkness, like a hand in shadows, a face in a dim doorway.

Melior slowly, very slowly, laid his forehead against the wooden armrest of the kneeler, and closed his eyes. It was all right, he could still see.

Do you know me? he said. I'm an old man. I'm very tired. You know that. Can you let me rest? How can I let you rest, yet give you your will? But I'm tired. How can I let you rest, yet give you peace? Rest gives others peace, but not you. Then cover my shame. I cannot see your shame. Why? I am blind to shame. But it is part of my sinfulness. Your sinfulness is very real, but I cannot see it. You can see all. I cannot see your sin. Why? Because you are a mirror. But even I can see the sins of others. No. No? No, they are mirrors too.

He waited, trying to think, then trying not to think. Time slowed down. An odd sort of echoing. He looked up, but the cupboard door had swung shut. His hand stretched out, but he changed his mind and pushed the cupboard door tight, turned the key. A cramp in his neck made him flinch with pain. On his way back toward the stairs he noticed a rather bad plaster statue of the Virgin at the far end of the small crypt, barely visible in the gloom. He could still see her, standing solemnly, slightly stooped, a crooked half-smile on her face, as he made his way upward into the vestibule, even quieter, even darker than before, with only night time, sleeping sounds.

Outside it was cold but the clouds were clearing; torn shreds sailed quickly away across the face of a half-moon. Melior stopped beneath the carved cosmos of the portals, far too distracted to notice them. His taper was burning down; he blew it out. With the moon there was sufficient light to make his way—now where was the path? He had not expected this. Of course he had hoped for inspiration here, a tightening of his perpetually slackening vows, a moment or two of peace, some intimation of Her presence—but he had gone far too many disappointing miles of pilgrimage to have presumed that he would find grace. He was buffeted by both excitement and exhaustion, yet his heart was not pounding, his temples did not throb, his eyes were not blurred. His thoughts swam. No, in fact, he had no thoughts. Instead there was silence, within and without. Of course it was now late in the evening, but could the town possibly be this quiet? He strained his ears: no child's cry, no barks of the hordes of mangy dogs he knew must prowl the streets searching for kitchen leavings, butchers' offal, greengrocers' trash. It wasn't possible.

But gradually a slow gathering of ringing filled his ears, as though a dozen very small, highly pitched bells were chiming at a great distance. Fascinated, he held still and tried to keep his very heart and breath motionless. He had a sensation of approach, of the bells coming toward him.

—Your grace.

His head jerked.

—Auxerre?

A cowled monk stood at the bottom of the porch, four steps below Melior. The man looked up, and the moonlight gave his young, clean-shaven face the gleam of mother of pearl.

—Excuse me, your grace. I am Gabriel. Gabriel of Ulm. Brother Auxerre has turned in for the night and sends his apologies. He asked me to see if . . . . I'm at the School; I'm a student, I mean. He asked me if I were passing by the royal portal. He thought . . . you had been gone for some time.

—And you *were* passing the west front? Besides, I've been here only a few minutes.

—Your grace, I've been waiting here for two hours. After confirming you were still in the crypt. Excuse me—I didn't want to disturb your prayers.

Two hours? Baffled, Melior sought to deflect the discussion.

—And is the palace of Our Lady too dangerous a place for a lone cardinal to say his prayers?

Hardly a palace, don't you think, your grace?

—Gabriel of Ulm, it's a fine old church.

—And also a diplomat.

—*Were* you passing the portal?

—Yes, I go to the crypt, many evenings.

—But only the sexton has a key, I believe, and no doubt the bishop?

—I have . . . managed to make a copy, your grace, if it pleases you. I guard it with care.

—Oh, it pleases me, certainly.

The moonlight was barely sufficient, but Melior

caught the heretofore rather solemn young man's smile. Not a relieved smile, though. His face was calm, open, but distant and self-contained. Gabriel kept his own counsel, Melior thought. Perhaps he had a good deal of counsel to keep. There was depth in him, an attractive combination of depth and youth.

—And what does Robert of Aulney, your master, teach the students about the sacred chemise?

—He teaches that the final approach to Our Lady, after faith and logic have done their labours, is over a small bridge suspended on cords of love.

—Does he? Or do you say it like that?

—Perhaps I paraphrase, your grace.

—Indeed. Will you show me back?

To his astonishment, Gabriel hesitated.

—If you wish . . . Lord Melior.

—And your wish?

Gabriel's left sleeve fell back as he raised a pale hand: a key, silvered by the broken wafer of moon. The gesture was so forthright that Melior was incapable of judging it either melodramatic or impertinent. But to put his will ahead of that of a Prince of the Church. The young man flirted with heresy.

—Go to your Lady, Gabriel, to mend your pious pride. I can find my way.

Gabriel bowed slightly; Melior felt his own face come under study.

The Cardinal hesitated, then descended the steps and stepped briskly toward the path that swept to the north of the cathedral. But the moon was lost, for the moment, in a patch of heavier cloud, and he had to slow his pace.

—Will I . . . he asked, halting and turning. But Gabriel

had gone in. See you at the school? he addressed himself, in a whisper.

*

The chamber was far from grand. It was located on the second floor of a long low building running near the east wall of the episcopal enclosure, a hundred yards from the palace. Other parts of the building contained the dormitory, storehouses, and scriptorium. Eight or ten paces long, hardly so many wide, the room did have fine, tall windows giving a view over the noisy hovels of the lower town and the city gates of the Paris road. Benches were set along three walls: for visitors, like Melior, for the doctors of the school who might wish to attend, for a few of the senior students who presumed to sit with them. Not grand, but spacious enough to hold half the students, who were there now, lining the floor at the feet of the lector in rows of brown cassocks, and standing along the back wall—an extra large gathering drawn, Melior hoped, by the eloquence of the distinguished grammarian Hugh of Paris—descanting today on a text from Dionysius the Areopagite—and not by any hope that the visiting prelate would enlighten them with his own commentary.

Melior was there to listen. He had heard so much about the cathedral schools of northern France, and this was his first opportunity to spend any time at one. Robert of Aulney sat comfortably at his elbow, eyes narrow but intent, a small quick man with a bit of plumpness: he reminded Melior of a wise old raccoon. Hugh stood at the front, a small table behind him that he never used, and a stand on his right bearing the priceless book, a translation from Greek into Latin—newly done at St. Denis itself, under Sugar's orders—of Dionysius Areopagite's *Celestial Hierarchy*. Most believed the work, by a student of the apostle Paul, had been given to Louis the Pius centuries ago by the emperor at Constantinople, and deposited by Louis at the Abbey of St. Denis. Rumour had it that Hugh—tall, thin, tonsured and goitered, simultaneously serene and energetic (like a disciple of Bernard, mused Melior: but this is no monastery!)—could worry out texts in Arabic, and Melior fully intended to confront him with the question afterward. Greek, Latin, and Arabic: a man like that, in Melior's Pisa, could, by himself, help to establish the sort of . . . . But at the moment Hugh was summarizing for his audience—the youngest students twelve or thirteen, the oldest over twenty, such as, yes, there he was, Gabriel of Ulm—the previous week's discussion of Macrobius' commentary on the surviving fragment of Plato's *Timaeus*.

What he now observed was so different from both the schools of his native Italy—Pavia, Bologna—dominated by law and Justinian's Digest, and the Benedictine abbeys of Bernard that swept the continent in still increasing numbers. In Cluny of Jumière silence was the greatest virtue; here it was a tourney of the mind. Already, once or twice, Hugh had nodded to one of his listeners to ask for his reaction to what was being said. And it was clear he listened intently to the response, fully expecting to find in it something of use, an expansion of thought, a fresh angle of approach. Yet Bernard need not rail against a Chartres as he railed against the scholastics, against

Abelard's arrogant brilliance or Peter of Poiter's "duty to doubt". Chartres, he was more convinced than ever after his morning stroll with Robert, had watched the great wave of scholasticism crash around it with a judicious eye, taking what could be used—lessons of rigor and logic, care in argument, the testing of each rung up the ladder of thought—while retaining the outpourings of the heart that filled its favourite texts (Genesis, Plato, mathematics) as the *finale* of all searching.

Now Hugh was leaning close over his book—his vision was obviously poor—absent-mindedly writing some unknown graffiti in the dust on his lectern, and straightening and gazing toward the windows to pronounce that *light, radiance* was the essential gift. But not, once one gave it some thought, such a simple gift to give as one might suppose under a spring sun. Not simple at all, because the divine giver is dependent on the beneficiary to complete his creation.

—Explain! A couple of raucous youths shouted from the back.

Melior was startled and irritated, but Hugh seemed delighted by the eruption. A school tradition, it appeared.

—Because the value of each object—and you, my lads, are all objects, if rather particular, unpredictable, and unruly objects—must be judged by the extent to which it partakes of light.

Brows furled throughout the room. Melior was trying to think.

—Explain!

—When we polish our jewels they shine. We make glass from sand and ash. Fire comes from darkest coal and gnarled wood. Thus they have light in them, whether our eyes are able to see it or not. This, you are all pointing out to me—yes, I've read your minds—does not explain how God is dependent on those he gives light to. And how all this is to be squared with his omnipotence. For Dionysius Areopagite, philosophy was a hymn. He sings what God is not, hoping to find him in negation, in what the thinker's mind cannot turn to quickly enough to capture, to glimpse behind him as it were. But in the darkness, in matter, there is light. Every candle tells you this.

—And with stained glass in profusion, Gabriel interrupted, Sugar tells us all: with walls of light.

—Thank you Gabriel. But I have still not explained. If anyone thinks I have explained, they are badly mistaken.

—Explain! tittered a young fellow on the floor, whom Melior had noticed earlier absentmindedly counting his lice.

Robert of Aulney sat up abruptly out of his meditative slouch at Melior's side; one of the boards of their bench creaked loudly. The boy looked out of a corner of his eye, then down at the floor.

—I shall, said Hugh, trying to look solemn. Can a candle see its own light, given eyes? William?

—Yes, master.

—You're certain.

—Yes . . .

—But can it see flame, the source of the light?

—No, master.

—Not unless a recipient of the light, polished by its own love of the light, turns back, to look at the source, to face the flame.

A low murmuring in the ranks.

—Mirror! said a startled voice.

Hugh bowed toward Melior.

—Your grace. Mirrors.

In the pandemonium of chattering scholars bolting out of the room, Melior heard two voices behind him as he tried to listen politely to Robert and Hugh discussing a fine point of the translation spread out on the lectern.

—Point. Gabriel's voice.

—Point, said another. Melior saw a young monk he'd never met chancing a quick look.

—The Cathedral is the centre of the bishopric. The bishop alone can ordain. The ordained alone can consecrate. The consecrated bread alone is the presence, the reenactment of the incarnation. The incarnation is the principal event of the cosmos.

—Point.

—The Cathedral, seat of the bishop and the temple of God, should also be a model of the cosmos, in both time and space.

—Point.

—The cosmos contains only one light; matter is suffused and radiant.

—Point.

—So why is the temple at Chartres a dank old pit?

—Because, boomed a profound voice—Auxerre, face flushed from a bout of falconry in the fields outside the walls, just coming in to meet Melior—because the pious are contemplating the Holy Trinity and carrying their light inside them. You'll be calling for icons next.

Melior watched, bemused. Gabriel remained calm, but his apparent tranquility betrayed an edge.

—Thanks, my lord Auxerre, for the party line. But, after all, what's the matter with matter?

Clever, thought Melior. But he turned back to Hugh, to mirrors.

14

I talk to you most, Liza, about the little things, details of my living as time passes through me in my flat, thinking about the letterbox at the foot of the stairs and the letters that I haven't found inside for weeks now. This and that. I will find myself commenting to you that the soup is a bit salty, or that the left shoelace on my track shoes has broken three times without the right one breaking once. Or I will be looking at the drafting drawings clipped to the work board—windows and doors—and telling you I'll probably never finish it, blowing that commission. Or that I have taken to drinking Jasmine tea, for example. I find I never make any other kind now, and I'm not sure when that happened. My cup is a huge mug, fired clay, chipped around the top from too many washings in the old enamel sink.

I've just come in from the living room, where I had flung open the front window onto a gorgeous mid-May day with a bit of breeze making the shadows of new leaves dance across the hardwood. It was the right backdrop for re-reading the central scenes of my chapters on Melior, which I had finally gotten down in a form with which I was happy. Some might say that he has become an obsession, as if that were a fault. With you, I never had to apologize; that's the true compatibility that I discovered when I found you. Everyone's mind is an odd place to other people, preoccupied with the not-very-important, ignoring what anyone else would judge crucial. Living with you, I lost all self-consciousness; I didn't need to plan whatever came into my head and out of my mouth, knowing it wouldn't seem out of place to you. So I figure everyone has an obsession or two, which to them seems normalcy, and which, unshared, is the definition of loneliness. Dear Liza, dear Liza, there was Melior, walking the grounds of the School deep in conversation with scholars and students, feeling he had found his place after the long journey, after the winter in smoke-blackened Paris. Whatever the official accounts said, and in spite of what he probably even admitted to himself, my argument is that it was the School that drew him to Chartres just as much as the shrine and relics of the Virgin, and certainly more than Saint Fulbert's venerable church, or his administrative-reform assignment from Rome. Awaiting the formal banquet in his honour, he kept the prize gift he had brought for Bishop Renaud and the acting chancellor of the School: a copy of Sugar's *De consecratione ecclesiae sancti Dionysii* which he had managed to obtain in Paris, where the Capetian court held no end of such wonders.

Trying to re-live it all without you here, remembering our first summer together in Montreal, makes it seem as empty of events as the early days in Eden. Memory doesn't know what to make of undiluted happiness. There must have been some problems, right? Something that laid unsuspected foundations? That would be reassuring on some levels: logic, narrative, psychology. But I don't believe this is possible, really, though maybe I should try.

When Daniel insisted on *quid pro quo* I gave him fragments. I told him how, without classes, Liza and

John's weekends and evenings were completely their own, and John's hours at the bookstore—filled with liberal reading breaks on quiet afternoons—were hardly onerous. It seemed as though we had known each other forever, but our life together was still new and unformed. Making it up as we went along, we kept the two apartments, not knowing why really—a sense of wanting to evolve, relishing the gradual transitions, plotting our path.

Of the times you decided to stay over I remember most the moonlight finding its way into our room from the alley, where it touched the leaves with lacquer, where it uncovered your slender body, naked, pale, looking to my bemused and delirious eyes like the horseback maidens in the forests of medieval tapestries.

Finally we became lovers. You knew how afraid I was; the latent male fear of wounding increased tenfold because of your history. I assumed you were afraid, and I was afraid of your fear. We were both so gentle with each other that we ended up creating a fine tension that was triply erotic. Again, logic suggested to me that you would have "hang ups." All I noticed was the pause, the plateau at each step; but if there was grief in your pleasure I could not detect it. Coward that I was, I did not ask.

But mostly, with spring here and thoughts of summer coming on as I try to think this through, with even *La Californie* empty now, the scriptorium and Melior waiting for me to begin again, I can't remember our early time together with enough clarity to fulfill my longing. I don't remember because we were living. Deaths stay more fixed in the mind.

Your summer job paid pretty well. The Master's

fellowship came through. We began to talk of a possible wedding trip the next summer in Europe. You thought Spain. I thought France. At some point one of us suggested a compromise, following the ancient pilgrimage route south through France to Compestello, and that became a sort of long-term project. So I managed to hang onto part-time hours at the store for the new school year to try to accumulate savings, while you found someone to sub-let your old flat. In September, we settled into my semi-basement near McGill. It was a wonderful autumn. We were spooked by our love. Eager for our courses.

Some nights, to my shame, I slurred more intimate bits of our story to Daniel. The letters from long lost Lee began to arrive less often, I said melodramatically. They no longer meant to be cruel. Their calm sadness was even harder to withstand. I understood that I had permanently changed her. I could do such a thing. There was nothing I was not capable of betraying. I tried to remind myself that I could even betray Liza. I would be safer, knowing that, keeping watch! But did I begin to prepare myself, to accept this? Did I begin to watch for the fates' revenge? Turn about is fair play . . . .

Speaking of watching—that was one thing I loved about you: You watched. You didn't stare; you didn't gaze or peer, or scrutinize the world—Montreal's streets, our friends and neighbours, films, art galleries. With an alert patience—not placidity—you watched it all, from a still centre. Not apart, yet not entangled and distracted. This was the core of your kindness. The core of your respect, for others, for yourself. But how to reconcile this with the damage? For you were damaged by the breakdown, the lost year. Once you told me what the collapse of nerves and the relentless voices badgering you were like: you had walked transfixed out onto a long pier—a thin line of tension, your will like a tensed muscle—into an ocean of storm: and waited at the end while the tide rose, the cutting salt exploded in the spray, the sun long gone and the pier itself breaking up, all the time looking outward, forced to watch and not turn away.

But when you arrived in my life, you remembered how to watch. You were a half-smile.

That summer in Montreal, loving your work, loving me, loving the city, you were happy. Twice you cried after we made love and I was too afraid to ask why. Silence was kindest. Once a month or so you screamed your way out of a nightmare, and I reminded myself that nightmares happened to everyone.

In August we made the long-delayed visit to your parents. I liked the hobby farm, down a south-western Ontario gravel road white in the August heat, chicory and scotch thistle marking the ditches with end-of-season blues and mauves, and up a curling laneway, behind a copse of maples. The old barn was the colour of unsettled weather, the steeply gable-roofed house was filled with carefully chosen objects: with window seats cushioned for reading, a library of built-in bookshelves, an antique sideboard, cherry wood in the kitchen. This came naturally to your parents, who were neither sons of farmers nor daughters of miners. My parents had carved out gardens and workshops in late middle age, working toward their own natures tardily, by fits and starts and accident. Your bedroom, where we spent a few moments, with a dormer looking out over a pasture, filled me with an odd jealousy and insecurity: you had lived before meeting me, without me. An amazing notion.

Your father seemed an uneasy man who didn't know what role to play when I was in the room. I sensed an unbridgeable loss between him and you that no one wanted, that you both knew was illogical. Your mother seemed to like me and was a bit sterner because of it behind her steel-rimmed glasses that suited so well her greying blonde hair. She was a speaker of clipped sentences and clearly pronounced words. Things were not to be taken carelessly. But cheerfully, in an almost professional way.

Do you remember sitting in the swing on the front lawn one evening, surrounded by heavy-boughed trees? That evening you looked at me so strangely, with terror in your eyes, and I wondered if the worst days were coming back to you; I panicked, and someone else inside me thought, my God, who is this? Who is she? An owl hooted in the treetop. Then it was over. We rocked quietly until the colour left the sky, and we went inside.

That was only a hint that the scars from your breakdown had not been truly healed. It is easy to downplay what is hidden; it is easy to forget a lot of things when life is good. But that isn't what I'm saying. I'm saying that I *did* understand this vulnerability. That's what I want to tell you. I knew you were vulnerable. That's not saying much. Most people are. But *I* knew precisely the attack point. I knew where the fissures, once opened, led. Because of that I worried that someone, something, would strike there. I remembered back to my words to

Lee after you and I met, and how telling the truth about us had battered her. I remembered the unwilling cruelty, and I touched the possibility—like a tongue worrying a canker—that the person who might some day hurt you where you were most defenseless would be me.

We bought a second hand washing machine and jammed it into a closet, renouncing the Laundromat era forever. We read in the evenings propped at opposite ends of the old sofa with our feet intertwined in the middle—or, as you'll remember, with your toes trying to see how long I could keep my concentration while they wiggled between my thighs.

One evening in *La Californie*, sentiment blossoming as the beer flowed, I told Daniel that at Thanksgiving we went to Vermillion for the long weekend. We had been making careful calculations. If I could maintain my hours at the store, what was left of my work-year savings and the portion of your scholarship you wouldn't now need to spend on rent, could buy us five or six weeks in Europe. I had bought my first book on Chartres— John James's focus on the master masons who actually made the cathedral stand up—and was working my way through it on the train. Your presence intensified everything. The world overflowed. I would find myself sitting at my desk staring with pleasure at a green book lying on a sky blue book, the covers clasping the white paper-edges, resting on varnished wood; or a building— and not always a distinguished one—would arrest me in the street. I would eye its lines, its texture, relish the sky behind it. Lines of poetry from high school English would swing into the front of my brain out of a long forgotten doorway—"the spellbound horses walking warm out of the whinnying green stable," or "and all her hair in one long yellow string I wound three times her little throat around." I was amazed I hadn't understood their unbearable loveliness sooner. It was the same for you. I'm sure it was. You were finding the texts of Freud—however vigorous your ongoing argument with him—full of never-before-noticed ingots. Sitting up straight with a start, you would say:

—John! Listen to this: "We are so made that we can derive intense enjoyment only from a contrast, and very little from the state of things."

In Vermillion the aspen were turning over their leaves in the chilly autumn winds, showing silver touched with yellow. The birch trees were pale lemon. The river was bluer. The pines were beginning to step forward out of thinning softwoods, wedges of dark green. The blueberries were gone. My brother Robbie was home from Alberta, one reason we'd made the trip—and that made Thanksgiving dinner all the livelier, the talk louder, Mom tired and distracted—her version of joy, I think, sad to say—Dad quietly content.

On Sunday night we volunteered to take two children—Katherine, six, and Nelson, three, who were visiting their grandparents the Watsons, our long-time neighbours next door, to a magic show the Legion was putting on at the arena. It seemed an innocuous enough idea. We took them each by the hand and walked up through the dusk across town to the double rink, built in the boom days of 1967 with Centennial project money. A long line already snaked outside. This was a big event by Vermillion standards. The Amazing Mangalia tour had done shows from Barrie to Thunder Bay.

A cold wind hinting of winter swept across the dark tennis courts and school grounds as we stood waiting to get in. Katherine was excited. Nelson didn't know what, exactly, magic might be, and I was trying to explain.

Inside, the set-up didn't seem conducive to mysteries of any sort. With the ice still out, the white boards and plexiglass surrounded smooth, dark cement, the penalty box was empty, and kids' voices and scraping chairs echoed off the girders. Old felt banners on the painted cinderblock walls proclaimed assorted championships. The stage consisted of plywood sheets laid across the tops of wooden stacking tables. A disorderly semi-circle of plastic chairs faced it, with a few volunteers unloading more chairs off dollies. A few dozen parents shepherded scores of unruly kids. A straggle of teenagers sat on top of the boards at the players' benches, displaying their indifference. We found a spot where the kids could easily see the stage.

The Amazing Mangalia came on wearing a scuffed tuxedo. He spoke with a vaguely Slavic accent. Any spell was immediately broken by malfunctioning mikes, capricious lighting and his officious asides to his two assistants, girls wearing black and gold leotards. Over and over spectators were hauled up the steps to pick a number, hold balloons that burst into doves, pull scarves from canes or rabbits from top hats. Nelson wondered what would happen next, bunnies or birds, but didn't seem to find their sudden appearance remarkable. Katherine, on the other hand, peppered you with whispers of *How did he do that?*

The Amazing Mangalia grew more imperious as technical problems proliferated. By the time he got to his final routine, he was in a foul mood. His assistants wheeled out a brightly painted box the size of an upended coffin. Mangalia called for a volunteer. Hands flew up. The magician stabbed a finger toward the back of the audience. Yes, *madame. Madame!* You! A stout woman headed for the steps and, before I could clamp a hand over his mouth, Nelson piped up loudly, "Will that big lady fit in there, John?"

Mangalia pulled his white gloves tighter with two theatrical tugs, opened the three front doors, top to bottom, and squeezed her in. Shutting the doors, he turned dramatically before realizing none of his gear was handy. The assistants emerged with two swords and metal sheets with handles, which resonated impressively as he flexed them. He spun to gaze sternly at the audience. He inserted a sword at the level of the woman's heart—then plunged inward. Another sword seemed to pierce her left side near the hip. Nelson was quiet, confused. I whispered in his ear that it was okay, she wouldn't get hurt. The two metal sheets, singing like saws, were slammed home at neck and thigh levels. An assistant held a black drape, which Mangalia tore from her hands and flung over the box. The capsule was rotated, a bit gingerly since one wheel seemed loose. With a flourish, Mangalia opened the top door. There was nothing there.

"She left," said Nelson, relieved. You, Liza, didn't seem to notice Nelson's unease; you were wide-eyed as a child. The bottom door. Empty. Doors closed, redraped, the contraption was turned again, undraped.

The magician raised his white palm for silence. A

teenager cracked from the sideboards, "She's a goner!" Mangalia sneered. Finally he tugged at the top door, the green one. It stuck. He had better luck with the middle, red one, and the woman's blue sweater and ample midriff were revealed. While he got the top open, she kicked at the bottom and stepped free, to the hoots and hollers of her friends in the back.

Suddenly the lights were thrown on. Mangalia barely had time to bow to the smatterings of applause before volunteers were stacking chairs and parents were stuffing children into jackets and heading out the runway behind the penalty box. The magician was left standing on the tabletops in a clattering, emptying hockey arena.

Outside, the darkness and silence absorbed us. The children were tired and quiet; we carried them, setting them down to walk from time to time when our arms ached. For me, an unpleasant sensation lingered. The night, after the clumsy and sneering magician, seemed damp and unwelcoming. I don't remember us talking at all on the way back. As we carried the children on the home stretch they both fell asleep. We dropped them off at the neighbours. At home, Dad was sleeping in front of the National, Mom was upstairs, perhaps reading in bed.

It was unexpected. We were puttering about the kitchen. I was completely unconscious of what was happening, about to happen.

The bright kitchen. Sink, clean dishes in the rack, the fluorescent light humming to the fridge, the window looking back at us. At some point (we were making toast), I took your shoulder lightly to turn you and kiss your hair. An unthinking, everyday act.

Your eyes swept past. Terror struck me. They came back, stared at me wildly. You clenched your hands into fists, then released them, felt for the counter, missing, almost falling. I knew abruptly that you were reliving the breakdown, and it was killing you, that it could kill you this time. For the first time, I *had* to know what the *cause* was; I needed a single answer. What *exactly*. Was it the lost child? Was it the night they all had you? Was it to do with the pain you caused your parents? Or were all of these too simple? But they were the realities, the events. Surely they are the cause? Where else could it come from? Or was the effect—the breakdown—now itself the cause of the fragility? I wanted you to *tell* me. I was self-absorbed. I had seen you cry before, flail at a wall, shiver in a cold sweat. But this was worse. I was afraid of it, of you. I wanted out.

It passed. I saw you again. But the need to know never passed. I'm not so stupid as to realize there may not *be* an answer, no pat formula. But the need remained. I could never give up the question. Failing to do so was a very real failure, I see now. Something, in the end, I chose to dally with. I never tended to the labour of ridding myself of that longing. It lurked in the corner, wanting to come out.

It may be part of love, wanting to know and share the darkest ghosts of your beloved, as if there were schools for the soul. Or it may be part of something else.

I don't know if you had sensed my feelings. Probably not. We ended up in the back bedroom, the door closed, because strange, barking sounds were escaping from you. I have never seen anything like your face, that moment in the kitchen. I hope you've never had to see yourself in

196

the mirror at such a moment. Perhaps you did, during the terrible year in and out of therapy and hospitals. On the bed, after you stifled the animal sounds with a pillow, your body stretched itself out hard and straight, jerked and leapt on the mattress as I tried in complete futility to cradle you. Your lips were curled back so hard, so far, so self-viciously, that all of your teeth seemed to be outside them. Your eyes clenched until your face was another shape. I was alone. A resentment rose in me, fed by exclusion.

I gave up and sat hopelessly on the edge of the bed. I had not understood your world at all. This darkness, this suffering, was not part of my cosmos. It came from another time and place. I was trivial beside it. I could only wait.

I waited apart, as if beside a closed hut or a veiled space, where a necessary ancient ritual—allied to torture—was undergone. You could be lost to me, irretrievable. But the spasmodic movements gradually subsided, the electric shocks withdrawing at their own deliberate pace. I was looking up at the shelves above the bed, dimly lit by a bit of moonlight, a bit of streetlight. The spines of old schoolbooks. A plastic blue virgin. A hockey trophy. I saw you as a bit of light too. But not the "creature of light's effulgence" of a Bishop Sugar, founder of Gothic, not a creature of reflected radiance, pointing a path back from shadow toward the source. No, only a moment of transmission, medieval and modern—a fragment of colour thrown on a stone floor by stained glass or an image on a screen, subject to a passing cloud, a burst of static. Once gone I, certainly, could do nothing to help; no more than I could put a picture back together out of a blizzard of white noise on a TV screen once the cable was torn from the wall.

You lay still.

Once Mother came into the back hall. I stepped out of the back room. She saw my face.

—Liza wasn't feeling well, but I think she's better now. I think she's dropping off, finally.

—Does she need something? Some aspirin? Hot lemon?

—No, it's okay. Good night Mom.

I went back in, as if to a cold fire, and sat down again to wait. You were not sleeping, of course. It was nothing like sleep.

A half hour later your lips moved, and I leaned forward, but the words were too dim to hear.

*

That was the last time we were together in Vermillion before our wedding in May. I had gone ahead while you wrote a final paper and did a job interview. You came up on the train with David. He had surprised us with his gift—a lovely earthenware chalice for the wedding mass he had found in an old pottery somewhere in the Townships. Claire, of course, arrived at the last minute, on Friday night, flying in from Vancouver where she'd been giving a paper at a conference on Structuralist Hermeneutics and the Text of Sex. Maybe I've just made that up. But it was something like that.

We had managed to keep the guest list down: your parents, with your grandmother from your mother's side, and your sister Jennifer (I guess she would have been articling in Kingston by then?); two close friends of your father, one a United Church minister who read the gospel. Mom, Dad, Heather and her husband Ron and kids, Linda, four or five friends of my parents, and David and Claire, who had the awkward task of lining up at the altar with us even though they had just had a horrible fight and were both trying to pretend they were through with each other for good. Robbie's job had sent him to Yellowknife for the summer.

The next day we drove south to Toronto with your parents and boarded the Air France Sunday night flight to Charles de Gaulle. And a week later, drunk on Paris's streets and galleries and exhausted by viewing so much art, we got on the train at metro Montparnasse for Chartres.

Even from a distance, dove grey stone and green copper roof soaring over the ripe wheat of the Beauce, its great mass hovering above the toy houses of the town, the cathedral was entrancing. And the broad approach to the west front following a ten-minute scramble through the upward, left-twisting cobbled streets from the station was exhilarating. We both loved at once the imbalance of the two superb steeples of different styles and different heights, two steps to heaven, up—and up. The exterior, so clear from there, is mesmerizing in its complexity, the architectural equivalent of a dozen three-hour symphonies with multiple choirs, and with trios, quartets, sonatas and fugues playing in various corners of the hall during intermission. Gargoyles, barely visible two hundred feet above us, flung themselves maniacally into space. The serene grandeur of the row of sixteen life-sized statues over a hundred feet above the cathedral's west porch was overwhelming. How to absorb this, from the perspective of Vermillion's squat houses and low, burnt hills? I was to go on trying to make it belong to me. The ancient Royal Portal, survivor of the fire, resolving as you draw nearer into an intricate and intimate congregation of two hundred figures, summing up the history of the world as it looked in 1150, included Gabriel, Euclid, Pythagoras, February warming himself by the hearth, August untying a sheaf of corn, the haunting *Majestus Domini* in the centre, Aristotle, the Virgin, shepherds and their charming, wide-eyed sheep.

But even this was only preface, an expanding and structuring of the mind—I see a brain laid open, as mine is again now on the streets of the Plateau—for the entry into the eternal cosmos, dark and delicious and jeweled, and eight hundred years old. Luminous, of course, though it was the richness of the dark inside that held me, with no breath, for long minutes. To be sure, the universal radiance poured down to find the object of reflection, light, clarity, the dazzling gleam on the surface of stone, grain, skin: creation as illumination was central to the school at Chartres, a doctrine that had seduced Melior long before he set foot in northern France. But not only radiance. That could be found outside. Just say mass in the midday sun. This was contained radiance, human radiance—worship as imitation. A home for the Virgin. A home for the tired human pilgrims who slept on a floor sloped toward the porch to facilitate sweeping and washing down after the filthy crowds departed.

The biggest spaces, you said to me, whispering, our feet on the labyrinth embedded in the floor near the front of the nave, are a lot like the smallest spaces. Did you notice that, John? All those numbers they've figured out for the galaxies, the distances to quasars. Ten to the fourteenth light years. Ten to the twelfth suns. Sizes like that. And the empty atoms: so small the scientists resort to the same vast numbers to describe their tiny-ness. The weight of quarks. The orbit of electrons. Ten to the minus fourteenth.

With you, there, I felt as though I were finally hearing the truth.

—It's as if the universe, everything, right out to some fiery radioactive glow on the edge—is that pulsars or quasars?—or whatever they're finding now—rushing outward into nothingness at fantastic speeds, glimmering with light from the first moment of creation, is an atom: you just turn it inside out, and it's infinitely small. A trace of weightless light slowly orbits an invisible speck, a half-whisper on a screen. John, you just reach your hand down a long sleeve, don't you see, and you take the cuff, and you pull . . .

You were right. Where were we? Inside Chartres, inside a gemstone. No, a frame for gemstones. That's what I see from my back room, trying to read the words on flying T-shirts on the clothes line across the building well. The stone of Chartres carved, cared for, was almost black—the colour of charcoal, old shale, Welsh mining towns. And suspended, impossibly high up, far above the beautiful-in-its-own-right stained glass of the main windows, and above even the archivolts, above the slender statues on jambs and trumeaus, even higher than the unparalleled lancets, in upper darkness, the jewels of the clerestory windows—amethyst and topaz and burning scarlet and deep aquamarine and lapis lazuli, the blues unmatched anywhere, an earthy yet brilliant sky-ness—threads of the robe of the Virgin.

And if I reached up, now, and found a hold, and pulled it all inside out . . .

I looked at you, and reached to touch your face.

After that—the great expanse now also within us, like a held breath—we lost ourselves deliciously for hours in the details. Each transept, its windows touched with the blues that dominated only those upper windows, was itself a mansion of glory. Each aisle of the ambulatory was populated with whimsies and beauties, crowded with carved lives on every shaft and tympana, the lintels veritable processions. A smartly parted beard on magi number three; a cheerfully anachronistic rosary spilling from the Virgin's prayer book as she dandles the child on her knee, all were magical. The choir was burnished with wood and silence. This was no mere house for the Virgin. This was a city, a society; intricate as life itself; arched order yet too variegated for explication. Enclosed yet infinite. An epic vision of the personal.

Everywhere we looked we saw the cold antiquity of the stones, and the charged light on the windows. There was also the old, bitter flesh here, a sense growing in me as I walked, staring up at the clerestory, its flatness contrasting the deep recesses of the long dim aisles, all light, all colour. But the cold stone was just as real; the worn flesh of the place telling you that humans made it with their hands and bloody pride and then died, coughing and terrified. I suppose this conviction was already in me by the time we came back to the west porch and looked for directions to the far older crypt: I wanted to be there while a milling crowd of workmen, their guild colours growing dusty at the edge of the site, stood and strolled and sat and spat, awaiting directions from the warden-of-masons, who was chatting and spitting with the Master, who, peering at the re-jigged lines on one of his charts, was still steaming after an unsatisfactory lunch with the Bishop, who thought he knew a thing or two about architecture and was incongruously demanding the step-effect from the new choir at Canterbury he'd heard so much about and the quadripartite elevation pulled off so gracefully at St-Remi in Reims.

Chartres was a miracle; I'd already decided that. I wanted to see it at its conception, find the gap, the fissure between the imagining and the realization. If a miracle could not get its hands dirty and yet survive then it wasn't human, or not human enough to matter to me.

Hard to explain. But that night, back in our room, as I excitedly spluttered out my first fumbling attempts to articulate what I felt, I could see you understood. I have never loved you more, or felt more afraid for our miracle. You even tried to understand when I said there was a slaughterhouse on the floor at Chartres, blood on the hands of the School even as it dwelt so persistently on mathematics and music—and that therein I had learned to love architecture. You realized I didn't mean this in any simple way, didn't mean the scholars were also butchers, Nazis playing Bach. I didn't merely mean that the funding for the edifice was in part the tithes of the poor (though it was), or that workmen died in its construction (they did: after all, even the great cathedral architect, William of Sens, once fell from the scaffolding of one of his English churches, barely surviving). I meant less than that, and more. I meant the violence-ridden parishes of the masses of pilgrims sleeping on the sloped nave floor amidst their garbage and leftovers and sweat.

It partook. You could feel it in the chilly old stones.

And it soared. Partook yet soared.

To save your faith in the deep radiance of the clerestory, you not only forgave the huddle and muddle below, you partook. It is how humans love, my dear absent Liza, how humans should love.

15

Memory has pretty much misplaced the year that followed. You took it with you. Maybe I take your memories back to my flat each night, so that you can't summon them either. Maybe I have you, and you have me, and all we have lost is us. But without you to help I feel incapable of recapturing the sensations of us together with any precision, just as I could never have lived them by myself. Meeting, creating, leaving, destroying: those moments I can bring to life, even if I have to sit long hours with pots of tea to make them come, sit until I'm spooked by an unseen watcher who sits with me: because they are the edges where we join and break, where I disappear into our life together and re-emerge again, little better off than Daniel: a remnant, a bit of air, a noise in the next room.

David and Claire were part of our lives, off and on. This was not only because we had found each other at their party. There was an unnerving symmetry that joined us. Once we both stopped at the same campsite above Tadoussac and unwittingly pitched tents a hundred yards apart. Once we ended up in the same metro car in London when we didn't even know the other couple was outside Montreal. And of course there was the summer they ended up in a room in Chartres, on their way back from Portugal, only blocks from the apartment we had leased for the month. I won't speak of David. Not now. In any event he was always an indefinable element to me—that was why we liked him?—made up of three or four cultural types which, found together, seemed completely original. (He was a rare Francophile American for starters—few of *them* from Binghampton, New York). An undergraduate major in Political Philosophy, he had ended up doing a doctorate in psych, with a dissertation topic I don't understand in detail to this day. Funny how little he spoke of it. I can hear your protests: but most striking to me was his fierce interest in social justice combined with psychology and psychoanalysis, where, frankly, justice seems to have little role. What can you say about a man who tries to write a thesis in clinical psychology—rooted in hundred of hours observing grade seven and eight classrooms in local public schools—designed to support the industrial-society theoretic of Habermas? One of a kind. Quiet at a high pitch, kind to a fault, brilliant as hell, and alternately hooked by and retreating in dismay from Claire Howes. A more serious dance, as it turned out, than we understood.

Must knowledge always be fascistic? he used to ask.

So I would tell him that for the twelfth century scholastics, the created world deciphered itself. He would smile. Think hard. And ask his question again.

I remembered these conversations when I came across the historian Duby discussing an era long before the scholastic faith in logic took hold: the year 1000, a time when the never-quite-definable forces and events that allowed Europe to slowly emerge from the anarchy and famine of the ninth and tenth centuries began to gather. Only a few dozen scattered doctors tried to hold together the shreds of the classical world. Their schools (such as they were, at Reims, Fleury-sur-Loire, Chartres) were repositories of a handful of laboriously

206

copied books; their letters to other masters might never arrive; a rare visitor would have voyaged for a month through great danger to hear a scholar read Greek. At that time, Duby wrote, all great art was sacrificial, a form of magic. It was a world filled with spirits. No spectacle, no rite, could draw a line between what was true, and what was merely real.

And Chartres? A full two centuries later. But I don't think the glorious edifice of the thirteenth century, with its splendour and proportion, its theological and political treatises in stone, can be separated from the ninth century crypt over which it was raised. Fate is not ruled entirely by one's foundations, but there is a structuring laid down, a framework that can be evaded only with great difficulty. When you walk on the scoured black stones of the nave, that vast resonating arc, the crypt is like the air just behind your head that you can never see, or like the thought that appears out of nowhere—an opening downward and inward. And below even the crypt, lost, the sixth century altar to the Virgin of Saint Béthaire. And the fourth century church deeper still, part of soil, burnt too, as ancient to Charlemagne as Shakespeare is to us.

Sacrifice? Not only. Central bay, north porch: I have stood and gazed at that spot long enough, in the hot Ile-de-France summer sun, that I can see it clearly from here. It surely represents some of the first stonework done after the fire. Abraham stands between Melchizadech and Moses. Here, more than anywhere else, my theory is validated. The statuary looks both ways. These slender draperies carry the standard symbols to identify the biblical personae (Melchizadech with his chalice, Moses elevating the brazen serpent), and bear the actual faces (and subtler emblems) of the rough and tumble politics and theocratic infighting of their day. Abraham—with the visage, and wearing the ecclesiastical emblem, of the fiercely anti-Melior (and anti-School) Bishop of Evreux, still bitter, I posit in my work, at the astonishing fund raising campaign that followed the fire, a campaign to raise a testament in space to a religious perspective he not-so-privately despised. That the glory was reflected onto the Bishop of Chartres and of course onto Melior himself didn't exactly cheer him up. Just to spite Melior, implies the Master of Chartres—or a sculptor drawing his own tangent?—Evreux would sacrifice laughter itself, Isaac. There he is, delicate as limestone can render. Evreux would sacrifice the optimism about human nature that cohabited with the worship of light at the School: this optimism was not his; he would give it up to his god. The longer I study the figure, with its left hand curved under Isaac's chin to rest long fingers against his neck, the gaze neither solemnly focused like those of his neighbours, nor elevated, nor light-and-suffering bearing like the nearby masterful embodiment of John the Baptist, the more I become convinced this Abraham felt a little too much relish for his terrible duty. No ram would save this child, this sweet summation of joy with hands relaxed across his waist, his innocent feet already bound.

Sacrifice? Of what, in honour of what, to what end? A child on a mountain, lost, in her baptismal lace. The full story came out gradually. The media's needs are stronger than love or silence. Unconfirmed reports. No comment. Off the record.

16

Liza, last night I finished writing the section on Melior. As recently as a few days ago I thought there would be more to it. Standing the typed pages up, I straightened and laid them in the centre of the desk, squared on the old oak surface to mimic calm, before emerging from the scriptorium, heart pounding, bent for *La Californie*.

I was hoping Daniel would be there. I had avoided the bar for a while, or gone early so as not to cross his path, worried he would be intent on finishing his story. Recently, I had wanted only the earlier Daniel of diverting and brilliant cynicism, with his obsessive sense of personal responsibility turned into a philosophical system completely unable to countenance current society—all this, hilarious and morbid by turns, for a half hour or hour, had been the perfect early evening tonic before the plod home. But tonight, convinced I had written my way into Melior's brain the night of the conflagration—and so been able to walk more confidently along his mental path through the crucial days that followed—tonight I was magnanimity itself. Daniel could tell me the end of his story; I knew a better one.

But I was delayed getting to the bar. My wallet, it turned out, was missing. You know me. I went through every pocket, scouted under the bed and couch, crawled about on closet floors, rifled drawer after drawer and then checked them all again. Finally, giving up, and figuring that *La Californie* of all places owed me a short-term tab, I decided to leave—only to find the wallet in the letterbox on the way out. Unnerving. How I managed to leave it there, I'll never know. Or perhaps I had lost it somewhere else, someone had found it, scouted inside for an address, dropped it off? At 7:15 I walked toward the corner through the balmy evening, coatless, sleeves rolled.

Daniel arrived even later. The night was tipped toward a time crisis from the beginning. Roger was at the bar as I pushed open the inner door, after a pause in the vestibule to scan the tables for Daniel. It felt nice to be inside. Yes, it was like a second home. Roger had a cup under the whining cappuccino machine but was sneaking glances at a book lying open on the counter in front of him.

I went straight over.

—Daniel been in?

—You know Daniel, John. If he comes, he stays.

He placed the foamy cup on a saucer. Something was irritating him.

—He been in lately? I've been away.

—Yeah, sure. Frankly, he's not looking too good. Spring fever in reverse, I guess. You know Daniel.

You already said that, I thought. Besides, it wasn't Daniel, I decided, who was the problem. When he came back from delivering the coffee, I ordered a café-au-lait. I would need to save my beer stamina for later.

—What are you reading?

He held up the volume with one hand as he fed a cup under the machine.

—Aquin? I mused. Cheerful stuff. A bit antique now, don't you find?

—I think you need to understand him to—*comment expliquer?*—to sit in those closed rooms with the FLQ.

Ecoute. "*Mais je suis sûr de l'avenir. Déja je sens la pression irrésistible du prochain épisode.*"

—Is that what's bothering you, Roger?

He slid the bowl to me, arching one eyebrow ever so slightly. It was impossible to surprise Roger.

—Is something?

I shrugged.

—No. I think it is the story about the baby. Normally, who cares about the newspapers? But this one . . . . It just caught me in a mood, I suppose.

—The baby?

—On the mountain.

—Something new? I was working all day.

He picked up a *La Presse* from behind the counter.

—*C'est rien, vraiment, quand on y pense. Je veux dire . . .* after she's dead . . . that's the only thing that . . . it is the only fact, no? That she's dead. *Mais . . .*

I read. They were confirming the earlier report that she had been strangled, and by someone with no desire to evade detection. The prints were clear. And an unconfirmed report: HIV positive. Born awaiting rampaging infections. But Roger was right. If she had been found in the woods under a shawl of leaves, even in a dumpster, the mind would veer away in horror, but in familiar horror. Another crime hidden, thrust away from view. But she had been laid out to be found, for presentation, as if a gift to the city and the sky.

Roger shrugged as I looked up.

—Is it beautiful, or horrible? I asked.

—Jesus, John. Neither. It's some self-obsessed masochist trying to make a symbol out of their mis-put, misplaced? sense of guilt.

211

—Or their tragedy, I pointed out.

—Come on. Maybe there is a cure tomorrow. There might have been one yesterday that hasn't been announced yet. It's not so fatal anymore. Maybe in a few years it will be like—what's the English?—*le diabète*. Just something you live with.

I didn't answer. A cure? Maybe.

—John!

I spun around.

—Take your chair, you coenobitic bastard.

Daniel already had his jacket off and slung over the chair back, and was tucking his tie into the pocket. His hair was disheveled, as if there had been a gale outside. His face gleamed—but not exactly with pleasure; with alacrity, wildness.

—Roger! he exclaimed. *Pour commencer, donnons-nous deux Noirs. J'étais en train de mourir de soif tout l'après-midi.*

While Roger fished for Black Label in his chiller, I made my way to Daniel's table. With no bottle yet in his hand, he fidgeted with his beard, then became distracted by a hangnail, which he began to chew. While this was an old habit, something was new tonight; something had changed.

—Where you been John? In California fucking my wife?

—On Jeanne-Mance, actually. Is Isabelle back in California? What now, a post-post doc?

—You've been fucking Jeanne-Mance?

—I thought she was in Pointe Claire.

—So hard to keep track of wives.

—I've just been working. Too hard. That's all.

—A mortal sin. Anyway, I too, Father, have sinned. You've been gone so long I've forgotten all the best details. But settle in. Mind if we do it here? It's so hard to get good bar service in the confessionals, eh Roger?

Roger uncapped the bottles. A little wisp like smoke rose from the mouths. He threw me a gloomy glance and headed to serve a new arrival at a table near the big screen. The Canadiens were into the second round, and *La Californie* would be crowded for the game tonight. It was already only fifteen minutes to the first beer commercial. The fellow ordered a cognac. I remember Daniel's impressed exclamation. Verve, he said, now that's verve. Hockey and cognac. I like it.

—That's my darling, Roger, just ignore us. What's with him? Anyway—he paused to down the top half of the bottle, setting it down with a little gasp of approval— if you remember, we left me slogging through the sands of California beaches with the baby carriage, ga-ga-ing surfers and watching the volleyballers bounce—or the volleybouncers ball?—while Isabelle examined the entrails of the human mind at UCLA.

—Can minds have entrails?

—You bet. What did you think this was about? Fluffy wingtips?

He was flying. As if extra energy were still required, he pulled out a pack of DuMauriers and lit one from a wooden match he snapped into flame with his thumbnail.

—Want one?

—I don't smoke. And neither do you.

—What is this? The Brady Bunch? I'm only allowed one personality?

213

—You're on the beach.

—I'm on the beach. Watching all the balls bounce. As it were.

He drew so deeply on the cigarette I expected him to come up choking. The tip stayed aglow, red fire creeping up white paper. He was on a different, higher plane tonight. Or lower plane. In this sort of terrible ecstasy he also seemed to feel his body more keenly, savouring the cigarette like a twenty dollar Havana, as if where he was going the mind and flesh fed each other, no longer kept apart. When he picked up his glass I was startled to see it was empty. I swore softly to myself. He had not drunk the second half. I was certain.

And how did Roger know? What kind of subtle signal had gone out? But there he was, uncapping two bottles of a blonde Belgian lager—Loburg, I think—standing two clean glasses between us, and even swapping a clean ashtray for the one Daniel had barely started to use.

Daniel was already off again, no time to spare. I numbly followed his waved order to fill the glasses, while trying to reel in the start of his sentence so I could follow along.

—I was perfectly aware that I was trapped inside a big glass cliché like a butterfly in a jar, about to get pinned. Cold Canadian in California, temporarily jobless (he ignored my glance), not-quite-so-new but dearly beloved wife and daughter, "searching for myself."

He chortled and, as he spat laughter at the ceiling of the bar—a high fan turned slowly there, dispersing smoke—hefted his glass and smothered his own outbreak with a slow, steady pouring. When he set it down, the top of the glass was a sheath of foam. It was quality beer. The bottle, which he balanced approvingly on his palm a moment as if to be served at a diplomatic luncheon, was still a third full. He smiled, lowered his mouth slowly over it, and tilted the bottle upward on a fingertip. For the first time, as he stubbed the cigarette, he took my bottle and emptied its dregs into his glass while waving for Roger. Admiring the pack for a moment as he tilted back the lid, he slid out two cigarettes, lit one, handed it to me—okay, I was thinking, okay, I give up—then lit the second. He looked at the glasses and bottles wonderingly. How could it be there was no beer to be had?

As the Hockey Night in Canada theme music launched, Daniel ran on.

—The Pacific surf crawling up the beach, little skirt of foam. The brown lads trotted down the sand with their pretty boards and plopping in, paddling out. Hazy sky and burning high clouds sand and glare and palms. A big fat volleyball popped back and forth over the net into that sky, like a video game. Superb chests and little bums in red trunks. Breasts tied up with spaghetti strings just about to come undone. LA behind your back like a high school full of ten million Romeos and Juliets without the anxiety of a non-sitcom ending. Roger! *Finalement. J'ai soif.*

He laid down his cigarette to pour the beer, forgot it, and lit another. Someone, two tables over, was worried about interest rates. I couldn't blame them.

—And you had trouble with the stroller wheels in the sand? Can't you get strollers with special beach wheels in California?

—John, John. Yes, no doubt. Yes. I had trouble with

the fucking stroller. And I knew it was all a cliché! I had my eyes wide, wide open. California couldn't touch me if I didn't want it to. I wasn't a child. I didn't merely want a spoonful of baby bear's just-right porridge! It wasn't an accident. I'm not a goddamned accident! I'm not a sample for probability theory or statistical norms! It's not a question of the mothering odds. I insist on will! I did it! You can't erase me from the equation!

The pre-game was on. I kept catching phrases like "come down to," and "will be key." The Canadiens were not dominating the deep slot, it seemed.

—I wouldn't dream of it, Daniel.

He was doing it to me again. Cardinal Melior was ancient history. Even you, Liza, were difficult to remember, receding down an avenue of trees.

I watched him drink, watched the piston of his Adam's apple. From behind me, I could hear the poolside scene, the dive, and someone pouring themselves a Golden on the big screen. Roger delivered two O'Keefe's. I pushed them both across at Daniel. His chin came down, and he caught my eye. He looked like a bird, a cold intelligence wondering what world I had dropped in from. Cocking his head to one side, he fingered the scarring.

—A pretty sight?

—I was just admiring your rate of intake.

—You need a pulpit John.

—Lay off.

—According to my mother it was a very near thing.

—Come again?

—My lovely scars. When I was five I succeeded in setting my parents' pillowcases on fire. Freudian thing, no doubt. I found the matches in a little drawer of their

216

night table, the night table where they always kept a candle and candlestick. Mother told her little boy it was for when the power went out. Understandable enough.

—Nice, as long as your kid doesn't play with matches.

—As long as your kid isn't me. Oh, I think the gods thought it was pretty damned appropriate.

Another match head exploded off his thumbnail. Daniel held the flame up and studied it while drawing a cigarette from the pack. He lit it with the last pinched millimetre of match, fire at his fingertips. My cigarette lay in the tray, a worm of ash.

Daniel stood up, letting his chair teeter a moment before it fell backwards with a clatter, interrupting the opening chords of O Canada. The café, almost full, was noisy; only a few heads turned.

—Just another dull old tune, now that Roget Ducet is dead and they left the Forum, he said. I need a piss. Get us some fucking beer will you, John?

He was holding an empty glass. As if bemused at the inattention paid his toppled chair, he held the glass at arm's length, winked at me, and let it fall.

17

Our fifth year together. A few blocks below the Chartres train station, rue Jean-Marie runs along the side of a gentle slope, and extends from a neighbourhood of small shops in the shadow of the cathedral—as the shops there have been for a thousand years—into Chartres' eighteenth-century petit-bourgeois residential district. It was late May. The lilac that softened the walls of the stone houses was past its peak, its perfume heavy, the clusters of petals shriveling and falling onto the lawns, a dusting of blue. I swung the bag of groceries I was carrying, strolling along as if nothing was about to happen, and looked back over my shoulder from time to time to see the great spikes of the steeples from slightly different angles. Radiants.

Something in the grace of the church was irritating me these days, though I knew my own mood was the culprit. I had gone out for coffee, and had also bought some fruit. I needed to get back. You were waiting. It was time to make love. I had never gotten used to the imperatives of the biological clock. We made fun of ourselves to keep our spirits up. Today was, as nearly as we could determine, your peak of fertility for the month (and the moon was kind enough to be rising emblematically over the railroad station roof). You had awoken that morning with the ache that suggested you were about to ovulate, so we had hurriedly made love before breakfast. We would try again before settling down with books and music for the evening, doubling our odds.

I was discouraged, and feeling off-centre. Where my career was going would have been a good question, if I had had one. And then we had started trying to conceive the previous summer, during our second visit to Chartres. The symbolism pleased us, and we had felt we knew, in the way we had known everything about each other from the start, that you would get pregnant more or less instantly. But now a whole year had passed. If we arrived back in Montreal this fall still unsuccessful we would have to resign ourselves to the battery of medical tests and probes. Even so, Liza, I can remember no conscious sense of dissatisfaction with our life together. Nothing hinted to me that either of us was vulnerable.

We had found a two-room apartment above the garage of a three-storey pile of Ile-de-France granite owned by a Chartres physician. As I approached it, the light, almost gone, reduced the steeples behind me to twin dark thrusts. The garage, separate from the house, was also clad in stone. But unlike the Valades' residence (steeply pitched, slate shingled, gabled) it was flat roofed. A short flagstone path led down the side to the metal staircase up to our apartment, which had no doubt been planned with a resident maid or gardener in mind. I could see a dim glow from the front windows through drawn curtains, and wondered if perhaps you had lit candles and would greet me reclining on one elbow, sipping wine—something to distract us from calendric necessity.

But as I let myself in I heard you talking excitedly; you were fully clothed at the kitchenette table, on the phone. What could be such good news, I wondered, kissing you on the cheek on the way by, and stepping into the alcove—hot plate, bar fridge, small counter and cupboard—to put the things away? Coffee. I had a half-kilo of fresh-ground, a dark French blend. I needed coffee. My research was proving adept at finding cul-de-sacs. Blind alleys were everywhere. I couldn't deny it. They were getting me down. And unhappiness was the one thing I felt no way of communicating to you. You were saying you would see them Thursday, whoever they were, then hung up and came in behind me.

—It's fantastic!

—Just like you, I said.

—Likewise I'm sure.

—Good news? Want some coffee?

—That was David. Remember, he and Claire were going to stay in Portugal all summer? They were tired of the six countries in six weeks bit?

—Claire wanted to seriously absorb ochre. She said she'd never given ochre the time it deserved. Don't tell me. She's bored already.

—No. She's decided the Québecois are fundamentally non-Mediterranean. She can't stand the olive oil and the garlic and sun and brown skin. Of course that's David's re-telling.

—What makes Claire think she's Québecois? She's about as pure *laine* as I am.

—Her French *is* flawless.

—Unlike mine. Well, so is Queen Elizabeth's.

—It wasn't a comment on you, John. Anyway, she's decided if the summer isn't going to be a complete loss emotionally, they need to be near cold water.

—Not Hudson Bay, I bet.

—Normandy. But—a week at Chartres on the way!

—Oh! And they're coming Thursday?

—David and Claire do *not* dally. David wanted to know if we could find them a pension. Ah, with two rooms free. Or, better still, two pensions.

—Oh no.

—I'm not sure if David is going to Normandy.

You seemed absorbed, even disturbed.

—Well, it's not like it's the first time, Liza.

You seemed sadder than I would have expected. Surely we were all used to David and Claire's post-modern relationship. We knew its only permanence lay in continual self-subversion.

—Sure, I know. Just something in David's voice, I guess. He seemed resigned or something.

—I'd have resigned a long time ago.

The joke didn't go over well. I softened my voice, but I was also irritated.

—This smells like good coffee. It's from that shop just around the corner from the pharmacy.

You looked at your watch.

—No. I think I'll read for a bit and go off to bed. I'm tired. You go ahead, John.

While I waited for the hot plate to heat I could hear you washing up, and then putting on a string quartet. You had forgotten our necessary rendezvous. Through the doorway I noticed the candlesticks were still on the shelf above the bed.

How could you have forgotten?

Thursday afternoon, wearing a heavy sweater against the chill inside the cathedral, I was sketching and taking

221

notes about the south-west chapel of the apse, lost in the quietude of the long, unfrequented passages deep behind the altar. In Chartres there is a realm within each realm, a re-opening behind each apparent closing-in. The chapel is close to the flight of stairs, which climb upward out of what seems to each first-time visitor the absolute back wall, the final depth. They lead to the fourteenth century Saint Piat chapel where the cathedral treasures are kept, including of course the veil of the Virgin, principal relic long before its reputation for miracle-making was immeasurably enhanced by its being discovered unharmed amidst the smoking stones in the days after the great fire of 1194.

The apsidal chapel is really just a slight scalloping of the apse's grand curve, but its wonderful windows kept me busy for a week. Nowhere else I knew allowed as well as Chartres such sensual pleasure in the midst of scholarship (and, for believers, I suppose, such pleasure in the midst of worship). Though the panes are complex historical texts, chock full of thirteenth century characters from shoemakers to Prince and Cardinal, my studies were always simultaneously inhabited by that liquid, pulsing colour. An angel's halo is neon lemon, the virgin's cloak (mirroring the halo's shape) the scarlet of wet oil paint. A huntsman's robes are the green of a forest in a sunburst after rain, his steed a rich, lacquered brown. Saint Martin, a cobbler, Christ Pantocrator, St Thomas à Becket, a King and a bishop and a monk and a murderer and a sick man and St Nicholas and an innkeeper and a ruffian—light soaks through all of them, and colour blurs (softened, like chalk) on the dark stones beside me. Behind them all, Chartres' ground and base: the blue, the never ending blue; this gallery of thousands held up, always, against sky.

I happened to be working on the window of Saints Margaret and Catherine, which begins with the donors—Marguerite de Lèves and her relatives—near ground level (they bequeathed the window to the diocese in 1220 or so, and is crowned tragically where Emperor Maxence is having Saint Catherine beheaded, with a twisted little demon looking over his shoulder from the top left pane, egging him on.

—Grim story, *unbelievable* window.

It was Claire Howes. Faded black cotton dress—knee length—over black tights, an antique copper medallion between her breasts. Extraordinarily tanned, black hair frizzy from the sun and salt. Her neck was craned upward; she had been following my gaze.

—Claire! You're early.

We kissed, both cheeks.

—Hitchhiked. The train route was too complicated. You'll go crazy in here.

—I am crazy. I'm hoping to go sane. How are you?

—Tired of the sun. I'm not a sun person. I've got the wrong genes. Besides, this is not the sun decade.

—Nonsense. You look great.

—That's me, content as a clam. So. Chartres again, John? Liza tells me you're spending too much time in here. Not getting your vitamin E.

I tried to laugh. Had you really said that? Too much time? But you *understood*, didn't you? A bitter little bud inside me—given my already bleak mood.

—Well, Liza likes to spend her time inside people's

minds, I said. I prefer to spend my time inside what their minds have made. I'm afraid when you get right down to it, I'm not very interested in the subconscious. This is *design, intent*; all around us.

I waved off what I knew she was about to say.

—I know, I know. Where does the intent come from? And the design is structured by cultural contexts of which the designer isn't always conscious. Granted. I don't know. Maybe we just like to tackle things from opposite ends. But, as it says in the liturgy, "what human hands have made." This is their model of their cosmos. They not only dreamt it, they built it. Great zones of symmetry filled with innumerable unbalanced and unbalanceable details. Noses and angels and bricklayers and flowers. I'm rambling.

—No, Claire said, solemnly, in one of those unexpected moments of utter sincerity she could shift into. It's all right. I understand.

I looked at her sharply. There was a rare wistfulness on her face, but it had not dimmed her habitual intensity. Maybe she did understand.

I folded up my sketchpad and rubbed the back of my neck. Surely I had brought my umbrella? Yes, it had been raining as I walked over that morning. Gone. I wondered where I had left it.

—So, where's David?

—He went over with Liza to see the room you guys found. The plan is to meet for dinner. I've got the name of the restaurant here somewhere.

Claire and David. Was this really a turning point? Or was the turning point entirely within me? And if so, what force was shifting the balance? My waiting for the story to have shape, for me to be punished as I punished Lee? You, and me. Biology. The odds. With you still absent, I have too much memory. And in memory I walk again with Claire down the slow slope of Chartres' nave, the clerestory windows' ever-deepening blue hovering in the dimmer interior on this dull day, and I am thinking that there aren't really any decisions, only days that fold in different places.

18

In Daniel's absence, sick of caution, I got a pair of DeKerckhoves, an absurdly expensive Belgian beer I picked based on the look of the bottle. It proved blonde, crisp at the edge, but with extremely soothing qualities: what the hell, Daniel might as well follow my lead for a change. Roger swiftly swept up the broken glass. There were only fifteen minutes before he would have to go, but I was determined to force him to sit still and stay focused long enough to get to whatever point he continually made a pretence of driving at without ever, quite, arriving.

I looked around me, tapping my hand against the tabletop. The two nearest tables were inhabited, respectively, by a party of four drinking Labatts out of quart bottles and whooping at each save, and a pale youth in black, including gloves with the fingers cut off, drinking espresso and reading (believe it or not) Sartre. *La Californie* was that kind of bar. Hell, the Plateau was that kind of neighbourhood; Montreal was that kind of city. Anywhere else, I thought, and I could just get up and walk away, leave it be.

—The pipes are callin', Johnny Boy!

Daniel balanced above me, like a man in a gale, approvingly reading the green label of the beer.

—Danny Boy.

—And I thought your name was John, all this time. Silly me.

—You should have known better.

—Anyway, dangerous to drink alone, much less talk alone.

—Why don't you join me, Daniel?

—Thank you, I will.

He spent some moments arranging the chair, pack of cigarettes, lighter, glass, to his liking. You might have thought he was playing chess, setting up the pieces. The pace of his movements suggested tension. When he was finished, he picked up the ashtray and held it to the light, as if interested in the refracting qualities of cut glass. Then he turned and located Roger by the front door taking an order and hollered a command for two Budweisers. His voice was startling, booming, and again heads turned.

I thought of pointing out that he hadn't touched his DeKerckhove, but as almost immediately he began to make short work of it, I sighed and refrained. Besides, time was wasting.

—So, get on with it.

—King of Beers.

—Hm? Yeah, sure, king of beers.

—Actually, it's horse piss, but it's late, and horse piss is easier to drink fast.

—So get on with it.

—It, John? It? Is that the full and rounded extent of the no doubt expensive erudition your poor Ma and Da bought for you at some esteemed institution of higher learn . . .

—Shut up, Daniel. It. What you're telling me. Your choice. You started. You finish. Get on with it. It's twenty after.

The beers arrived, and Daniel tried, melodramatically,

to kiss Roger's hand in gratitude. Pouring took another ten seconds. In frustration—my Belgian was still looking pretty and golden in the television twilight—I took two of Daniel's cigarettes, to save him time, and lit them both. He took his, screwed up his eyes through the smoke of the first deep drag, and spat out a sentence.

—Still don't get it, do you? Christ.

—No, Daniel, I don't get it. Still. Again. Yet. I don't get anything.

—I take it you're no great reader of clues. Maybe you should ramble on incoherently about dear Liza, instead.

He dusted imaginary ashes off his wrist. You've got me there Daniel, I thought. I am the world's worst reader of clues, at least those from this century. And so I must whisper to Liza from here, all the way from here.

—Don't flatter yourself, Daniel. These jumbled bits you spatter out between swills don't exactly constitute a masterpiece of detective fiction. Just a mess.

—My-my. Constitute, no less. He drank.

—Jesus. Take a breath.

—I won't need many more.

—Beers?

—Breaths. He paused. Roger!

—So soon?

—I need my Roger reg-u-lar-ly. Tra la la. So. Having made a short story long . . . after all, there's not much to a life, is there? A key moment, two if you're lucky, which you're not, when you do something that matters . . . having made a short story long, now, I'll have to make a long story short.

—Good. It's time for your bus.

Roger appeared, looking at me dubiously.

—Fuck my bus will you, John? Get that Roger? Fuck my bus.

—*D'accord*, said Roger.

—Short version: in the middle of an intellectually stimulating, socially enthralling, and career-ly essential post-doc, Isabelle gets pregnant. Number two. Unluckily for all involved—without warning Daniel bolted upright and, hefting his sloshing glass to the heavens, yelled—*I was indeed the father!*

—Congratulations. Sit down.

Daniel relished my flippancy. A contented leer crept to the corner of his mouth. He sat.

I glanced at my watch. This was nuts. However little I knew about Daniel and Isabelle, him not making it home—again?—couldn't be anything but a terrible idea. How often did he dash onto the last train? How often did he miss? But Daniel was charged now, electric. It would be difficult to move him.

—But not a serious problem, right? Right, John-John! Right! No serious problems. Isabelle is too brilliant for morning sickness. Too fit for back pain. She ploughs onward, getting bouncier and shinier every single, lovable, curseable sunny California day. A regular turbine, my Isabelle. Baby's not due till June. Post-doc ends in April. Plenty of times for a nice, valedictory, always-to-be-remembered-with-snaps-in-the-family-album drive home across the continent to cozy Montreal and its humping green hill, a healthy delivery in good old St. Joe's with nice doctor Jenny doing the honours. Hallelujah and pass the smokes.

I had to get him out the door. I had a certain responsibility, for once. Hearing this to the end didn't

229

seem so necessary after all. Another time. Not tonight. The vibes were wrong.

—Here. A puff for the road. I shoved the pack across.

He glared at me, but the glare lost its focus almost instantly, diluted in alcohol. Then he sprung a broad grin.

—But there's no road tonight. Just here. No road.

Then he did something I'd never seen even Daniel manage before. Two sweating bottles of Heineken stood on the table at his elbow, rivulets coursing down their sides. I hadn't noticed their arrival. A miracle, I thought grimly, like loaves and fishes. Daniel took one in his left hand and raised it to his lips while picking up the other in his right, where he held it ready until, as his chin came back down from emptying the first, he switched drinking hands and poured the second down his throat. He set down the bottles with narrow-eyed pleasure. With both hands he took hold of his side of the table as if preparing to flip it on its back. I automatically reached for my edge, to keep it down.

—Daniel, you're crazy, I said in exasperation.

—You . . . you . . . never, ever say. She. Shut the fuck up. And what was it you told me about your missing w-wife the other night, John? Shits, its, whatever. Shit's so hard to remember. Rape victim, mental in a pinch wasn't it? So why would you shout her down when the going gets rough? Put her back in the bin.

—You goddamned asshole. She wasn't raped. You're as mixed up . . . as you always are. Jesus, Daniel. That's enough. I'm out of here. I never said she was raped. You can spill your bitter tales on somebody else. I have no idea why I sit here . . .

230

He was hopelessly confused, Liza. He was making it up as he went along.

—So see, so see, so she does it! Finishes her research and teaching her course between . . . between . . . pro . . . professionally pouring out a slew of job applications for fall, cleverly landing a position back at UQAM, doing assorted daily workouts to tone up for pushing our . . . our second perfect baby into the world. Our second perfect. Ladling quality time on Kate. We pack up. So we pack up our things, our books and paintings and nicknoks or knickknacks or whatever you Anglos call them and strollers, we have a few good-bye parties . . . *salut! salut!* . . . with the friends we'd made—lot of psychos actually—everybody pats Claire's tummy for luck and we do it, load our stuff into the car, gather up a fistful of roadmaps, wedge poor Kate into her car seat with a jumbo pack of crayons . . . every fifteen seconds for four thousand bloody miles she'd say "Da! Wook!" and I'd crane my head around to see the latest talented scrawl. Canadian as American apple pie.

He stopped a moment and scoured his face with his hands, scratched at his beard, tugged out an eyelash, raked his hair—then went on, waving away Roger, who had arrived at the table, having given up on me doing my duty. Roger didn't leave though. I could sense him hovering behind me. I picked up my backpack and put it on the table; I shoved Daniel's cigarettes closer to him and closed the flap on the pack. Time, gentlemen. He was unmoved.

—But John! What happened then, John?

He smirked, then lilted his way through the next phrases.

—Isabelle and Danny and little Kate zip through

231

California and Nevada and Utah, into Colorado and north through a Dakota or two, and Minnesota and Michigan and Ontari-ari-ari-o.

—Daniel . . .

—*Tête-toi*, Roger. *Vraiment*. Doodled along the 401 in blissful familial splendour and put up at the in-laws a day before pulling up at the front door of our very own Outremont duplex, all tired and happy and stretching our legs.

—Outremont still? Not Pointe-Claire?

—John, said Roger behind me. *Vraiment*.

—And went down *en famille* to the lovely and sensitive Family Maternity *clinic*, in St. Joseph's catholicizing hospital, *Daddies invited too! All the latest attitudes assembled under one roof!* Where a positively Neanderthally simple tiny blood test . . . . He stood up, face blazing, his chair clattering to the floor as punctuation.

—And . . .

—HIV positive.

—What?

As he swung in an aching, slow motion pirouette, a few of the other patrons actually stood up to back away. He stalked toward the door and half-leaned, half-fell against it. But the door, which opens inward from *La Californie's* inviting little vestibule, didn't budge.

19

On the plaza in front of Chartres, Claire and I paused to appreciate the late afternoon golden light on the front of the cathedral. The low angle of the sun threw the statuary into relief, carved with shadow.

—We'll be way too early, Claire. The restaurant's only another three or four blocks from here.

—Stop for a coffee? A glass of wine? That'd be nice.

—Actually, I said, molding my voice into neutral, the place we got for you and David is just about as close. We might as well go by there and see if Liza and David have left yet.

—Wine with you sounds better. But if you insist.

I wasn't clear on what their plan was; whether David was going on to Normandy with Claire, or to Paris, or back to Portugal; whether they were both staying in Chartres only a few days, or if David would remain behind while Claire bounced onward.

The pension had a lousy location. But on short notice, in high season, you couldn't be choosy. Located south of the town centre, tucked behind a three-storey garage that serviced transport trucks, the modern two-storey building was one of the few in town from which you couldn't glimpse any part of the cathedral. But we did know Madame Groulx. We had been forced to spend a week under her watchful care the previous summer. From the doorway, as I rang the bell, I could see her silhouette watching TV in the downstairs common room, with her Pekinese, as usual, perched beside her.

—Oui monsieur. Encore, bonjour.

—Bonjour madame. Nous voudrions voir si ma femme est toujours ici. Mais je devrais introduire Claire Howes, pour qui nous avons réservé la deuxième chambre.

—Oui, la deuxième. Oui, elle est toujours ici, et le monsieur, en haut. A ma connaissance.

Up the stairs we went. Madam's *"connaissance"* was undoubtedly accurate. Off the second landing, we reached the room. The door was closed. I was unthinking, asking Claire about where they had stayed in Portugal as I twisted the knob and stepped in.

You were on one end of the couch. David was half-seated, half twisting across you so that his face was away from Claire and I, toward your breast or shoulder, so that I never saw his expression. Now, I would like to take whatever he was feeling into account, but the moment has passed forever, however much its power remains behind. Your hand cupped his cheek. Your other hand was tenderly stroking his hair. It paused. Your eyes met mine. They showed me some concern, a trace of surprise; they were troubled, clouded, but (I can sometimes see) not startled. They were not difficult to read, though. I felt certain at the time I understood them clearly. The certainty stayed with me; the knowledge felt complete and carried me forward for weeks afterward, a fullness, a conviction. Where did the certainty come from? Your gaze was suffused with emotion, a richness of emotion I recognized but which, I abruptly felt sure, I had not seen recently. I was all reaction, and, in that sense, pure. I don't remember any reflection, much less words. Claire, though, is never at such a loss.

—What's this? she burst out sarcastically, the Pietà?

David's face, when I saw it at last, was red from crying.

A part of myself I had willingly prepared said, My turn, my turn. I don't know if I spoke this out loud. The hollow pain was right, and inevitable.

You didn't say anything. I couldn't look at you. I saw a window, an industrial brick wall beyond it. I was vindicated. The nightmares in the early days with you, the strangeness, the uncanny familiarity. Liza, we had been living in a suspension of disbelief. The damage was not necessarily very great; a part of me understood that. But the belief was no longer perfect. And once the faith is no longer complete, there is the strong desire to destroy it altogether. I often wonder where this desire comes from. It is culture, I suppose; it must be something we have taught ourselves, our most common route to damnation in the romantic West.

—John, can you give us a minute? you said.

—Sure.

I still had the knowledge from your eyes. You loved him. So I thought: a whisper over and over within me. Outside, the long summer day had hours of light left; the sun was gloriously suspended above the western horizon, a furnace lighter than air. The streets and shops and cafes held an elemental longing, a drawn-out note. I don't remember seeing where Claire went, what she said or did. Public hours were just ending by the time I reached the west porch, where the doorway was ringed with circle after carved stone circle thronged with humanity and angels. The gatekeeper wouldn't let me go in.

20

Robert of Aulney's pudgy hands lay palms-up on the bishop's brocaded tablecloth, as if expecting something. But this was simply his habitual pose. He sat next to Melior. He was fifty-four, an old man, but his face was remarkably smooth, as if some inner pressure, some slight inflation, filled out his skin. Gabriel of Ulm was across from him, invited at Melior's request, scowling at his Lordship Bishop Renauld's most recent remark (after which the bishop's puffy eyelids began to flicker shut, his wine-mug half-way to his lips). Behind him, on hands and knees, one of the serving boys was trying yet again to re-light the fire in a draughty grate. It was a cool, breezy evening. Auxerre, on Melior's left, was still picking at a plate of chicken bones, bits of meat and bread clinging in the steel wool of his beard. Even seated he made the rest of the men feel undersized. But his unrelenting hunger had not dulled his ears.

After wiping his chops with the back of his hand, and indicating to a server to lug a flagon his way, his eyes darted intently to the face of Gabriel and then to Robert and then to Dominique of Bruges, a middle-aged monk at the now dozing bishop's left elbow. Dominique was slow of speech, with a tidy tonsure and formidable knowledge of biological and medical treatises, from Galen to Avicennes. Melior caught Dominique muttering to himself, apparently as miffed as the younger Gabriel at the bishop's contented dismissal of Sugar's always-unfinished, always later-to-be-perfected, so-called *chef d'ouevre* at St. Denis: "no gravity, no solidity, no history."

236

—Pardon, Dominique, queried Melior. I couldn't make that out.

Dominique noted the slumber of his liege-lord and spiritual patron and tugged on his right ear twice.

—I was only saying, those who haven't *seen* St. Denis, as I haven't myself, but by all accounts . . . well, those who haven't, I was saying, or about to say; those who haven't seen St. Denis with their own eyes are perhaps best, perhaps best to consider, to reserve judgment.

—*I've* seen it, said Gabriel. He was taut as a strung bow.

Melior turned to Auxerre.

—I haven't. I'd love to hear what Gabriel has to say about it, wouldn't you, William?

Auxerre demurred.

—If it pleases. But Gabriel's passion is eloquent on his face already. I will say only that in my opinion God is worshipped in the chambers of a man's heart. I have nothing against a pretty church mind you.

Gabriel could not restrain his anger.

—*Pretty!* Pretty, forgive me sir; pretty has nothing to do with it.

—Then I'm sure you'll tell us all what it does have to do with.

—With your leave, my lord.

—Go ahead, Gabriel, said Melior. He was smiling, but felt a fine nervousness.

—It has to do with belief. An explanation of our faith. Bishop Sugar's abbey is a work of theology, but a work of theology not restricted to the privacy of the page, or a few breaths of air, a mortal man's breath. It is a work of theology that also gives believers pleasure because they apprehend the theological truths with their senses as well as with their minds.

—And what would you say is Abbot Sugar's, that is, what is his theology? queried Dominique.

—Simple in a way. That the visible world reflects the invisible. That matter is given form by light. And light is divinity. He *shows* you matter in the great windows, but matter that is now visibly full of light. Sunlight pours through solid matter. Matter is real only to the extent to which it partakes of light. I'm not saying it's a new idea. Genesis verse one.

Auxerre grunted.

—Sugar hardly invented stained glass, lad.

Gabriel let the "lad" go.

—But the change, the newness, is all in the shift of emphasis! Don't you see? The young monk was frustrated almost to insolence. *Before*, windows interrupted walls. In Sugar's new choir—and it's finished, finished well enough—the tracery of the windows floats on a *luminous* wall. It is the *supports* that are interruptions.

—Grosseteste, mused Dominique, pulling at a loose fold of skin below his goiter. Brilliant fellow. Defined light, defined light as the . . . as the mediator between bodied and immaterial substances.

—Exactly. Sugar is *building* that theology. Must we forever ask if our actions, our longings, our goals give homage to this world or the next? Can't it ever be *both*?

Your fervour, thought Melior, is precisely defined now. But he said something else aloud.

—Love, he murmured, staring above his tablemates' heads at a stretch of bare stone on the far wall, grey between two bright tapestries.

238

—Pardon? asked Auxerre.

—Breezy, said Melior, pointing to the slowly billowing edge of the wall hanging. Nasty wind outside I think.

At that moment, in a coincidence that chilled Melior when he later recalled it, one of the heavy shutters behind him burst open and flipped outward on its hinge to crack against the castle wall with the authority of a battering ram. Bishop Renaud sat up and called for wine. Two servants ran toward the night air. A gust swept around the grand dining hall, threatening the tapers. At the window, the serving boy wrestling with the casement seemed to suddenly lose his will. He stood like a cautionary illustration pointing at the devil. He gave a long, low whistle.

—Milords, he said, his strong brown arm gesturing into the darkness, his hair flying, his cassock snapping smartly in the wind. There's a fire below, in the town.

Not the devil though: only the six-year-old son of a smith in the ironworkers' guild's sextet of streets—alleys really, where wooden huts joined to shops joined to sheds abutted the roofs of further shops. The forges were tucked for protection just inside the city wall with the permission of a long-ago grant from the city Alderman following a Norsemen's raid, which had carried off every iron master the town had with the result that the Alderman couldn't get his horses properly shod for weeks. The boy had helped his father all day and had the smudgy face, red hands and limp, steamed hair to prove it. When dipping six sets of his father's tongs in the water barrel to cool, he dipped only five, and inexplicably set the sixth, un-dipped tong unsteadily on its hook. From there, a little later, it fell, and lay on a dirty woolen smock in what soon became a bed of curling smoke.

The fire moved fast, far faster than the hapless and uncoordinated efforts of the townspeople against it. There was no organized fire brigade, no one officially in charge. Fire was a terrible fate for the wooden town, but it was not a fate it had any notion of evading any more than it would have planned against plague or earthquake. Like plague or flood or drought it came from God and served to remind everyone from bishops to smiths' sons of their sinfulness and frailty—and their smallness, most of all their smallness. There was nothing masochistic about this: the habit of mind constituted the only known method of deriving meaning and consistency from the cosmos given the data available at the time. The alternative, a senseless universe, was even less bearable. By the time the smith's workshop was fully ablaze, his family's adjoining hut was burning to the ground from the roof down. But the family was brought out safely, and the craftsman had even dashed in and staggered out clutching his precious anvil and kicking a ball peen hammer before him for lack of a spare hand. Life would go on, diminished. Much of the smiths' quarter of Chartres was ablaze five minutes later. By the time the bishop's dinner guests had hurriedly gathered cloaks and assembled on a palace balcony to have a better look, a thin red line, like liquid metal, was flowing over the roof tops below and spurting up toward the higher parts of the town, and toward the diocesan walls.

—Light, thought Melior, feeling detached from the scene, which, from this distance, was still a silent drama.

240

With leaps and jets the fire came at them, homing. Odd. While near the town wall the fire spread relatively slowly, swelling outward one building at a time like a pool lapping at dry sand, this one stream of flame seemed to flee purposefully upward, lava ascending a ridge, driven by pressures from below.

Bishop Renaud was not, in fact, a stupid man. He had assessed the blaze and gathered his wits. He had left the spectators on his balcony, and was already at his desk in the audience chamber, penning a series of orders, with which messengers were dashing off as soon as his seal came off the wax. A few minutes later monks and stable boys and doctors of theology were labouring at the three walls located inside the demesne's walls and ferrying the barrels of water on mule carts to the wall facing the fire. Unlike Gabriel, the bishop had no doubt about the worth of the lordly, ponderous, and venerable cathedral, and had dispatched twenty students with buckets and brooms to the north porch to serve as a second line of defense should the unthinkable happen and the fire breach the wall and enter the quadrangles.

As Melior watched, the wind blew demoniacally stronger. The timing of it all—the wind kicking up harder and harder now, in the late evening, when usually it died down—exasperated and infuriated him. The intensity of the inferno was clear enough, the visual message was evident: not everyone was escaping in the snarl of alleyways through which it howled. But again, the emotion persisted only a moment. Then his calm returned, like a curse, and he watched as though from a distant mountaintop. The others seemed to have left. In any event, no one spoke.

*

Later, he could remember confusion, darkness, smoke. Little else. How long he had watched from the balcony he could not say. But at some point, in the middle of the night, with half the town below either on fire or already reduced to embers, with the other half spared by the wind's whims, he made his way back through the palace into the yard and along the side of the cathedral. Sparks had scaled the stone surrounding the diocesan buildings and were igniting a watchman's hut while three cowled figures beat at the flames. As the rags they battered with were lifted away, only darkness lay beneath them. Then, each time, fire sprung up from nothing and they flailed again. From nothing, he thought, *ex nihilo*. Silhouetted figures hurried across the courtyard lugging chests and cupboards. Renaud had ordered the emptying of the palace—a difficult decision, as this left many fewer to fight the fire. A burst of gale. Melior was almost blown over, but recovered himself to gaze in wonder as the guard hut burst into a fireball, flinging pinwheels of flaming tinder onto a stable, onto the awnings of the School, onto the roof of the porch of the palace.

Then he saw it: a finger of red lay a hundred feet above him against the sky, on the steep wooden roof of the church. It ran up the ridge, a reverse trickle, then folded outward, an opening fan. Then the great slope, the cornices, the gargoyles were illuminated, flooded with red and orange light. The roof became an illusion of transparency, molten, glowing. Within ten minutes, when he stood inside at the front of the nave, the inner vessel was already a house of smoke and dim running

242

figures. A wall of roiling, unbreathable air stood between him and the entrance to the crypt. A monk stumbled out of the darkness and fell to his knees beside Melior, hacking and choking. He helped the stunned man up and pushed him toward the vestibule.

A hooded man, Melior stood, blind, waiting to be told what he was waiting for. The roof glowed, as though it were the door of a furnace. Then there was a great crack, a rumble, and a rent appeared in the veil as tons of ancient, iron-hard timbers broke free and fell ghost-like through the smoke to crash across the entrance to the east transept. He didn't know it then, but two monks died there trying to salvage the missal—illuminated a century ago by Denis of Norman-près-du-mer—which was chained to the side-altar. Melior held on to his fear, didn't move, pulled his hood closer around his face.

A figure swam out of the dark and smoke. Melior stopped the wraith, his hands on each shoulder, peering. Yes, it was Gabriel, but he was barely conscious, his eyes clenched shut, face smeared with sweat and soot, an eyebrow singed. He was weeping. Melior slapped him across the cheek and shouted furiously into his face. *Out, out!* Gabriel came to himself and, startlingly, Melior could still see determination there. They went out together, where they found a small group of students from the school preparing the last mule carts to flee out the south gates of the cathedral precinct, to leave all of it to the fire's light.

21

For an hour I was able to feel very little. My thoughts flailed so wildly they dissolved before they formed. But at last the habits of the rational mind, as we like to think of it, started to resurface, and I found myself reviewing the scene with something like calm, if only for brief moments. There had to be some explanation. That's the way these disasters were resolved: the misunderstood was illuminated, and everyone was okay, lesson learned. On the other hand, we were supposed to meet at the restaurant—our entrance was unexpected. The expression on your face had to be taken into account. You didn't seem horrified, or guilty. Puzzled, disturbed: a bit distracted, as if your train of thought had been interrupted. But there had been an earlier expression, briefly glimpsed, just before you looked up, as you gazed down at David. Sadness, but also tenderness. Love? What kind of love? It's a spacious word. I was trying to get it straight, remember precisely. Had David been crying? If he had, what did that mean? Did it make a difference? Did it change things? Seeing it as a spectator, your expression had been very beautiful.

I kept coming back to that emotion in your gaze, but also to the sense of what followed. The sense that you were distracted, taken away. In the end that seemed harder to dismiss. Harder to dismiss because I intuited it as something beyond your will. You couldn't help it. You were adrift, just a little ways from shore, but adrift. It was impossible to reconcile that with my belief in what we meant to each other. Ordinariness. Something in me sought a sort of revenge—the revenge of the duped. And, in fact, it all made sense. It all fit together. It was the miracle that had been strange and unnerving. Surely I had understood all along it couldn't be real, couldn't last. And it had been built on my abrupt severing with Lee. When you stepped back and looked at that, if anyone else looked at my actions, the way I had swiftly turned her life upside down was unforgivable. The structure of the world: its pacing, its momentum, its movement and counter-movement. We accept it. It had now come to claim me in its logic. Yes, it all fit together.

That changed me, at least for a time. For long enough to do the damage. But not fatal damage, surely. Later this spring, or early this summer, you will come back to me. From the cathedral, I walked back toward the apartment. I had loitered an hour on the benches in the shadow of the main portal. The grey stone buildings of the town's narrow streets were filled with bright recesses—cafes, chic clothing shops, purveyors of fine whiskies or cigars or cheeses. Around another corner I passed, in the failing light, a wine bar, luminous wood within. Four tiny tables sat outside, each with two chairs. Claire was at one. Well, it was a small town. She lifted a sunset-tinged white wine.

—My second glass. Catch up to me John. You need someone to talk to.

She had signaled a waiter; within a few moments of taking the chair opposite her, white Bordeaux appeared before me.

—I'm not good at sentiment John, she said as soon as we set our glasses back down. Isn't that horrid? Don't answer. It's horrid.

245

—I don't follow, Claire.

—Sure you do. I've already played this scene out. I know how it should go, and I know that I can't do it.

—I'm not up to this, Claire. You're talking code.

—That's how the scene starts. I know how awful you're feeling, but all I know how to do is analyze it. Tear it to pieces, in fact. With a little laugh at the world's expense. The naive, innocent world.

—Interesting concept, innocence.

—Who are we talking about?

—A concept.

—My little role would be to help talk you through it, a bit of therapy, and you would help me with my own grief . . . now there's a melodramatic phrase! Is Claire having grief? See? I keep turning on it, around and around. Maybe another glass or two. I'll need to be pretty blind to see all this clearly.

—I'm sorry, Claire. I've been dealing with my own problems. We tend to assume you and David . . .

—Are merry gallants.

—Something like that.

—Not so merry.

—I'm not sure I want to talk about this, right now.

—Drink your wine, John.

The lamps were coming on. The cobblestones, polished by the day's passing traffic, glistened in the light, as if damp.

—David and Liza aren't lovers, John.

—I don't think so either.

—David told me so.

—Would he tell you the truth?

—I would know if he was lying. He's a lousy liar.

246

—Does it matter?

—Now who's the cynic? Sure it matters. It's not all that matters, but it matters.

—No, I meant if she wants to be his lover but isn't, it hurts more. That turns opaque something we had that was transparent. But without destroying it. But if it isn't *whole* anymore, it still exists but it just feels . . . ruined. Better destroyed. Then it has noble memories. You can remember it nobly. Whatever. I'm talking shit.

—I just had a horrible memory of someone saying something about having to kill all the people in a village to save it.

—I know. It's a pointless sentiment.

The wine was working. I felt, although of course only for the moment, that it was best to end what was no longer perfectly and fully alive, or to at least pull back, be wise and cold. The second glass had been better than the first. Night was deepening. Claire's eyes were aflame as I looked up, her face darkening.

—John, I feel awful. You feel awful. But we're okay, aren't we? Don't be stupid. Don't ruin it. Are you two going through a rough patch?

—Liza and I don't have rough patches.

—Lucky Liza.

I heard her voice and its emotion as if for the first time.

I looked at her, gazed past her face, looked back to my glass. It was the worst possible time to try to make this new calculation. I had no idea how it added up, or what I wanted the sum to be.

—Sorry, Claire.

—Sorry for what?

I took her clenched hand off the edge of the table,

with no plan. I turned it over, palm up. I unfolded each of the fingers; I held up her hand, examined it, laid it down, touched the palm, noticed for the first time that no part of the body was so deeply scored and creased. We leaned across the table at the same time, and our lips and hands explored each other's face at the same time. The taste of a different mouth: nothing stranger, nothing more exhilarating.

We sat back. Claire was turned, a quarter away from me, looking up the street.

—You foolish man.

—You sweet woman.

—That doesn't help.

—No.

—The wine's on me.

—You want me to go.

—No, I want you to come with me; but I won't let you. Even if you had wanted to.

—Yes, you would. I have no idea what I want.

—Please.

—Okay, Claire. Claire?

—Go away, dear John.

Liza, when I came in you were sitting on the sofa. My thoughts would not rest. Claire kept coming into them. That seemed worse than the kiss. You apparently hadn't been doing anything; there were no books near you, no music on, no food out. I had prepared a saving equilibrium, but it was weak, apparently, and your first words destroyed it.

—Why did you leave?

Flatly, coldly.

248

—Why did I leave?

—Why did you leave?

—Jesus. I didn't really think my presence was required. And if I'm not mistaken you asked me to.

—You know I meant for a moment, not for hour after hour.

—Call me crazy, but when I come into a room and find my wife holding visiting male friends in her arms I sometimes act rashly.

—How can you joke about this?

—Oh, I'm not joking Liza. Believe me. I don't think Lee thought you were a joke either.

I sensed anger was a superficial show. I had already stopped believing in it. But I was inside a certain role now, and I didn't know the lines to break out of it.

—Liza.

Nothing.

—*Liza.*

—What.

—Maybe I misunderstood.

—Maybe.

—Well it's understandable, isn't it? Aren't you going to explain? I just want to know, that's all. It startled me. It still does.

—You mean you don't know, John?

—I don't know what you feel.

There was a sensation of not knowing my own voice. The remnant of nightmare.

—*Why* don't you know?

—Liza! It's not like I stood there carefully considering the situation and came to some sort of rational conclusion. I saw what I saw. Right in front of my eyes. With no warning. Maybe I misunderstood. But if I did, can't you at least have the decency to explain what it was I saw?

—Decency?

I was standing facing a wall. It was unthinkable to look at you. I couldn't have gone on. In front of me, on a shelf, there was the small black and white photograph we took everywhere. Simple, not very professional (my sister took it), but we liked it best. Me in my suit, you in the wedding dress you had made yourself; standing in a little copse of trees between two shoulders of rock, pre-Cambrian shield, with the river shining behind us. After another few moments I realized it had been some time since I had spoken, that you hadn't answered. What had I asked? Yes. An explanation.

—*Well?*

My word was too harsh, a command.

—No. I can't.

—You won't.

—I think it's the same. If I have to explain, John, it means you believe there may be more than one possible explanation; one of them is that there is something between David and me other than our friendship.

—No, no. It's not . . .

I turned, panicking. There was fear and pity in your eyes. I guess the pity won. I wish it hadn't.

—Oh John. Nothing at all. It's really over between David and Claire. Probably you won't believe that either. I certainly didn't at first. But it is. I guess we let ourselves think they didn't . . . *love* each other, really. But that wasn't true. Now it seems obvious, doesn't it? David's a mess. He was crying and crying and crying. He needed to tell somebody. He certainly can't talk to you. He was sobbing. I held him. Now please go. I want to be alone.

—Don't *say* that.

—Go. Please.

—All right. Another long walk won't kill me. I'll let myself in later. I'll . . . see you in the morning.

—Yes.

—Later on, let's go to the church. We'll climb the west tower and look at the fields.

You didn't respond. I let myself out. As I walked, I gradually realized I wasn't sure I believed you. And by accepting betrayal, it gradually turned out I had done the betraying. As I have calculated it during these long months, this was only the first step toward the breakdown, not the cause. But accepting that you may have been lying to me made talking it out so much more difficult, the conversations shallow, my bitterness building. Betrayals are situated too firmly in time, incarnations of instants. They won't be ravelled up again. I had demonstrated the ability to believe you had betrayed me. Betrayal was part of my belief system.

22

It was no fit room for a Cardinal, but Melior was too exhausted to care. With the cathedral a smoking ruin, the chapter house a roofless shell, and the episcopal palace damaged (and in any event stripped of all accoutrements of comfort in advance of the flames), Bishop Renaud's administration had commandeered two large inns which stood side by side in the southern quadrant of Chartres, the only section of the city untouched by the fire. Unlucky merchants, weary after trekking to the town from Burgundy or Vosges or the great fair at Vincennes, had been summarily bustled out of their rooms, as had a few wealthy pilgrims—who had arrived too late in any case. A few unfortunate long-term tenants living in the cheap rooms under the rafters had also found themselves unceremoniously evicted. They were muttering in their stew in a few cow-stalls at the back of the inn yard, where the owners let them sleep at quarter-rates until the fuss blew over.

A softer chair *would* have been welcome after an entire day on hard benches in the inn's dining hall, converted for the plenary sessions of the extraordinary diocesan council. Melior rolled his head in a slow circle against the gristle of tension in his neck. His room was furnished with a hard chair, a table that appeared to have arbitrated a few knife fights, a slab of wood on two trestles covered by a far from clean straw tick, a cold grate. He idly looked about for another taper. The place was gloomy. What did it matter? More than the church was ruined. He had failed today, and he wasn't used to that. He was too old, evidently. His tongue had lost its guile. His plans for a magnificent new edifice, an exalted place of worship that would replenish both himself and the School and—he had even allowed the fantasy—the very soul of France and Christendom now that the wars seemed to have ended after so many decades, the plagues receded, the Albigensians weakened—had been dashed. The hopes were more than thwarted; they were humiliated, turned into something unclean, unkind.

The meeting of the rarely convened Diocesan Assembly had opened sombrely and never really recovered. His efforts to find that fulcrum where the mood of a gathering can be tilted, then spun, turned in another direction, had faltered, time after time.

The greatest enemy around the table was despair, depression, listlessness, a sense of being abandoned. But usually *that* field of battle was his forte, and he had entered the lists with confidence . . . . The protecting powers of the Virgin, where had they been? Far from being diverted, the fire had seemed to make a beeline for the cathedral, surging up the slopes of the lower town until, pausing at the walls of the bishop's sanctum, where it faced three score students and servants and friars armed with water barrels, brooms and blankets, it had received an unexpected boost from a wind surging to new strength. It had leapt the wall, taken scant notice of the palace—leaving it scarred but largely intact— ignored the school dormitory and a mass of succulently flammable sheds and storerooms and shacks and privies—and fallen on her temple.

There were also, of course, philosophical differences among the thirty-odd men around the table—

prebendaries, auxiliary bishops, chapter-men, abbots (independent of the diocese in theory, but politically powerful, crucial to have on-side), doctors of the school, Melior, two delegates from Louis' court and one from the city aldermen, capitularies, and a dozen key vidames, essential to any fund raising effort. The Benedictine abbot agreed with the followers of Bernard present that silence was the pathway to salvation, and the old church had housed a cacophony. Divine disfavour was evident enough, was it not? One could do reverence to the Virgin here even still, even with her great relic annihilated, for the site itself was holy, sanctified by the fervour of a millennia of pilgrims. But an intimate chapel, well and strongly built, tranquil, lightly ornamented so as not to distract the mind: that was what the current situation, so soon after the disaster, called for. Audacious effort now, given the mood of the people, given their battered faith, was folly, arrogance, and would be paid for in failure. Of course, the diocese would need a new cathedral. No doubt. But there was no rush for that. Look after the pilgrims and Our Lady's needs for now, and think, over the coming decades, of gradually accumulating the funds needed for a new church, substantial, in keeping with the importance of Chartres, but quiet within, turning the faithful to contemplation.

Bishop Renaud was having none of that; Chartres was a major seat, its honour required a new building such as to make its status clear to the many who would find advantage in denying it. But Renaud was lethargic, his faith and confidence genuinely dampened. They should, first of all, put their house in order, he went on. Their guest Melior had recommended some excellent administrative reforms, and should the agricultural revival continue and trade grow, with time, perhaps, God willing . . .

Gabriel—how had *he* gotten into the Assembly?— gave it his best effort, knowing his lowly status was causing most of the gathering to take a mental siesta when he spoke. Surely this was the Fortunate Fall! he pleaded. The message was clear; and it was not one of despair. Wake up. Opportunity is the greatest gift. The old cathedral, beloved as it was, had been hopelessly inadequate for such a great shrine. (But the shrine is now without its jewel, one of the Lords from Paris mused aloud.) Gabriel rejected his lordship the Abbot's implication that only Benedictine architecture turned the mind and spirit toward God, that only simplicity— nay, emptiness—was edifying. He spoke of the idea that a long nave shows the distance one must travel to grace; that contemplation was indeed of great value: contemplation of eternal splendour, of the real cosmos, a *stupor* or *admirator* that the theology of architecture and the architects of theology could induce in the souls of many thousands. The very notion of incarnation, Gabriel went on—are we not the heirs of St. Anselme? Silence is wonderful: light and speech are better. To shrug off—and redeem!—the fall, through building, creating . . . .

The young monk sat down, aware he had long ago overstepped his bounds, his face burning, his forehead flushing, his eyes flashing beautifully.

But the weariness came back, the lassitude settled again over the gathering like an oppressive humidity. Melior talked about the budget numbers. He mentioned building projects in surely lesser locales—Noyon, Laon, Lausanne. The people's faith was in fact unbowed. They expected leadership. The charred shell was an affront to God. The preserved Royal Portal was like a beacon—a superb cornerstone from which to begin. The relic, the chemise was gone, but the presence of the Virgin surely remained?

Did it? They seemed unsure. A few eyes brightened, but only a few. He tried another tack. The feast day of St. Amelia was only a week away. A grand procession could lead to the cathedral site. A feast of repentance and renewal. A meeting of all the townspeople. A solemn mass on an altar in the ruins. Solemn pledges. Rekindled fervour?

The city was in shambles, pointed out the alderman. The guilds were devoting any energy they could find to helping widows and rebuilding shops. Fund-raising on a major scale would have to wait. Renaud sniffed and asked if the alderman was now speaking for the guilds? Last he remembered, they were mortal enemies. The alderman replied that he was speaking for the people. The vidames could always help of course—the regular revenues, carefully nurtured, could in time warrant hiring a master, justify plans and diagrams and budgets. But the peoples' pockets—crucial even in a rich diocese—were empty, their hearts dispirited. We might meet again in three years, or five. Talk then from a realistic perspective, with clear eyes.

Melior could consider it nothing more than a miserable compromise. The Bishop agreed, at Melior's (startlingly harsh) insistence, to strike a committee to examine possible building options, evaluate revenue bases, sound out public sentiment, get some costings from those in the know at other building sites, ask around about the best masters and if and when they would be available—and report to him in writing. The committee would not be formed until the next spring—other priorities intervened—and would be expected to conclude its work in one year, almost two years from now. It was the best he could get. And he barely got that.

Melior did hear, as he was meant to, Gabriel's furious whisper to a classmate in the corridor just after the meeting broke up. "We'll *start* to build a half-decent carbuncle, if we're lucky, in time for the baptisms of our parishioners' grandchildren."

Now, hours later and alone in this wretched room, Melior paced the chamber, ducking at each end to avoid the beams of the steeply pitched ceiling. Stopping at last at the warped sideboard, he poured a goblet of wine from a decanter. It was heavily mulled, to avoid spoiling, in the French manner. The spices galled him; he kept thinking there was a decent grape underneath their camouflage. Perhaps someday he would learn to like this stuff. A year in France had so far not been enough. He went to the casement and opened it, thinking that even the sound of carters' squeaking wheels or the quarrel of pigeons from the inn yard would be welcome. But outside, the evening was preternaturally quiet. It had been so in these weeks since the apocalypse, as if everyone were still exhausted, turning in early. Still, this quiet? He was trying to remember why this blanketed, hooded sensation, this absolute quietude, seemed familiar, as if he had been here before, listening in just this way for something to interrupt the too omnipresent soundlessness, a

257

soundlessness as if *there were nothing there*, no sky, no sleep, no dreams, no thoughts.

The tap at the door was very quiet, a slight cough of the wood.

Inexplicably, Melior panicked. Should he speak up? Who was there? He sensed . . . no, it was just a ghost of breeze carrying a bit of ash to his window, the remnants of the fire still sifting down over the town.

—I am here, he said. Odd, he thought. Why did I say that?

—My grace, said Gabriel, stepping in. He pulled back his simple brown cowl as he did so. His beardless face glowed in the light of the low fire in Melior's grate, as if he had been running, perspiring. The hair, light brown; the eyes, light blue and, at this moment, fixed on Melior with an expression both deferential and determined.

—Gabriel, it's only you.

—Only me, your grace? I'm sorry. I . . . you're expecting visitors.

—No, no. Your knock startled me. That's all. I was . . . praying.

—Excuse me.

—Sit down, please. Is something wrong Gabriel? You've rushed here. What is it?

—No, your grace. He looked puzzled. Melior's heart, on the contrary, was now rushing; he was nervous. The silence! Even while they talked it was all around him, at the back of his neck, just behind his head.

—Your face, said Melior awkwardly. He mimed wiping his brow.

—My face? Oh. A warm evening indeed, my grace.

—Please, sit down.

—If you, that . . . if I might stand, Cardinal Melior, I would be in your debt.

—Stand then, Gabriel of Ulm, said Melior, trying to soothe his odd fear with a jaunty tone. Melior stayed near the window, three paces from Gabriel.

Gabriel laid a small parcel he had been carrying on the bureau to his right. Melior noticed the pallor of his hand. Gabriel spent too much time in the study hall and scriptorium. He must recommend to the master that he second the young man to one of the monasteries in the region for a few months, one of the less corrupt ones, where they hadn't yet indulged in servants to fulfill their vows for them. Some work in the fields would balance the mind while refreshing the flesh.

—If you could spare me a few minutes, my grace.

—Go ahead, Gabriel.

—I'm sure you already realize. If I felt that the council today was only a disgrace . . . but for me it was also a tragedy.

—Disgrace is a strong word if you examine its meaning.

—Your grace, Chartres is the temple of Our Lady. I have felt her presence.

—I know. I know. Melior almost whispered, turning his back to stare out over the town, at its few lit torches.

—Guibert of Nogent wrote that the Sacred Tunic, and the name of the Virgin of Chartres are venerated by the entire world. And Guibert is a *skeptic*.

—It's true. Of course it's true. Chartres' fame reached Milan centuries ago. You have the writings of Guibert here?

—Yes. The *De vita sua*. Two copies.

—Two. Wonderful. Wonderful. Melior shook his head.

—I will bore you, your grace, but please give me leave. The tunic was given by Charles the Bold himself, over three hundred years ago. But he presented it to the Bishop here because, according to our scholars, the Virgin's disciples had honoured her here long before there was any church here at all. Some believe there was a sanctuary here *before* the Immaculate Conception, in homage to the oracles of her birth. Even our local liturgies, my grace: *domine civitatem istam carnotensem quam primam apud Gallos de mysterio tuae incarnationis instruere voluisti*. Divine providence sent *first* to Chartres the veneration of the mystery of the incarnation. I know. A bold claim. But I believe *you* know it is true, your grace. And it is the mystery of the incarnation that leads us to our respect for Our Lady, and it is the mystery of the incarnation, that spirit can touch flesh, that lies at the heart of our own desire to *create*, to *make something*, to believe that stone can uplift, that our energies can give grace to a vessel re-enacting the cosmos. If we believe in the incarnation, we venerate Our Lady. If we believe in the incarnation, we believe we can give back to God worthy efforts to embody love, grace, spirit. And to make that effort *here*, at Chartres, *for* the Virgin . . . . I can think of no other task for my life.

—And Gabriel of Ulm, Melior said to the casement, after a moment. After the fire, even after the fire, you have no *doubt?*

—Do you, your grace?

Melior turned slowly to face the young monk. He felt a door thrown open inside him, blown inward by a strong wind. Gabriel's gaze was even steadier now, without a flicker, and Melior felt as though they had exchanged places, traded roles.

—Is doubt not allowed?

—Not allowed to become another kind of certainty. Then . . . then, what lesser animals we are. No. I have chosen my truth. The people must be told, from the Bishop on down. They must be told Our Lady has graciously presented us with a miraculous occasion— and thus a duty—to raise to her glory and the glory of God a fit abode for her great relic, an abode that is the work of human hands transformed, transfigured, into paradise. You were right at the council. I don't know why I hadn't thought of it myself. You were a perfect tempter, my grace. A major feast day lies before us, one particularly loved by the townspeople here, as if God had arranged everything to make sure we had no excuses, to make certain an opportunity exists, an *exit* from our dilemma.

—Gabriel, Melior said abruptly, not wanting to hear this. The point of your visit, please. I'm supposed to meet Auxerre. I'm late.

Gabriel was genuinely perplexed by Melior's sudden harshness. He hadn't encountered it before, not in person. But he ploughed on.

—A major procession through the streets, with the crosier held before it, and the banners of Chartres and all the orders that share this great diocese, with abbots in full array, with the Bishop and his entire chapter in solemn parade, with nuns and monks, with doctors of theology wearing their velvet hoods in colours according to their rank, and leading them all, as is his right, a

Prince of the Church, in the raiment of a Cardinal who has thrice sat in holy plenum to select the successor to the throne of Peter.

Velvet words, thought Melior. His tongue is inspired, as mine was not today—or bewitched. He turned his back again. And again, at the window, he could smell smoke.

—A fit abode for her great relic. There is no relic, Gabriel! The relic is ash.

—Such a procession, your grace, could move the exhausted townspeople, the cautious Lord Mayor, the lethargic aldermen, the divided chapter, the politic bishop, to *action*, to move now, exploiting the great revenue-generating powers of this diocese, to employ the greatest masters and the finest masons guided by the inspiration of the school, to raise a cathedral unlike any other, a history of now and a model of eternity, a home for the relic and an inspiration to millions.

—A home for the relic.

—The procession *could* do this, my grace, with the right climax. *That* would be your role.

Melior heard the whispering of cloth. As he turned he saw Gabriel unwinding the package he had laid down upon entering. In the silence he heard a persistent, distant knocking. He shook his head, trying to still the sound. Already lying across Gabriel's outstretched arms was a long and somewhat narrow piece of very old, very faded, very worn cloth. Of pale grey, it was, on first glance at least, indistinguishable from the sacred tunic of Our Lady of Chartres.

—Gabriel, Melior whispered. *I* saw the crypt. What was left of it. A jumble of black stone.

—Can anyone be certain, certain that if the stones are cleared away . . . ?

—No cloth could survive that heat. Some of the stones themselves had partly melted.

—The sacred tunic is not mere cloth.

—Where did you get it?

—I was walking in the marketplace, past the cloth merchants, lost in thought. There it was. I opened my eyes and saw it. Old, the right size, the right colour. A gift.

—A temptation. Where did the merchant say he got it?

—From another merchant. For a pittance. Part of a large batch. Unwanted.

—Where is this other merchant?

—A traveller. No one knows his name. From the south.

—A lie.

—Your grace, the *council* was a lie, a heresy, a denial! A Peter pleading he knows nothing. The truth is much bigger. You know the truth. I saw it on your face, the first time I met you, outside the Royal Portal. You had seen Our Lady. She had seen you. Am I mistaken?

Melior licked his lips. Gabriel's face swam in front of him. The voice was hypnotic.

—No.

—Sometimes you must cover your doubt, as you would cover the sin of your brother, to save your love. Sometimes you must lie to save what you believe in.

—That is the way to damnation, Melior whispered.

—Maybe. Or salvation. I think the way to damnation is to spend too much time worrying about the fate of our souls.

263

—*That* is heresy. You are my tempter.

—I'm sorry, your grace.

—Who can be my confessor now, Gabriel?

—Sins . . . all sins . . . need not be confessed. They can be shared, quietly, then covered, to be allowed to shrink to their proper size.

—Not to fester.

—Some think so. This, I think, is to give them too much power. Sin is weak.

—You are very wise, for a young man, Melior whispered. Or I may be completely wrong.

—And a heretic?

—Probably.

—What shall I do? I am at your service.

Melior understood that the decision had already been taken, and with a sense of utter relief he commended his soul to a judgment beyond his ability to anticipate or understand. That was how he phrased it many years later, on his deathbed, to the assembled body of Cluniac monks, deep in the Italian countryside.

—You should take the candle on the table, Gabriel, there, and singe the edge of the cloth and allow other parts of it to blacken, and all of it to be permeated with the smell of smoke. Then you should leave here, and take it with you. Tomorrow I will order the careful excavation of the crypt.

23

Dear Liza, having come this far, I still am not sure whether what matters most, what needs to be confessed, is thoughts or deeds. Does what was running through my mind matter? Our modern minds are repulsed by the notion we would warrant some celestial reward due to faith even if we act badly. But at the same time, we locate the roots of all actions in the mind, in the dark downward spiral of consciousness, the semi-conscious, the unthought. And the dark gods? No, of course there are no dark gods. No Lucifer or Bacchus or Erinyes. No medieval Virgins, shadowed in their own way. The mind builds the will, right? Fomenting our acts in the world. Our mind is constructed of nothing but experience and genetic code. Or at least so we are now told.

But what about whim, and fear, and blasts of fire from nowhere, and the brain twisting on its own convulsive behalf? Breaking, breaking down. Are we so certain the brain isn't another spasming muscle? It seems to me that's what the current version of theology rejects most firmly: that there are blasts of fire from nowhere, unexplained and without origin.

I can't remember all that I was thinking when we got to the church the next day, struggling within our own silences. The line between thought and sensation, the murk of feelings—I can't locate it now. I kept "forgiving" you. A conceit. And deciding I had torn it all even further. I was pulled between accusation and confession. I have one conclusion though, for now at least. I believe I failed us because I could not enter a large enough time frame; I was trapped in a short span of attention. I felt our perfection was ruined. Ruined by you. Ruined by me—both in advance, by basing it on my cruelty toward Lee, and now, by kissing Claire. But would a dim subterranean urge toward Claire have surfaced, become meaningful, without the shock of seeing David and you?

I couldn't see forward to us being perfect again, or perfect enough to be an object of our longing. We could stay together. We could be happy enough. We could re-create. But I couldn't project myself forward to us again finding the clarifying, liberating sensation of beauty. Could I face a future without that hope?

This bred bitterness. I don't know where it came from, my dear. I didn't know it belonged to me. From the fire and brimstone. But I couldn't throw it off. If I couldn't have the vision entire, I would destroy it; no cheap counterfeits. These weren't exactly thoughts—put so baldly, they lie. They were recited from elsewhere, as if told to me by someone else. I certainly remember realizing that this was the wrong conclusion, a disastrous immaturity; I remember reminding myself that I would always regret it if I could not find a way to restore our relic, in whatever shape we could manage, to the place of pilgrimage. And, of course, such an unwarranted conclusion would not have lasted. If I had not hurt you so badly that day, bringing on your illness and that leading to a deeper withdrawal, I like to think little or nothing would have come of the entire mess.

But those were thoughts. And should we recite thoughts or deeds?

Inside the cathedral together, we still had trouble

finding any useful words. A strange tentativeness immersed us; there was no confrontation, no reconciliation. We entered through the Royal Portal and crossed the labyrinth set into the floor at the top of the nave. The great vault held a mountain of stone aloft, penetrated with the fathomless blue upon blue of the clerestory windows. We passed along the north aisle to the entrance to the tower.

Alone in the flat on Jeanne-Mance, I go through this scene over and over, reciting it to myself, to you, to us, to the quiet rooms, telling it to you a slightly different way each time.

The last thing I said before we slipped into that vertical space and ascended the tight spiral of stairs was: Liza, I think I've figured out what annoys me and enchants me about this place. Nothing elaborate. Nothing universal. No "key to Gothic." Simply my own fit with the wards of this giant key—I flung my arms—all around us. Liza, you already know it. Chartres has ornamentation where no one can see it. You can wriggle your way out onto a ledge, a flying buttress cutting the clouds in half over your head, until you can see under the little stone canopy of the miniature classical temples you find there—two Ionic columns with pediments—that cap each buttress. There, meticulously executed eight hundred years ago, is a stook of wheat, heads tasselled, string twining the straws—carved from granite. There are gargoyles visible only from aircraft, with detailing that went un-photographed until telephoto lenses were developed. You know what it reminds me of?

—The conscience, you said, the human conscience.

—The psychoanalytic approach, Liza? I said it with

an edge of accusation that surprised me. You looked sharply away, took a step from me, and half turned as if to gaze back the two hundred feet across the vast transept. I looked above you, not at you, my heart pounding unreasonably, losing myself for a moment in the scarlets and royal blues of the upper storey grisailles, in the lilies of France, among the castles of Castille in the borders.

You turned back.

—Like a conscience without the possibility of confession, John, musing on its regret over something no one else will ever know about. Why bother? Morality? Faith? But were the builders all believers? You said you weren't so sure.

—I was only going to say, I lied, that it reminds me of Dad. That's mystery enough. He varnishes the bottoms— the outside bottoms—of the drawers of the dressers he builds, just because he likes things done right. So why do them right? Why bother? Why not do them wrong? Faith? Morality? Or lack of faith? Turning away from the unending, unraveling mess? Anyway, let's go up.

So we stepped inside, the familiar staircase a tight spiral, with low risers and worn edges; our hands searched for balance on the ancient column that ran up through the centre, sometimes they rested on rough walls interrupted by alcoves with tiny, blackened oak doors I had never seen opened, or by six-foot-deep wells leading to narrow iron grates allowing distorted grids of sunlight into the narrow space. Half way, you stopped.

—John? you said, not turning, still facing upward.

—What?

But you only started to cry. No sound, but I could see the small convulsions of your shoulders, at the back, where Renaissance artists attached the wings of angels.

I reached out, guilty even though I hadn't done anything yet. But you had already gone on, so I followed you up, my thighs beginning to ache, chasing you around that black, hand-polished stone column. You didn't look back. The combination—your crying, your running—frustrated me, then irritated. It was an implicit and unjust accusation. You can't blame me for what I want to say! I almost shouted after you. We're not accountable for our thoughts, are we? After all, we can hardly control them; they come to us, ghostly swerves. You, of all people, know that. It's what we do we have to answer for, for thoughts made flesh.

At last: the upper door, space blossoming around my head as I ducked and stepped out onto that exhilarating belvedere at the climax of the north tower. The sun was in the last trees across the plain, showing us their thinness. Beyond the town the wheat was the same deep gold. The green roofs surrounded us, geometric moors, climbing higher still to the cap of the nave, angling down to the Saint Piat chapel, spreading—at shallow angles it seemed from here—like great wings to cover the transept. Here the gargoyles were local monsters, close enough to glare directly at us, on a human scale. You stood a dozen feet away, facing me. Somehow this surprised me, pushed me further into hopelessness. The thoughts I had been nurturing—or had they been nurturing me?—would, finally, not be lied to. From then on it was only words, fire. It was terrible knowing you were fragile. And terrible wondering if I wasn't.

—I guess people never really change, Liza.

—Look at me, John.

—You're a Freudian. It's the foundation of your beliefs. People never really change.

—You know more about my work than that.

269

—Who said I was talking about you?

—So it's you who never really changes?

—Sure. Losing things. Knocking things down. Great architect. Yeah.

—You were talking about me.

—I was talking about me. Me who ruins things. And about you. Lover of men. Sure, I was.

You didn't react. Lover of many men: I had saved the harshest words I could use against you, saved them for years, horrified at knowing what they were, certain I would never want them, but possessing them all the same. And now you said nothing. You stood there. Your eyes didn't change. I saw no flinch. Nothing.

But it just took time. A seeping. When you broke the silence your voice was changed.

—I thought I knew. You.

—Maybe you don't. Maybe you haven't been looking. I can't see that you've been looking. Christ, Liza, you know what you are for me: if you stop looking, I'm nothing. And we're supposed to be looking for each other, trying to have a baby because we're longing for that, and when I go looking for you I find David soothing his heartache in your arms. I'm supposed to not mind? It's not a question of jealousy. It's a question of whether or not my world exists, or whether or not it's just something I built out of air.

—Maybe you should try seeing me, John. Did I look like I was in love with David? Did you see that?

—You looked just fine.

—John, look!

The mind has its own resources. My doubts and fury were mine. The faith was outside of me, and now it was tarnished. Throw it down.

—Oh, I looked. I stood in the doorway with Claire smirking beside me. Don't tell me to look, Liza. I'm all eyes. I'm all eyes in a hall of mirrors and I'm getting tired of wondering whether there's anybody out there looking back. I looked. I saw you, Liza. Something comfortable in your face.

Your eyes had lost their focus; I was looking at static. You weren't there. So I said it.

—You're not real, Liza.

Now it was complicated. It was your fault.

—You're not real, Liza.

The muscles of your jaw were twitching, a lump under the skin. You didn't look like my miracle any longer.

—You're not real, Liza.

24

On his third or fourth try, pulling at imaginary handles on unyielding walls, re-steering toward the exit, Daniel hauled open the door of *La Californie* like someone opening a vault, and fell into the vestibule, smashing his head on the jamb between the outer door and the window. I went after him, Roger behind me. He was up again with surprising speed and quickly outside, standing there as I reached him, swaying like an aspen in a stiff wind. The spring day was long gone. It was freezing. The outdoor café tables down along the side street were desolate. I took Daniel by both shoulders. A welt was coming up over his left eye, starting to redden. I shook him, hard; harder.

—Go home, for Christ's sake. Just for God's sake *go home*. What's the matter with you? What-is-the-matter-with-you?

He was dazed, his eyes glassy.

Roger put his hand on my arm. I realized I had been shaking Daniel again.

—*Tu ne savais pas?*

I ignored him. Daniel resurfaced one last time from wherever he used to go; his eyes flashed back at me.

—So. John. And what do you have to tell *me*?

—What?

—Tell me the whole story, you keep saying. Well. Tell me something! The story.

—You were the one who started it.

—What are you going to tell me?

—Tell you? I don't know. I could . . . all I could do is

show you my letter to Liza. I write to her all the time. Sometimes on paper, sometimes in my head. We had arguments. I said things I never should have said. She had some nervous problems. Her family asked me to . . .

—Liza?

—They asked me to give her time. You know, time. Alone. That is, without me. For a while. She's coming back soon. Next week, the week after.

—I think you told me all that.

—No, Daniel, you're imagining again.

—You could show me.

—My letter to Liza?

—You really know a Liza? No lies?

—Yes. Now go *home*, Daniel.

—Home, John? What do you think I did when the darling baby was born, John? Can't you guess? Guess, John!

—It's late for guessing.

—I dressed her up in her baptism gown and strangled her, and everything was quiet, and I put her in a baby carriage and put the carriage on the mountain. To make it all clear. Jesus and Mary Mother of God you're slow on the uptake old boy.

He reeled out of my grip and moved in a stitching, butterfly motion across the street, veering toward the *dépanneur*. I couldn't move. I watched him fall, face first, halfway across the street. There were no cars. He was charmed. He seemed to barely glance off the ground, rolling upright like a child's punching bag. Then he was on the far sidewalk, feeling his way along the front of the *dépanneur*. Inside its front window you could see the flashing light of the TV on the shelf above the cigarettes, and the flitting blue and red, yellow and black, of the Canadiens and Bruins. When Daniel got past the entrance, and around the corner to proceed along Bernard, he disappeared from my view.

—Roger. Oh, Christ, Roger.

—John, listen.

—Roger, we should . . .

—John. Daniel's been coming to *La Californie* for at least two years. Since I started here.

—So? Jesus, Roger.

—So. The baby they found on the mountain . . . that was what? Six, eight months ago? And the baby was little, right? A few weeks, a month old.

—He didn't go to California?

—I don't know. But not lately.

—But . . .

—He told me once the child fell down the stairs. While he and Isabelle watched, locked out when they ran down to get groceries out of the car. She fell down the inside stairs of a walk-up apartment while they stood helplessly outside trying to break the glass out of the door. Maybe. I don't know. He told Céline a different story, about smoking in bed, causing a blaze, not getting her out.

I walked slowly over to the nearest table and pulled out a chair. It was icy under my hand. Roger hesitated, came up behind me.

—Look John, I've got to go back in. Everybody's thirstier when the Canadiens are winning. Daniel, well . . . . Who can say? But not the baby on the mountain. No. He claims it. Okay. But it belonged to someone else.

—He'll never get home tonight.

I started to cry.

—Don't you see, Roger? Tonight, there's no chance. A little thing, right? Trivial. But where is the seam, when does it come apart? How much more can a marriage take? Love needs looking after. He'll never get home. Did you see him crossing the street? Anyway. Look at the time. He'll never get home.

—John, said Roger swiftly. There is no Isabelle. I thought you understood. There's no house in Pointe Claire. He turns right on Park Avenue, that's all I know, taking a bus, walking. Park Extension maybe. It's not my business. But somewhere north. There's been no Isabelle for a long time.

I was spinning. The table needed holding down. The streetlights were about to explode into flame.

—That's *crazy*. What are you trying to do to me? Why wouldn't you have told me? Why didn't you tell me? *Fucking* bastard.

—Haven't you ever had to cover up for somebody? Cover up the worst stuff? Pretend it wasn't there?

—What about Céline? Does she know all this?

—It was Céline who checked. There is no Isabelle Lafontaine living in Montreal. Or Pointe-Claire. There is one Isabelle O'Brien. Céline called. She's sixty-five, never heard of a Daniel.

—You could have told *me*. I was crying again. I *care* about him.

—So do I. But he's not stupid. You're no actor. He'd know.

—Is he lying? Or is he crazy?

—I can't tell.

—But Roger . . .

275

Roger had gone in. Forgetting my bill and my jacket inside, I stood and walked toward Park Avenue, determined to catch up to Daniel. At the first corner, though, my feet took me left, toward the walk-up flat and the empty letterbox, letting him go. It would have been so cold on the mountain. The stars would have looked so cold. I wanted to reach down, make sure the little eyes were closed.

25

Dear Liza, this morning was the start of a glorious late spring day, spurring me out for a ramble through my neighbourhood, trying to get the scents down, the angles of light; poking my head into the combination pool hall-café, checking out the upside-down goat in the window of the Greek butcher shop, verifying that the shoemaker on Bernard was still at his machine, sewing his lasts. Finally I walked to the corner of Esplanade and St-Viateur, to *Marche Latina*, my favourite grocer, to pick up some fruits and vegetables, some feta (they hew you a slice from a huge block floating in brine), a six-pack of St. Ambroise, some of their unmatchable pork chops. All the way back to the apartment I was thinking about how I could explain the scriptorium to you. You'll misunderstand. You'll think I've been misleading you.

That moment on Chartres' battlements did too much damage. I know it wasn't the only pivot. The earliest are probably forgotten, or I never even saw them. In the days that followed I'm sure there were moments, opportunities for healing, when I failed you further. Part of me expected you to be your old self again any moment, the self that looked at me. I suppose it was only a matter of time before a breakdown. It began more like a slip, an accidental slide to a point just slightly out of focus. But it persisted, a downward listlessness. Then, one day, more cruel words from me, and weeping that would not stop, eyes that would not come clear. Your parents gave me the name of a therapist; they helped me with the caring for you.

Your mother's e-mails say that you are feeling quite a bit better now.

A few of the Greek ladies on Esplanade were turning the soil in the little vegetable gardens they conjure between greystone and sidewalk, scheming for ridiculously successful vines sagging with tomatoes, cucumbers climbing all over their stakes, a nip of thyme and a tuck of oregano in the corners, sweet peas twining it all together. I got out my key and let myself in, past the letterbox and the drift of advertising circulars, up the narrow flight to another locked door. I heard a creaking from inside. I was afraid again, my heart too loud. I thought the door might be unbolted, that someone might be there. I turned the knob gingerly, but it was locked. Inside, setting the groceries on the kitchen table, I put on water for tea and passed into the back hallway, and opened the door to my lair.

I remember you less and less. That's not what people say: they say they will never forget. Of course I think of you, almost constantly. That isn't what I mean. It's that the precision is gone. At times I remember your clothes better than your body, or an expression rather than the actual flesh of your face. That flesh, on my hand: it is hard to believe it still really exists, that one could touch it.

I see you vividly only in flashes, when some object or colour or situation veers my mind through the thousand veils between us. You've gone and left me alone. I'm not sure I believe any more, though I am willing to pretend with all my heart. The gods have taken the world away and given it to a realm I don't control. Even the dreams, so persistent for months, are beginning to dissipate. I told you about them, in the early letters. It was part of